PRAISE FOR
MY MISTRESS' EYES ARE RAVEN BLACK
AND TERRY ROBERTS

"Terry Roberts' new novel is a literary thriller of the highest order: lyrical and suspenseful, with characters you will long remember. This is a heart-pounding, timely, and completely immersive read. It's also Roberts' finest hour."

—Silas House, author of *Southernmost*

"[*My Mistress' Eyes are Raven Black*] is pure entertainment–think Raymond Chandler or, perhaps, an Appalachian James Lee Burke. At the same time, the book confronts the reader with important questions about American immigration policies and race. Set at Ellis Island in the early 1920s, it is nonetheless sharply relevant in today's America."

—Wayne Caldwell, Author of *Cataloochee*

"Terry Roberts has a knack for exploring the forgotten corners of American history—and then shining a light on the moral ambiguities he finds there. And he knows how to tell a story. This one has all the right ingredients: fascinating setting, winning characters, mystery, real suspense, and romance. I thoroughly enjoyed it."

—Julia Franks, author of *Over the Plain Houses*

"In *My Mistress' Eyes Are Raven Black* Terry Roberts expands his fictional world as never before, from the mountains of North Carolina to Ellis Island, the heart and soul of America. Roberts tells a story of mystery, intrigue, murder, bigotry, and romance. With homage to the masters of crime fiction, Cain, Thompson, Chandler, and the Hammett of The Thin Man, this novel has thrilling action, and humor, as it addresses both the racism and humanity in our culture, in 1920, and the present."

—Robert Morgan, Author of *Gap Creek* and *Chasing the North Star*

MY MISTRESS' EYES ARE RAVEN BLACK

MY MISTRESS' EYES ARE RAVEN BLACK

A NOVEL BY

TERRY ROBERTS

+ KEYLIGHT BOOKS
BOOKS
AN IMPRINT
OF TURNER
PUBLISHING

Turner Publishing Company
Nashville, Tennessee

www.turnerpublishing.com

My Mistress' Eyes are Raven Black

Library of Congress Cataloging-in-Publication Data

Names: Roberts, Terry, 1956- author.
Title: My mistress' eyes are raven black / a novel by Terry Roberts.
Description: Nashville : Turner Publishing, 2021. | Summary: "Summer, 1920.
  The immigration and public health authorities on Ellis Island in New
  York Harbor are slowly recovering from the war years, even as a new
  influx of European and African immigrants is flooding the Great Hall. A
  young, pregnant, Irish woman, Ciara McManaway, disappears from the
  Isolation Hospital on Ellis Island. Stephen Robbins, a specialist in
  finding the missing-persons as well as things-is sent to Ellis Island by
  his boss in the Bureau of Investigation to locate the McManaway woman.
 Set in the years following World War I, when racial tensions in the U.S.
  are growing and the science of eugenics is widely accepted, My Mistress'
  Eyes are Raven Black explores just how far human beings will go to
  protect racial purity and condemn those they fear."– Provided by
  publisher.
Identifiers: LCCN 2020054655 (print) | LCCN 2020054656 (ebook) | ISBN
  9781684426942 (paperback) | ISBN 9781684426959 (hardcover) | ISBN
  9781684426966 (ebook)
Subjects: GSAFD: Mystery fiction. | Suspense fiction.
Classification: LCC PS3618.O3164 M96 2021 (print) | LCC PS3618.O3164
  (ebook) | DDC 813/.6--dc23
LC record available at https://lccn.loc.gov/2020054655
LC ebook record available at https://lccn.loc.gov/2020054656

Cover design: Emily Mahon

9781684426942   Paperback
9781684426959   Hardback
9781684426966   Ebook

Printed in the United States of America

To the memory of my mother,
Helen Sampson Roberts
and
in honor of my sister,
Julia Roberts Greene

Give me your tired, your poor,
Your huddled masses yearning to breathe free,
The wretched refuse of your teeming shore,
Send these, the homeless, tempest-tost to me.

—EMMA LAZARUS

From "The New Colossus," inscribed on the
pedestal of the Statue of Liberty (1903)

PART ONE

CHAPTER ONE

The Nameless Man always had this eerie ability to pass in and out of a room silently and almost invisibly. That evening at the Algonquin Hotel on West 44th Street, when he reentered my life, he materialized with his usual thin and ghostly attitude. That and the ironic smile that told you nothing about his thoughts.

I was in and out of the dining room that night, ranging from kitchen to front desk to restaurant tables, even out to the dark and rainy sidewalk, moving with a quiet smile and nod, slipping through brief encounters with staff and patrons, priding myself as always on seeing without being seen.

But the Nameless Man saw me long before I saw him, and you could tell he enjoyed beating me at my own game.

He was seated at a small table for one that the maître-d' must have shoved obligingly back into a corner not far from the famous Round Table. It was dark in his corner, and he'd asked for a candle. Hamlet the Cat lay splayed out on a sidebar, and I had just rubbed his belly and was on my way to the kitchen to check on how much fish was left when I spied a pale, nondescript face beneath brown, nondescript hair combed straight back over a thin, nondescript head. He wasn't invisible, but you got the feeling he could be if he chose.

"What the hell?" I said to myself, and then again, louder, so he could hear me. He was chewing his steak slowly, savoring each bite, and it took him a few heartbeats to reply.

"You like this job?" he asked, waving his fork to signify the entire establishment. "House manager of the famous Algonquin?"

"I must," I said. "I was doing something similar when you found me."

He nodded. "Way down yonder in the lost state of Carolina," he said and considered another bite, but he paused with his fork halfway to his mouth. "You loved that old hotel," he said. "But this . . . this is beneath you and you know it, petting the cat and servicing your female guests."

"Not a hell of a lot of servicing going on." I shrugged. "Although I did rub an old matron's tired feet one night, with God and the bellman as my witness."

He grinned while he chewed. Swallowed. "Just as I thought," he said. "Bored."

"I get to listen to Dorothy Parker, Alexander Woollcott, and their crowd every day at lunch," I said. "Right over there at the Round Table. How could I be bored? Besides, I think Miss Parker wants to date me."

"She wants to do more than that," he said and almost smiled, which for him was a grin. "How are you fixed for money?"

"Could use some of that," I admitted. "I play poker with the Round Table crowd too. I may have helped finance the *New Yorker*."

This time he did smile. "You need a job, Robbins. A real job that doesn't involve rubbing some fat broad's feet or shuffling anybody's cards."

A few months before I would have asked what. And where. Maybe even why. But I was swinging at the end of my own rope by that August night, and the rope—suddenly, unexpectedly—felt frayed and slick with sweat. So I nodded at the Nameless Man, sat down, leaned back in my chair, and gave him a grin. "Tell me," I said.

He paused and then looked around the room without seeming to.

"It's after five," I said. "Have a drink . . . on the house." I was curious to see if the Nameless Man would drink. Apparently, he could

4

eat, as I'd seen him chew up half a dozen bites, but the Volstead Act had been in effect since the fall before, making all booze illegal, and he was, after all, a government Nameless Man.

He nodded. "Scotch," he said. "If you can still manage it."

I smiled and whispered to a waiter.

"How about you?" he asked.

"Not yet," I said. He thought I meant *not yet* that night, but I meant not yet in my slowly falling apart life.

After his drink came in a nondescript coffee mug, he told me the tale.

"What do you know about Ellis Island?" he began.

I watched his face as he said it. It had gone blank, impersonal. Even his eyes darkened by a shade or two. His face was getting down to business.

"It's where the poor, unwashed, and unlovely come into the country. Probably where both our ancestors tried to sneak in."

"Mine . . . yes," he said. "Not yours. I checked. Yours probably came a long time before."

"You know more about them than I do then," I admitted. "But I know Ellis Island has a new boss, the former police commissioner, I believe, but I couldn't tell you his name."

He nodded. "His name is Wallis, and he doesn't factor into this, at least not yet. Anything else?"

I considered. "Not much. I've looked at it from the docks. Watched the ferryboats bring over the folks who made the grade and somehow slipped through the door into this bright land of ours. Most of them were scared to death, from what I could see."

Again a nod. He'd laid down his fork, with his steak half-finished.

"That's about it," I admitted. "You going to deport me?"

That earned his thin-lipped smile. "Where the hell would we deport you to? North Carolina?" And then, after a pause, "We have a problem on Ellis Island. A disappearance. A young woman from Ireland who came over in steerage and who apparently expected to be met by her uncle, who would lay claim to her and launch her new life in this country."

"If she came over in steerage, why does anybody care what happened to her? She's poor, right, half-starved. Why did she end up on your desk?" This last bit was a stretch for me with the Nameless Man, as I wasn't at all sure just what department of the US government his desk sat in.

"Her uncle, the old geezer who was supposed to claim her, is a United States congressman from the great state of New Jersey. A man named Brendan McCarthy, who looks like a leprechaun, only he's six feet tall and carries a silver-headed cane."

"So friend McCarthy is raising hell because an Irish lass he was responsible for has slipped away?"

The Nameless Man shrugged and sipped from his mug. I got the distinct impression he was weighing just how much to tell me. "He claims her for his niece. We think more likely she is, or was, his daughter. And yes, he's raising hell all over Washington, even pounding on my boss's door."

"Who's your boss?"

He ignored the question. "I work for the Justice Department, which means you do too. The Bureau of Investigation, Department of Justice. Doesn't matter who." Again that pause to consider. "And she didn't slip away."

"Who didn't slip away?"

"You know who. The Irish girl. She never left the island. Dead or alive. She didn't leave as a stowaway. She didn't leave as a man or a child or somebody's wife. She didn't sprout wings and fly. It's been a month, and she's gone into thin air."

"You want me to find her?"

He sipped from the mug and shrugged. "Brendan McCarthy wants us to find her," he finally said. "I think the fish ate her weeks ago."

CHAPTER TWO

There was more to the conversation that night. We talked about why he'd picked me for this (because I myself was a stranger, an alien, and so I could see further in), whether his Bureau of Investigation would pay me (they would, better than managing the Algonquin), whether I would need to live on the island (which was up to me). And that last part, the living away from home part, led him to ask me if I was still with Anna Ulmann. It was an almost human moment between us, and I was at a loss as to how to answer.

"Hard to tell if I am or not," was the first thing I said. "And even if I am, I think some time apart might be good for us," was the second thing. "What the hell is your name anyway? Since you can call Anna by name, what the hell is your name?"

He ignored the question long enough to pick up his knife and fork. Then, while he carved another bite, "Try Will," he said. "That might work." He had occasionally been *William Smith* in our exchanges.

"My God, is that really it? What your mother named you?"

He didn't answer. By that point, he was chewing.

I had come to New York in the summer of 1918 after being recruited by the Nameless Man. What I had really come to New York for was to find and love a woman—Anna Ulmann, whose life seemed so indelibly written into mine that I could either find and cleave to her or hang myself.

And I had found her. Anna . . .

For a year or so, life had seemed like the middle part of a ballad. She earned a decent living as a photographer, and I did one thing or another. Worked in various hotels until I had gained enough of a reputation to land as manager of the Algonquin. Twice I did small jobs for Nameless Will. Once, I took three days to find the corpse of a missing person he had an interest in. The other time, I searched a mansion on Central Park, not far from the house I shared with Anna, and found an envelope full of photographs secreted behind a wall. In each instance, I unearthed what he wanted because I could close my eyes and imagine things other people couldn't see, plus I had learned to talk to people in that huge, buzzing hive of a city. On the street corner, in the train station, in the kitchen of a great house. Just talk. . . . Ask and answer, laugh and tell a joke. Keep sticking your nose into other people's business until somebody offers to cut it off or points the way in. Or both. But the irony was that as I learned to talk to everyone else, Anna and I lost the habit of talking to each other.

We tried. We loved each other, and so we tried. But sometimes in the riptide of close relations, a shared language is washed away, becomes a lost language—read perhaps or written in an ancient manuscript, but not spoken. And if spoken, misinterpreted. She had miscarried our child two years before, and somehow the ghost of that lost generation hovered between us.

By the time he, the Nameless Will, reappeared that evening in August, Anna and I were barely speaking at all. Trading pleasantries at breakfast, telling abbreviated versions of our day in the evening, leaning away from each other in a sort of quiet desperation, and reaching past each other with our words.

She wanted more than anything in the world to be a renowned photographer—certainly more than she wanted to be a wife or mother. I yearned to go home to North Carolina, where I understood the weather and recognized the songs of birds. Neither of us could quite say what we wanted, but deep desires were welling within us—dark, surging waters that tore us apart.

The next day at breakfast, I told Anna most of what Nameless Will had told me. The missing girl and her uncle congressman. The swarm of people—men, women, and children—who passed daily through Ellis Island. Those who, for a laundry list of reasons, might be detained or sent back to Europe or even Africa.

"What reasons?" she asked in that curious way she had. "Political?"

"Not really. Crooked spines, missing limbs, trachoma . . ."

"Trachoma?"

I gestured at my face. "Disease of the eyes, contagious. They send them back for anything and everything. Senility, feeblemindedness, pregnancy. Oh, and polygamy. You can't get into the country if you admit to polygamy."

"Maybe the missing girl was a polygamist," she said, with just a hint of her old humor. "Looking for some husbands in the land of opportunity."

"Maybe. But they didn't send her back as far as anyone can tell. She arrived on the island, was sent to the Contagious Disease Hospital, and then she disappeared."

"How long will it take you?" she asked. "To find her, I mean."

I shrugged. "A week maybe. If she's to be found at all."

"Will you spend the nights there?"

My answer was out of my mouth before the thought was fully formed. "Some of the time . . . I may have to in order to see what goes on in such a place at night." It didn't seem like much when I said it. After all, I had often spent the night at the Algonquin or gotten home so late that she was already tossing in her dreams.

"Will you miss me?" Anna asked.

"I miss you now," I said. "Sometimes when I'm in the same room with you. The same bed with you."

"I know." She got up and went to the stove, where she poured herself half a cup more coffee and then, unexpectedly, brought the pot to the table and filled my cup as well. "I miss . . ." she began and then didn't finish.

What? I thought. What do you miss, Anna? Us? Sleeping naked together under winter blankets? Laughing together at the simplest things?

She interrupted my thoughts. "If you're gone for a week," she said, "or maybe two, that will give me time to prepare for the show at the Anderson Galleries. I need another five images, maybe ten. And I need to print everything in large format."

"Do you want me to stay away for two weeks deliberately? Or longer? Would that help?"

She didn't catch the tone of my voice for a moment, so absorbed she was in thinking of the walls of that gallery, the singular place to exhibit art photographs in the city, those walls naked until she adorned them. But then she looked up and, seeing my face, realized the deeper run of what I had said.

"Yes, it would help," she admitted. As she said it, the tears came.

CHAPTER THREE

I was on the earliest ferry out the following Monday morning, with a hastily packed valise of clothes and a letter of introduction to some distinguished soul named Augustus F. Sherman, secretary to the commissioner.

I landed at the dock just in front of the long, covered passageway leading up to the ornate doors of the main processing building. I admit to being impressed. It was not unlike the first time I saw Grand Central and realized that the world contained wonders—especially for me, a runaway mountain boy from a cove so isolated in the Southern highlands that it could have been on another planet from this place I had come to.

I let myself be carried along in the tide of busy, gossiping employees into the main building and then followed the better-dressed contingent up the stairs into the Great Hall. It was my first time in that high room and so early in the morning. It was mostly empty, an enormous, hollow place that foretold a thousand voices pitched in dramatic tones. It seemed to echo with tears and laughter from the day before, even as the new day beckoned across the harbor from the east.

I asked a woman dressed as a peasant sitting on the wide staircase where I might find this Augustus F. Sherman, and she looked up from the papers she was sorting. "Who are you to be asking?" she said, her face wary. I had assumed she was an immigrant left over from the day before, but her attitude and the tone of her voice had too much authority for that.

"A newcomer," I admitted. "I'm to be his assistant. Working with the appeals process."

She snorted. "Well, it needs all the help it can get," she said. "Secretary Sherman is upstairs on that balcony level you see above the hall. I'm told he's a late riser. You won't see him before midmorning."

"What do you do here on the island?" I asked.

"Who are you to be asking what I do here?" Her accent was from the middle of Europe, the syllables curt. The effect would have been harsh but her voice partly softened it. Her face, too, seemed chiseled until she smiled. High cheekbones and crystal-blue eyes.

"Stephen Robbins." And then, after a pause, "It's the first time I've stepped foot here, so I suspect I'm nobody."

She laughed and stood up. Then she reached out and cranked my hand up and down with a firm, dry grip. "I'm nobody too," she said. "Just a social worker." Her eyes flashed with humor as she said it. "Ludmila Kuchar is my name, and I have been here two whole months."

"Will you show me around," I asked, "before the Honorable Augustus what's-his-name puts in an appearance? Give me the lay of the land?"

She studied my face intently, judging me somehow against some internal rule. "I'm a busy woman, Mr. Steve Robbie, but I'll direct you to some of the island." She glanced up at the large, ornate clock at one end of the hall. "The first boat will be here in twenty minutes, and my day begins with a slam and a jump."

"Show me just a little bit then," I said and smiled reassuringly.

The first boat of the day was late, and so for almost thirty minutes, Ludmila Kuchar paraded me at a breakneck pace from the complex of buildings where the initial processing occurred down a long corridor that connected the three parts of the island.

"It is like the giant letter E, yes? You say that, don't you, in your queer Southern English? The letter E?" She didn't pause for me to answer. She walked so fast that I could barely match her stride for stride, all without seeming to pause for breath. I could only nod yes to her giant E.

"At the top of the E is Island 1, where all the drama takes place and where I do my work. Number 1. It is much tears and terror, love and kisses. Everything the human heart"—she reached over with a loosely closed fist to tap my chest—"can know. It is here that the immigrant comes into America.

"And here, in the second finger of letter E is Island 2, the main hospital, where the truly sick go to heal. To suffer their fevers, to retch and moan. If they do not get better, they go back. They go back to the empty world they came from. To Bohemia they go back, to Russia and Germany they go back. Africa."

"But—"

"No but. If they don't get well, they go back, broken and lost." She suddenly smiled, her face turned to me without slowing her pace. "But if they get well, ah, then they go ashore. Then they become . . ."

"What about . . . the isolation ward . . . ?" I gasped as we turned down the long corridor toward the last leg of her letter E.

She paused as if suddenly realizing how much time had passed. "We turn around now," she said and pointed. "There is the last finger of the hand. Island 3, where the patient is set off away from everything and everyone, where the contagion, if there is any contagion, does not spread. Some unfortunates go here and seem never to return."

"They . . . die?"

"Die or sent back. I do not know. Some are sick there for months."

"Are some released? Are some allowed to stay?"

"In America? Yes. After the days or the weeks, yes. But that is not my job, you understand? My job is with those in the Great Hall. My job is to help the ones who go straight through to . . ." She shook her head impatiently, searching for the words. We were almost back to the Great Hall where we had begun, and the dozens of people around us were scurrying to their posts. A ferry packed with immigrants was easing into the dock. "How do you say it?" she asked me.

"You help them survive?" I guessed. "To not be cheated? To land unharmed?"

She smiled again, with all the intense, glittering blue of her eyes. "Yes," she said. "Unharmed survived."

"Who in the world do you work for?" I asked.

"The YMCA," she said proudly.

CHAPTER FOUR

Augustus Frederick Sherman was fastidious. Dressed in a solid black suit, well cut to fit his portly form and brushed just that morning. Thinning silver hair and an old-world goatee. A well-polished monocle at the end of a black ribbon was pinned to his lapel; he held it in his hand and waved it for emphasis.

He regarded me from behind his desk as if I were one of his aliens and he was trying to determine my type . . . Norwegian, Austrian, Sicilian.

"From whence do you hail, Mr. Robbins? From your accent, I assume it is one of our Southern provinces?"

"North Carolina," I said evenly. "Though the accent might fool you. I'm mountain bred, and we're a different animal entirely from the rest of the state."

"German then," he guessed. And then he stood up, leaned over his desk, and peered through his monocle. "No, no. I don't see it. Not German. Not with that round head. There's Celtic blood in your veins."

I had to laugh. "You have exactly the same tone of voice, Mr. Sherman, as Uncle Jeter used in judging horse flesh."

"Was he a sufficient judge, your uncle?"

"One of the best. Always came out on top in the trade lot."

He sat back down. "Then I say Celtic. Of mixed bloodlines."

"A mongrel by any measure," I admitted. "And a runaway in my youth."

"Oh my! Then may I say Irish? The Irish have a hard time staying put anywhere for long."

I nodded with a smile. The old man—for he was old in the summer of 1920 when I met him—was irresistible. "Not just Irish," I said. "You'll have to be more precise than that."

"Oh well then. It's obvious. Scots-Irish. Last port of call for your ancestors was Dublin, or more probably, Belfast."

I smiled.

"You have the slight build. And dark skin for those eyes. Black Irish some would call you."

I smiled and nodded.

"And may I say, a truly wonderful scar on that face of yours. Were you in the war?"

I didn't smile this time. "Only indirectly. A mountain sheriff gave me this just before he died."

He bowed his head slightly by way of sympathy and glanced at the letter of introduction I'd given him. "And so you come to us as the hired investigator. A hard man."

"Hard and soft," I said, "as the occasion requires."

"See," he said, "there you have it. The Scots and the Irish, mingled blood." I didn't reply, and after a moment, he continued. "So you are here to find out what happened to Ciara McManaway."

I nodded but didn't speak. Now that he was wound up, I didn't want to interrupt him. "I'm afraid that you've caught us somewhat with our pants down as regards Miss McManaway. I know that's a vulgar phrase, but I suspect you'll understand what I mean. . . . Her name appears on the manifest for the ship that brought her from Cork. Her name appears again in our records on the day she was initially examined here." He gestured down toward the Great Hall two stories below us. "Apparently, the doctor who examined her suspected she might be pregnant, and so she was sent first to the hospital for confirmation and then to the isolation wards for long-term convalescence."

"And then?"

"And then she disappeared entirely."

"How long did the process you describe take? From the ship to the initial examination to the hospital to . . . ?"

"To the isolation wards. Two or three days perhaps."

"Perhaps?"

"You have to understand that we're still getting back on our feet after the war. In the years leading up to 1917, we were fully staffed and fully operational. Then, during the war, the influx from Europe slowed dramatically, and the government set us to guarding anarchists and socialists while they were awaiting deportation." As careful as Mr. Sherman was with the English language, some serious disdain had crept into his tone when he described the war years. As if he took it personally.

"I gather that's not what Ellis Island is for? War and deportation, I mean."

"You take it correctly. This beautiful facility is meant to bring into our great body politic the new blood that keeps it vital and flourishing, not act as some giant sewage station to flush the unwanted from our shores."

This was a little much—he was starting to speechify—but I nodded encouragingly. "If Ciara McManaway was pregnant, and you sound as if you're not sure, why was she sent to the isolation wards? I've never known a swollen belly to be contagious."

He chuckled. "I take your point. No, pregnancy itself isn't contagious, but the lax moral code that led to that condition is. And as you can imagine, it's not part of what we want to encourage here on the island."

"So you put her away where no one can see her."

"Not just her as an individual, but any young woman whom we examine for entry into the country and discover is in that condition. If she walks through those doors into our Great Hall obviously pregnant and has no husband, no father for her child, and—this is important—no one who is already here to claim her, then we send her back."

I stifled the urge to tell him just what I thought of his policy. "Send her back or send her into isolation?"

"If she's far enough along in the gestation period or if we think the return journey might endanger her health, then we care for her in the isolation hospital until her delivery. You must understand, Mr. Robbins, we are not unfeeling monsters on this island—it's just that we are charged with the implementation of very strict policies. And after all, the situation we are discussing happens very rarely."

"Once a woman in this very rare situation delivers her child, what happens to her?"

"By special dispensation of federal law, a child who is born here on Ellis Island is not automatically a citizen. After the birth, both mother and child are returned to the country of origin for their own health and safety. So you see, we take very good care of those for whom we are responsible."

"But not of her," I said.

"Her?"

"Not Ciara McManaway. You lost track of her completely."

CHAPTER FIVE

When he learned that I planned to live on the islands for as long as it took me to find the missing woman, Sherman offered me quarters on the third floor of the main building. Which I politely declined.

"I want to stay as close as possible to the last place she was seen. Or at least the last place where there's any record of her. I assume that's the isolation wards?"

He nodded and peered at me. "Yes, yes," he muttered reflectively. "On Island 3." And then suddenly he chuckled and rubbed at his goatee in pleasure. "You're in luck, Mr. Robbins. Unless I'm mistaken, there is no one currently in our measles pavilion, which is in an out-of-the-way corner on Island 3. The second floor is where we normally keep the dangerously insane who also suffer from contagious disease. I trust you don't mind a few metal doors and bars on the windows."

"I can stand it for a few weeks."

"Ah . . . so you think you're actually going to find Miss McManaway, do you?" It was the first false note in our interview, this sudden wink of cynicism.

I shrugged. "It's what I do. Find things."

"Including people?"

"Sure."

When I stood to collect my valise and go, I noticed a series of framed photographs on the walls of Sherman's office. Photographs of an astonishing variety of people, of all colors and costumes, male and female. My breath caught in my throat; this sort of display always reminded me of Anna, and our parting had been neither fond nor reassuring.

"Did you take these?" I asked.

Sherman rose and walked around the desk to stand beside me. He gestured with his monocle at one photograph of a line of men facing the camera, all wearing the same getup. "Russian Cossacks," he said. "All arrived together on the same ship. And when I asked them to pose, they all retrieved their native dress from their trunks along with those gorgeous knives you see at their belts."

Beside the Cossacks was a photo of four blond children wearing wooden shoes. Beside that, a group of very dark-skinned Africans, two men and a woman, wearing native dress. "What are the odds," I asked, "that you might have taken a photograph of the McManaway girl, or that there is an image of her somewhere in her travel papers?"

He shook his elegant head brusquely. "I took no photographs of the passengers from her ship." His tone was dismissive. "There were no interesting subjects among them."

I had to ask for directions from a guard and two nurses before I found the psychopathic ward up under the roof of Building E on Island 3. The hospital that made up Island 3 was basically one long line of medical pavilions separated by anywhere from thirty to a hundred feet of grass between them, all joined by a long central passageway covered against the weather. Most of the pavilions were two or even three stories high, allowing space on the second floor for more patients when, before the war, the island had seen enormous traffic of human souls. Some of the buildings also had nurses' quarters on the third floor, which housed those specially trained to care for immigrants with measles, tuberculosis, or influenza. As I wandered around in search of the insane ward, it became obvious that most of the second- and third-floor wards were standing empty now with dusty sheets thrown over the beds. Lots of locked doors and barely cracked windows. At least twice, I thought I could hear mice or rats scurrying in the next room.

I knew I had found my new home on the second floor of Building E when I came face-to-face with metal doors under a stark sign that read **Psychopathic Care Unit – No Unauthorized Personnel Allowed**. The space within was broken up into individual cells along a barren hallway, almost as if designed for solitary confinement; more jail than hospital. I chose the last room on the left because it let light in from barred windows on two sides. The room smelled faintly of disinfectant, even though a thin layer of dust had settled silently over the desk and chair. Out the southernmost window, I could see the Statue of Liberty lifting her torch into the sky not half a mile away. I threw my valise onto the sagging frame of one of the two beds and left a note for any staff person who might wander in even though the place looked and felt deserted. I put both my federal ID and my letter of introduction from Sherman into my jacket pocket, figuring I would need those in my wanderings.

Then I went out to have a look around that part of the island where the missing girl had last been seen. More than anything, I wanted to get a feel for the place, especially the nooks and crannies where things and people went to disappear.

Before the afternoon was done, I had poked my nose into a dozen wards and been turned away from several more. I had chatted up a half dozen nurses, most of whom seemed more bored than anything else. The two doctors I talked to both pointed me toward the hospital director's office, which was hidden away in the main administration building. They said that I would have to talk to the man in charge of all things medical, a Dr. Knox, who ran the place and lived with his family in an old Victorian structure at the tip of the island.

I avoided Knox and his house, having had enough of the administrative personality for one day, and after poking around the various wards went out into the open space between the Island 2 hospital wing and the Island 3 isolation wards to think.

It was late afternoon, after five, and a cool breeze smelling faintly of salt water was blowing steadily in from the east. The long summer evening was upon us, and I felt the need for grass under my feet and smoke in my lungs. I sat my weary self down on a set of concrete steps and set fire to a cigar. I'd been there less than ten hours, and it was already more than a little overwhelming. As if I'd landed in a different country, with dozens of buildings and hundreds of people, a small city unto itself, with a large part of the population flowing in and out over its borders like the waves that broke over the breakwater rocks that rimmed the island.

The five or six acres between the isolation wards and the regular hospital—between Islands 2 and 3 of Ludmila's giant letter E—was mostly a large lake of shallow salt water open to the ocean on one end, slowly being filled in by barges hauling earth and rocks from subway construction in the city. As I sat and smoked, letting my mind drift through what I'd seen and heard, I watched as a steam shovel dumped the day's last barge load of wet sand and rock up against the embankment where I sat. A woman's shoe floated lazily in the dirty, gray water beside the barge, and I remembered the Nameless Man's offhand remark that the fishes must have dined on Ciara McManaway by now.

CHAPTER SIX

When I returned to my room in the psychopathic ward, I found a woman dressed like a nurse seated on the bed beside my valise, painstakingly going through my clothes and other belongings.

"Find what you're looking for?" I said from the doorway.

She spun around to face me and then grinned. "No," she admitted and blushed ever so slightly. "But I know who you are anyway."

Her voice had the quick, skipping syllables that suggested somewhere north of the Mason-Dixon Line but without the harsh, nasal tone of the city. When she stood up, she was almost as tall as me, broad-shouldered but thin-waisted. She had a ruddy complexion, with dark-brown hair and chocolate eyes. Full brown lips. The nurse's uniform didn't do her body any favors, but the way she turned—first her shoulders and arms, then her hips—suggested a feral awareness behind the starched white cloth.

"Who am I then?" I asked.

She took a step toward me, but I didn't move out of the doorway. "You're the federal op that is looking for the Irish girl. Robinson or something like that. Your clothes don't have your name sewn into them."

I laughed at the thought. "No. My clothes come off a rack or out of a pile on the counter. Nothing there about me."

"The letter you've been showing around the wards says we're to offer you our full cooperation, answer any questions, unlock any doors. The girls tell me that you're good-looking except for the scar, but damn if they don't each remember your name differently. Ryan or Russell . . . Richards maybe?"

"What kind of full cooperation are you willing to offer?"

She put her head back and laughed. Her eyes gleamed with humor, full of light to be so dark. "I'm so cooperative," she said, "that I have a bottle of bootleg gin in my room and two glasses. Which means something, by the way. The whole damn island is dry as dust."

"Why would you share it with me if it's so rare? You don't even know my name."

"Mine is Lucy Paul, in case you're interested. American Medical Association. Ethicist, activist, and general, all-around pain in the ass. Sent to find out why the current death rate in the hospital here is so much higher than before the war." She reached out to shake my hand.

I stayed between her and the door, but I did step forward and take her hand. The skin was dry and warm. Rough from hard work and constant washing, but not calloused. "Robbins," I said.

"Stephen," she replied. "Your first name. Every single woman in the wards remembered your first name."

"Is that stuff you said true? Medical Association? Investigator?"

She nodded. "True as hell. How about you? Federal operative? Missing persons expert? Sticking your nose into every cupboard and closet that you can put your hand to?"

"Every single cupboard that isn't locked, Miss Paul."

"Lucy. And you can let go of my hand. I won't run."

This time I laughed; I hadn't realized. "Tell me why you were going through my things, and I'll turn you loose."

"It's my job. Anything unusual belongs to me. And you're unusual enough that I need to know who you really are and what you're up to. And if you're who you say you are, we can work together." She squeezed my hand. "Savvy?"

"Maybe. I am Stephen Robbins, just as you suspected." I let her hand go, finally. "And I am looking for one particular girl named Ciara McManaway."

"Dead or alive?"

"Sure, dead or alive. And since I've been here a day, and you've been here . . . ?"

"Six months."

"Six months! Then you know a hell of a lot more than I do."

"Good. I'm glad you see how it is. And Stephen . . ."

I raised my eyebrows.

"Why stop with your Irish girl? Between the missing and the dead, we have two or three disappearances a week around here."

CHAPTER SEVEN

W hat do you mean, disappearances?"

"People suddenly dying who have nothing wrong with them, or at least nothing fatal. And sometimes, like with your Irish girl, disappear entirely. Physically, corporeally gone."

Her face had lost its earlier luster. Darkened along with the tone of her voice.

"They can't just disappear. It's an island, for God's sake." My mind raced with the possibilities. Bodies sent ashore on the ferries that were in constant motion during the daylight hours. Or maybe . . . "Maybe the ones who disappear aren't dead. Maybe they're taking themselves off somewhere or being taken."

She nodded. "I know. I've thought of that. White slavery . . ."

"Are the missing always girls . . . women?"

"No. Mostly women but also some men." She shook her head roughly as if to clear the uncomfortable thoughts like spiderweb out of her mind. Then she forced a wan smile. "How about that drink? I can scrounge some lemons out of the infirmary kitchen and some ice from the nurses' quarters . . . make the gin worth the effort."

I rolled my tired shoulders slowly. I could feel the weight of the long day in my neck, creeping up into the back of my skull. And beneath the skull, there was the thought of Anna, who was somewhere doing something extraordinary without me.

"I need a drink," I admitted finally.

What Lucy Paul didn't know is that before Anna, down in the mountains of North Carolina, I'd had my own struggles with the bottle. Never incapacitated, or at least so rarely as not to count, but struggles enough. Then came Anna and the complexities of a life reborn. I had all but stopped drinking, my body and skin taken up with another kind of lust, another form of satiety. Now, though . . . here and now . . . a drink seemed like something the gods had provided for my pent-up soul.

We couldn't mix up our lemon juice, sugar, ice, and gin in Lucy's room because she shared it with three other nurses, one of whom was off shift and reading in bed. So we built our drinks in the back corner of the infirmary kitchen and carried them out into a grassy park on the harbor side of the island. The wind had picked up as the afternoon dimmed down to dusk, and Lucy led me to a picnic table between two of the measles pavilions. The windows all around us were closed, protecting the patients within against the evening air. Our little spot felt almost empty, isolated even.

Even so, we fell to whispering, in tune with the sudden quiet of dusk.

"That's a fine scar you have there, Stephen," she said at one point. "I assume you got it during the war."

"You might say that." I sipped at my gin. It was cold and tart against my tongue.

"But not over there?" She waved her mug loosely to the east, toward Europe.

"No. . . . I got it down in North Carolina, in the mountains where I'm from."

"Whatever it was turned that patch in your hair gray. How did you—"

"Stop asking questions long enough, and I'll tell you."

She giggled, the gin having begun its play.

27

"I was the inspector general of an internment camp in a place called Hot Springs. My charges were—"

"Two thousand German noncombatants. Sailors and such. I read about it after I came back from France." She glanced at me.

"That's right. That's my Hot Springs. My hotel. My Germans."

"And you were in charge?"

"Try not to act so surprised."

"I'm actually not surprised. You have a certain way about you."

"Well, I was in charge right up till the local sheriff decided to take one of my Germans away in the middle of the night, and the two of us got into a—"

"A tussle?"

I laughed out. "Sure. A tussle. And he gave me this with a gun barrel across the face. Broke my nose and my cheekbone."

"I read about that too. Didn't you kill him for it?" She seemed more intrigued than dismayed.

I shook my head. "I stood trial, which is probably what you read about. But no, I didn't kill him."

She studied my face with those cocoa eyes, the dark irises growing in the dusk so that the whites of her eyes seemed to disappear.

"A woman I know shot him down when he was about to finish me off."

She smiled. "I like your way with women," she said, "or rather their way with you."

"How about you?" I asked. "You in the war?"

I asked it randomly, just letting the gin talk.

"I was an Army Medical Corp nurse in England and France." She raised her mug as if in salute. "I have a nice scar too, but I can't show it to you."

I returned her salute with my own drink. "How did you get from nurse to investigator? Or was that something you made up to justify plundering my things?"

She didn't laugh. "No, Stephen Robbins, I didn't make it up. My scar isn't from a German shell. It's from getting stabbed by a British doctor who I caught stealing morphine." Mist was blowing in now off the harbor, and she shivered from the sudden chill—inner or outer, I couldn't tell. But then, suddenly, she brightened again. "It's a small scar, though. He tried to stick a scalpel between my ribs."

"Did you kill him for it?"

"No, but I should have. Stealing morphine wasn't all he did. All he tried to do."

"You cup is empty." I reached across the table and poured half the gin left in my own mug into hers.

CHAPTER EIGHT

Lucy Paul walked me back to the psych ward before we parted ways, stopping on the first floor of my empty building to collect an armful of blankets and a pillow for me from a locked closet.

She came all the way up to my hallway under the Psychopathic Care Unit sign. Led me by the hand down the hallway to my room and reached inside the door to punch the button beside the door that turned on the bare electric light bulb hanging from the ceiling.

"Don't worry. I'm not coming in," she said before I had a chance to ask. "I just want to make sure . . ."

"I can take care of myself."

"I bet. It's just that . . . this whole place at night . . . when the wind whistles around the corners and rattles the windows. I like sharing my gin with you, and I don't want you to disappear into the mist before morning."

We were standing mostly in the dark, with a metal door swung shut behind us. I had the strangest impulse that I should kiss her—or rather that she wanted me to kiss her—in the growing gloom. But the ghost of Anna stood between us, and I didn't reach out. The moment passed, and she was gone.

That night I dreamed of . . . *mountains.*

I was on foot, high in the hills of home. Boots on my feet and my father's deer rifle in my hands. That old denim barn coat, worn through at the elbows, and a slouch hat so stained by sweat and faded by sun that it fit the contours of my head like a second skin. Lost, I believe I was, in the dream and in the woods, searching for the faint trace of a trail down through the deep walls of a hemlock and laurel cove to the creek below. And along the creek to the river. Despite the rifle in my hands, I wasn't tracking meat for the pot but rather being followed. . . . Being trailed from behind by something larger, older, something vicious . . . something I didn't want to meet. I was dimly aware in the dream that this was something I didn't even want to see.

And if I didn't find my trail, didn't make my way down to the river and the old turnpike that snaked beside it, I was in danger. My rifle wouldn't protect me, nor the knife in my belt. The danger that stalked me was darker, stronger meat than that. This danger breathed the air and walked on two legs. And should it catch me, I might never wake . . . might never seek light again.

The next morning—only my second on the island—I tracked Dr. Howard Knox to his lair in the last building on Island 3. His secretary, a bored young woman with platinum blonde hair and dramatic makeup, let me cool my heels for ten minutes even though I could hear the good doctor through the half-open door to the inner office. He was talking to someone in a high, nasal voice, someone he must have liked well enough, for his conversation was interrupted from time to time by a chortle at some shared joke.

I couldn't make out who he was talking to, though, because that person's voice was so quiet that it came through as little more than a hum. Maybe male, maybe female; impossible to tell.

I caught the secretary's heavily shadowed eye, nodded my head at the office door, and mouthed, "Who?"

She only shrugged her pretty shoulders and mouthed silently back at me, "What?"

I smiled. She smiled. I decided she wasn't real. Maybe a mechanical doll.

Just at that unreal moment, a stout, middle-aged woman in a perfectly starched nurse's uniform came through the door from the inner office, still talking over her shoulder to the doctor. "Later this afternoon," she hummed, her voice still so soft that it could have been bees buzzing or faint, faraway music.

She ignored the secretary, but as she passed, she favored me with a smile. And in that smile was the essence of a mother's love. Or more like a grandmother's love. Complete and unconditional. That smile went straight from her mouth to her eyes, which crinkled with unfeigned affection. Later, when I had seen more of it, I would think of that smile as a visible beatitude or a blessing. In the moment, it felt like such an expression of affection that I turned unconsciously toward her face, as toward the sun.

And then she was gone, through the outer door and down the hall, her spotless nurse's shoes squeaking on the heavily waxed floor. "Who was that?" I said aloud to the mechanical doll.

"Who?" she echoed. And after a pause, "You mean Miss Taylor?"

I gave up on her, stood without being invited, and walked into Dr. Knox's office. I paused just inside the doorway and cleared my throat to get his attention. The doctor was tall, with a long, thin, pale face, made even longer by a steeply receding hairline. He stood and reached across his desk to shake my hand. His hand was also long, with the thin, pale fingers of a surgeon . . . or a safecracker. "I believe you've been waiting," he said. "I apologize."

I introduced myself and shared both the letter from Sherman and a glance at my federal badge. Knox was suitably impressed but quickly pointed me elsewhere. "Do you know what it is to have an administrative post, Mr. Robbins?"

I thought back to the giant hotel in North Carolina and the internment camp we had built around it. "I'm afraid I do," I admitted.

"Then you'll know I rarely leave this office. The papers pile up around me, and when I look up next, high tide has come and gone, and my wife is ringing the bell for dinner." He didn't meet my eyes while he said this.

"I'm sure your secretary is a great deal of help to you."

He glanced at me sharply to see if I was serious. I wasn't, and he knew it.

He grinned in reply. "No, but she's . . ."

"Entertaining to talk to?"

He paused and grinned again. "Of course. But back to the matter at hand. The truth is I want the disappearance of the McManaway girl dealt with even more than you do."

"Is the good congressman holding your feet to the fire?"

His face, if anything, became even paler. "Worse. He's putting heat on the new commissioner to clean house. I've already gotten called over to Island 1 for a tongue-lashing."

"You like it out here in the harbor, Dr. Knox? Don't want to leave?"

"Yes . . . I've been here since the end of the war, and I'm still trying to bring everything back. Plus my research. Once we have both hospitals back up to operational strength, I can get back to my research."

"What do you study?"

"Intelligence."

I waited.

"I am developing ways of measuring intelligence that are free of cultural or linguistic bias."

"Do you experiment on immigrants?"

He didn't hesitate. "Of course I do. Many of those who are sent to us in the isolation wards are not capable of functioning in American society and will become wards of the state. If I can discover ways of identifying them, think what a service that will be."

I nodded, wondering if he, like Sherman, would automatically assume that certain races were more intelligent than others. I thought that probably he would.

"Who has been here long enough to understand the gears and levers of this place?" I asked. "Who was here during the war, for example?"

He thought for a moment. "Talk to Miss Taylor," he said, "and her nurses. Every hospital I've ever worked in, it's the nurses who know."

"Miss Taylor is the sweet-looking woman who just left?" I asked.

He smiled and nodded before looking down again at his littered desk, meaning to dismiss me with the gesture.

I didn't believe him that all he did was shove papers around all day. That was too easy an out for him. But I did believe him about the nurses. They were women, after all, and women always know where the hidden things lie buried.

CHAPTER NINE

Blanche Taylor was more than happy to talk with me. Her "office" was at the opposite end of Island 3 from Dr. Knox's and as different as two such spaces could be. Dr. Knox's was what you'd expect from a hospital administrator—the walls and floor an institutional gray, the desk an army-surplus green, the furniture so utilitarian that my ass hurt from just sitting in the man's presence.

Head Nurse Taylor's office wasn't an office; it was the living room from your aunt's house remembered from childhood, only more comfortable and more inviting. She did have a table covered with clipboards and a few files, neatly labeled and arranged. But the table was pushed up against the wall beside a sofa, which was upholstered in bright floral patterns. There was a rug and coffee table before the sofa and remarkably comfortable chairs, one to either side, upholstered in the same bright flowers from some faraway tropical paradise.

She sat back in one of these chairs as we talked, her legs neatly crossed at the ankle in spotless white hose. My impression of her in Knox's office was that of stoutness, middle age or beyond, and I still thought her to be fifty at least. Older than me by ten years. But there was something about her that let you know she had been a stylish, even attractive young woman. Her hair was a distinct brown turning slowly to dark gray, swept back from her forehead. Her face was creased but by the wrinkles of many smiles, the tracks of past laughter. Her blue eyes twinkled like crystal.

She seemed made for her nurse's whites, and its tight, starched contours didn't seem at all stiff on her. One small but telling detail—a brooch in the form of a large silver cross was affixed to her uniform just in the middle of her chest where the top button would normally be.

Again, I was struck by how a calmness radiated from her, and I was reminded of the last time I had visited my mother back home in the high mountains before she died. My mother had seemed to be half in this world and half in the next, and because of that, a certain light shown obliquely through her wasted form as through a prism.

And so it seemed now with the woman in front of me. She was anything but frail, and yet, there was an ethereal quality to her that was mesmerizing.

She had prepared hot tea when I came in, and we were each sipping our cup as we talked. She seeming to cherish each swallow of hers; me wishing for a shot of something hard to give it some spine.

"I didn't remember ever seeing Miss McManaway," she said sorrowfully, "but then there are so many."

"So many unmarried, pregnant girls?" I asked.

"Oh, not that. The good Lord preserves us from that sad fate. No, I mean that there are so many wandering souls that require our care. Our love even. Does it embarrass you if I speak of love, Mr. Robbins?"

I shook my head. "I've heard that it's a force in the world."

She absolutely beamed. "Oh, it is, it is. A force beyond reckoning. And my nurses and I mean to be a veritable army on its behalf. We are paid for our work, I will admit, but I promise you that once I saw this island and what it means, I would come here *gratis*, without a single thin dime of payment."

"I know what *gratis* means," I said. I was trying to maintain some of who I was and why I was there in the face of her almost blinding sweetness.

"Of course you do. Your erudition would make your mother proud."

I nodded, ignoring *erudition*. "What do you think happened to

Miss McManaway?" I prodded her. "After all, she was in the care of you and your nurses. For a short time, at least. . . ."

Tears, honest-to-God tears, beaded up on her lower eyelids, and for a brief moment, I was ashamed of having needled her. "I don't know, dear Stephen. I don't know, and how I have agonized over that. It is in the form of a confession that I tell you this. Just as I have prayed for insight into her case." She sat her teacup carefully on the low table between us and raised her arms in the air. "I have spent some hours on my knees, I can tell you, pleading with my God to send me a clue, an insight, anything."

"Who was the last person to see her alive?"

"Again, I don't know. I believe our own Nurse Thompson may have been, but I'm not sure because it's so hard to pin down when she went missing. I did interview Nurse Thompson, who would have examined her. Even with that, I haven't uncovered much of value. But of course, you should retrace my steps. With your refined skills as an interlocutor, you may see through our scanty official memories into a deeper vale of truth. . . . Mr. Robbins, can I ask you a personal question?"

"Ask away. Just don't expect an answer that will suit you."

"How did you come to this line of work . . . this detecting? You seem like the nicest young man."

"I am not," I said. "I'm not so very young and even less nice."

Her face lit up at this scrap of humor.

"But I am stubborn, Miss Taylor. And I have a gift for finding things—things that are missing."

"Second sight, perhaps?"

"Second and third and fourth even. Especially if the missing thing is in human form."

She sat her cup down again and clapped her hands together in delight. "Then it is the gift of a benevolent God that you have come to us. A blessing you are."

I smiled in return, unable to penetrate the inches-thick skin of her love for the world.

CHAPTER TEN

Nurse Taylor was a study in contrast to her assistant, a much younger woman who had a mincing femininity about her, whose every gesture as she led me down the corridor in search of Nurse Thompson seemed to mimic those of her elder. The problem was that this woman, Nurse Adams, had to be one of the largest women I'd ever seen. Not fat, not by an ounce, but as tall and strong as a German wrestler. Where Nurse Taylor's face seemed to radiate calm, this woman—I began calling her Helga in my mind—seemed to send out a constant nervous energy, like a radio station that never goes off the air. She outweighed me by at least sixty or seventy pounds, and her feet struck the wooden floor in violent determination as we walked. I had shaken her hand when Nurse Taylor introduced us, and her right hand had swallowed mine, almost as an adult's would that of a child.

She was friendly, talkative, explaining the purpose of one ward after another as we went in search of Thompson, and I asked her if she was assigned to give tours of the isolation wards for visitors. "Before the war," she replied. "Everything good was before the war."

"Everything?"

"Except Miss Taylor. We all love Miss Taylor."

"I can see why. She's like the magical aunt we never really had." I was mocking the head nurse, trying to distance myself from the effect she'd had on me.

But Helga was oblivious to my tone. "She is, isn't she. You can tell what she's like the very first time you meet her."

"What else was better before the war?"

"We got a much different sort of immigrant before the war."

I looked up to study her profile as we walked. "What do you mean? Were they better than what you get now?"

She emitted a shrill whistling sound, and after a moment, I realized she was laughing. "They spoke English, or at least most of them did. French, Dutch. Some Germans before the kaiser closed the borders and then later when we seized his ships."

"Were they white? Is that what you're saying?"

She nodded so hard that the nurse's cap shook in her thick hair. "Mostly. Mostly they looked like you and me, Nordic like you and me. But more than that, they weren't these Eastern Europeans, these Russians, these Polacks, Ukrainians, Lithuanians. I bet you ain't even heard of Lithuania." The whistling sound again. "Plus these Black Africans like we occasionally get now. And you know the worst of all?"

"I can't guess."

"The Gypsies. Romanians, or so we're told. Filthy people, wherever they come from. Nasty, dirty people with no way to tell who is married to who, if they even get married. And the children run wild."

"Well, hell, that's a discouraging state of affairs. Who did you used to get?"

She stopped suddenly, her shoes squeaking on the waxed floors. Turned to face me, except that she had to look down to really face me. "The nice, pale British. The sweet French, so passionate with their cheese. The Germans, nice people if you ask me, leaving aside the kaiser and all that trouble he started. And the Irish. The sad, merry Irish, always singing. Always crying. Even the Irish aren't that bad."

"More like us?" I asked, beginning to sense the map inside her very large head.

Again that passionate nod, the cap almost pulling loose from her hair. "Yes, Mr. Stephen . . ." She paused to blush. "It's Stephen, isn't it? Yes, more like us. You can understand what they're saying even when you don't speak their language. They ain't so outlandish, if you know what I mean. Even their diseases are something we're used to, something we can deal with. They's one man and one woman together makes a family." The whistling again. "And you can tell whose children is whose when they line them up and tell them to behave."

I was fascinated with this giant woman. She was like a bubbling fountain—a *loud* bubbling fountain. "Not like those fiendish Gypsies," I said, just to encourage her.

"Oh, my goodness God. Them Gypsies. You couldn't tell who went with who in that crowd. One man might have two women or three. One woman trails a string of men like fish she's pulled out of the ocean. And the children, my God, the children. They run in packs and steal anything that ain't nailed down to the ground. Scalpels, drugs, sheets off the beds."

"Do you get many Gypsies on Island 3?"

"No." She poked me in the shoulder for emphasis. "No, they're too healthy. But if we did . . . let me tell you, Mr. Stephen, we'd know what to do with them."

"Send them back . . . to Romania?"

"Maybe." She winked. Miss Nurse Helga winked. It was slow and ponderous, like a leather shade being lowered and raised again over a window. But it was an honest-to-God wink. Conveying what? *"Maybe* we'd send them back," she added. More whistling.

She turned to proceed. And when she did, she took my upper arm in her giant's hand to propel me forward on our search.

We finally found the elusive Nurse Thompson in the influenza ward, where the immigrants who arrived at the island sick with the flu germ were cared for. And just before Adams, my dainty giantess, left me in the anteroom to the flu ward, she leaned far over to whisper. "My name is Ethel," is what she said.

Sounds like Helga, I thought as I smiled up at her. But didn't say.

CHAPTER ELEVEN

Nurse Thompson was a man. And yes, I was caught off guard, for while it is more common now, in 1920, his slight form came as a surprise package. He was a small man in almost every way. Carefully groomed, precise, with thinning sandy hair that kept falling in his eyes while he talked.

The thing is that he didn't talk, at least not so that you could hear him. When he spoke, he leaned toward you with an earnest, open face and moved his lips. There might be a whisper of sound, you could hear a word or two, and you felt as though you mostly understood him.

During our first exchanges, I would say "come again" or "would you repeat that," and he would smile in his friendly way and patiently repeat himself just as before. You had to stare directly into his face, mostly at his mouth and eyes, to have even a prayer of understanding him.

When he came out into the anteroom of the flu ward in response to Ethel Adams's summons, he removed a surgical mask and gloves and threw them into a trash bin with a lid and then carefully washed his hands, all in a routine that felt more like a prelude to conversation than sound medical practice. He then shook my hand with a dry, firm grip that wasn't threatening but decidedly masculine, perhaps even friendly.

After the initial pleasantries—during which he actually read my note of introduction from Sherman rather than just glancing at it—I asked him to tell me about Ciara McManaway. He smiled, leaned toward me, and replied. Here is what I think he said:

"She was a sweet girl. Twenty-two years old according to her papers, but I think probably younger. She wore very loose clothes, but upon examination was obviously pregnant. Fifth or sixth month." He held up fingers to help me grasp the five or six months. "Her teeth were sound, which is unusual for the Irish. Her face full and freckled. Her hair a dark red, almost wine-colored."

"What color were her eyes?"

"Green." He pointed at an army blanket folded on the table to emphasize the color.

"Was she sick or just pregnant?"

He shook his head no. "Not sick." He smiled at the irony of this.

"Why was she in the influenza ward if she wasn't sick?"

He wrinkled his forehead in consternation and then mouthed, "Oh. I rotate through several wards in the hospital. Where I am needed."

"Like a utility infielder?"

He grinned. "Exactly. And because she was pregnant, which is fairly unusual here, she was alone in a ward by herself. And so I would leave my other assignment three or four times a day and go check on her. Pulse." He pointed at his wrist. "Eyes. Throat. Blood pressure. Take her something to read."

"She could read?"

He nodded.

"Is that unusual?"

"The immigration officials don't let them in if they can't read at least a little in their native language."

"What happened to her? Where did she go?"

Here he paused. For the first time, he seemed unsure. "I don't know." He shrugged his shoulders in painful admission. "One morning when I went into the ward where she stayed, she was gone. Her bed was made, her shoes and her rosary were gone. It was as if she'd been processed and sent on to another location. Her paperwork was there, on a clipboard, but the girl herself had disappeared. Nothing."

"Did you ask about her? The other doctors, nurses?"

"Of course." He was emphatic. "And they were as surprised as I. We searched. We notified the other medical units on Island 2. We called in the guards. A day went by, then two, then three. Nothing." His eyes narrowed with emotion. "I kept asking Taylor and Adams, but nothing. Nothing."

"Where are her things?" I asked. "The clothes she came in? Her personal possessions? Her papers?"

"Nurse Taylor must have her file," he mouthed. "But her clothes . . ." Again he paused, longer this time. And a smile teased his lips. "The carpetbag she was so careful with. There I may be able to help you." He pointed at himself and then at me to emphasize the assistance he was offering.

After checking in with the other nurse on the ward, he took me down to the administration building at the center of the island. There, he showed his ID to the lazy guard on duty and we were passed through to a long room in the basement, each wall of which was full of cubicles, perhaps three feet square. They were all numbered starting with 101. He took me to cubicle 313, which contained a thick woolen garment of some indeterminate color, gray or brown. When we pulled the garment out, it took on the character of a heavy shawl, smelling of salt and sweat, onions and potatoes eaten shipboard, and beneath it all, the must of peat fires on stone hearths. Behind the shawl was a stained carpetbag.

"I'm taking the bag," I said. "I need to dig into it in private, peel it back layer by layer."

The guard seated at his desk at the end of the long room sat up straighter, yawned, and began to take an interest in us.

"I don't think he will let you have it," Thompson replied. "You must have the claim ticket and permission from the authorities."

"Even if she's dead?"

He seemed surprised. "She may not be dead. She may return for her possessions."

I resisted the urge to tell him exactly how dead my instincts said she was. "Can't you remove it? You're her nurse."

"Not without Taylor's chit. Her note . . . her . . ."

"I know what a chit is, damn it. I don't want to go through her things here."

"But you can trust the—"

I interrupted him in a fierce whisper. "No. No, I can't trust the guard or the authorities or Nurse Taylor." I leaned in closer to whisper. "Somebody made that girl vanish. Somebody who knows their way around this place front and back, first and last, day and night. And until I know who, everybody is a suspect."

He pointed at himself and mouthed, "Me?"

"Yes, you. Although you don't have enough power and say-so to make much of a suspect." I smiled at him. "Besides, you are far too kind a man to make your own patients disappear." I glanced around the baggage room. "I'll come back tonight," I said. "When the guard is gone."

"The door will be locked."

"Not to me," I said.

CHAPTER TWELVE

Lucy Paul sat at my table in the nurses' dining room at supper, pretending she didn't know me—or at least didn't know me any further down than did the other women. The meal was so plain—a gray stew with little beef and hard white rolls—that the saltshaker went steadily round the table from hand to hand.

Lucy found me afterward back at our spot from the evening before, where we'd shared a drink and our stories of the war. This time she was wearing dark slacks and a pale-yellow shirt. Low brown shoes. They were her own clothes, and she looked comfortable in them. The slacks, though, caught my eye and held it. They were tailored to fit her, and the back side of her was worth fitting.

"Where's the gin?" I asked. And when she didn't smile, I added, "You look like you could use a nip."

That brought just the hint of a smile. "I need more than a nip," she admitted. "But I wasn't sure you'd be here, so I didn't lug everything down. Come with me, and we'll manufacture us both a drink."

"I have something else for us to do first," I said.

"Better than gin?"

I smiled at her. "For people like you and me, it is. We need to break into a locked storage space and steal a woman's bag."

Then there was the real smile, the glimmer in those almost black eyes. "I knew I liked you the moment we met," she said.

The door to the luggage room was padlocked, so the set of simple picks and skeleton keys I had built up since working for the Nameless Man were useless. Lucy stood by the door and looked disappointed while I walked out a nearby door and began scavenging around the site where a crew had been constructing a recreation hall for the stranded immigrants. In five minutes' time, I found first a hammer and then a metal file.

I drove the thin point on one end of the file under the hinge holding the lock where it was nailed into the doorframe and then with a little bit of gentle force, pried the base of the hinge free from the frame.

"Do this sort of thing often?" Lucy whispered as I eased the door open.

"No," I whispered back. "If I did, I would have come prepared. . . . Stay here and distract anyone who wanders by. Stand in front—"

"Hell no," she all but hissed. "I want to look through the bag with you. If it's a woman's, you won't even know what you're looking for."

"I'm taking the whole thing. We can go through it together in my room."

She pinched my arm. "No gin for you if you're lying," she whispered.

The storage room was so dark, I could just barely make out the numbers over the cubicles. When I found 313, I reached inside the black space and jammed my hand painfully into the back wall. I felt about almost frantically, but the cubicle was empty. I said a few choice syllables my father had taught me outside my mother's hearing and started back toward the jimmied door. It had been only six hours before that both the carpetbag and shawl were safely tucked into 313, and now . . . I was still cursing when I found them both, sitting on the floor beside the guard's desk just beside the door, the bag set squarely against the edge of the desk and the shawl folded neatly on top. I grabbed both, and a moment later was standing in the hall beside Lucy.

"Take them and start back to my room," I whispered. "And make damn sure you don't get lost between here and there."

"Trust is such a rare thing," she retorted. "What the hell are you going to do?"

"Hammer the hinge back in place so that anybody who's used to seeing it there will never know we've come calling. The same rickety latch and the same rusty nail heads."

And then as she was about to step away, I grabbed her arm. "And don't start without me." I was the one hissing now. "I want to see just how the stuff lies in the bag when we open it."

Although I ran along the darkened corridor, I still didn't catch up to her before the empty second-floor hallway of Building E, which ended in my room. And there I found her perched on my cot, with the shawl around her shoulders and the carpetbag held firmly in her lap. Her hair was pulled back in a way I hadn't seen it before, and her tanned face had a look of fierce determination.

"And just who is it that you think I may be?" she asked, with a not-half-bad Irish brogue, still slightly breathless from lugging the bag up the steps to the second floor.

I had to laugh. "I don't know for sure, but I'm guessing Ciara McManaway, late of County Cork."

"And so I might, if you be the lad I love, come to take me to that bright and shining shore."

"I may be the lad ye seek. It all depends on what you have in that bag you have clutched to your chest."

She suddenly stood up and let the carpetbag slide to the floor. "Never mind about my chest," she said. "I think I saw her."

"What do you mean, you think . . . ?"

"I didn't know it until I saw the shawl . . . hell, had it wrapped around my own shoulders. And saw the red wool of the bag. It nagged me all the way back here from the storage locker, and I did what I always do when I'm trying to recall some lurking thought. I try to re-create, reenact it. That's what I was doing when you came bursting in and broke my concentration."

"You saw her sitting just like that, with the bag in her lap. Is that what you're saying?"

She nodded ferociously. "You better shut the door, Stephen. Or better yet, shut the door at the end of the corridor at the steps, so we can talk."

Together, we did more than that. Catching each other's mood, we wedged the door at the end of the hallway shut with a sturdy chair under the knob and then set an empty metal bucket in the chair, sure to make a clanging if anyone were to force their way in. Then we searched each of the rooms on the ward to be sure they were all empty before returning to my cell with its barred windows.

I let Lucy have the cot, and I sat on a wooden chair that I had carried in from the nurses' station.

"When and where?" I asked.

"When and where did I see her?"

I nodded. "Or think you saw her. You don't sound sure."

"I saw her only once, if she's who I think she was. Sitting just so, prim and proper, with her knees together and this bag clutched in her lap, as if it was the only thing she owned in the wide world."

"Where?"

"In the waiting room outside Blanche Taylor's office, on a hard bench where they keep immigrants waiting who they don't trust or like."

"Waiting to see Taylor?"

"She must have been. It's the only explanation."

"Well, damn."

"Why *damn*?"

"Taylor told me that she never saw the girl and didn't know what she looked like."

CHAPTER THIRTEEN

"W hy would she lie?"

"I don't know," I admitted. "Protect the hospital maybe. Protect someone else here who she's attached to. Protect herself."

"Her reputation, you mean?"

"Maybe."

"It's hard to imagine. Everyone on the island thinks she's a saint. I wasn't here, of course, but apparently she all but ran Island 3 during the war, before Knox was assigned here last summer."

"Something's curious about that old woman," I said. "There is nobody on the face of the earth who really is as kind and cheerful as she seems to be."

We spread the contents of the missing girl's carpetbag out on the bunk across from mine. Then I made an inventory while Lucy picked up each item in turn to examine, smell, turn inside out, and hold up against her body, carefully re-creating for me some sense of what Ciara McManaway had in her possession.

> Two dresses—one of thick wool (gray) and one of linsey-woolsey (dyed black)
> A cap or bonnet—of faded blue cloth
> Two pairs of step-ins—stiff and somehow . . . harsh

"They've been washed in salt water," I guessed out loud as I wrote.

"Smell them and you can tell." She held first one pair and then the other to her nose.

> Make that *Two pairs of step-ins—washed in brine*
> *One handkerchief—embroidered linen, carefully folded*
> *One plain kerchief (red, faded)—washed in brine*

Lucy had, suddenly and quietly, begun to cry.

> *One pair of socks—wool, washed in brine*
> *One undershirt—linen, carefully rolled up, unused*

"Why are you crying?"

"I'm not crying."

"Why are your cheeks wet?"

> *A hairbrush—with a tangle of red hair (thick and dark, I added)*
> *Two tortoiseshell combs—stuck in the hairbrush, both with broken teeth*
> *One silver brooch in the form of a crucifix*

"I'm crying, damn it, because there's so little here. It's her entire life, and there's so little of it."

> *One leather purse with a silver clasp—empty except for a brass coin*
> *One New Testament—stained with . . . salt water*

"What's missing that should be there?"

"Everything." She was still crying, and you could hear the catch in her voice. "Not only are there no stockings, there are no shoes. Which means . . ."

"She had only the one pair she was wearing."

"There is no jewelry, except for the crucifix, which looks to be older than God." Her voice was strained now, cracking almost. "And . . ."

"And?"

"And there's nothing soft, nothing to comfort her. Her underpants would have rubbed her absolutely raw every time she put them on. She could read, maybe, but there are no books other than her Testament. No photographs. The only nice thing is this undershirt, and she must have saved it for the New World because it's never been unrolled, and . . ." She held it to her nose. "It smells like soap and lavender."

Lucy sank down to her knees before the cot and lay forward from the waist, spreading the upper half of her body over the worldly possessions of Ciara McManaway. "This poor, poor girl," she said quietly, her voice muffled by the mattress and the clothes.

I stepped across from where I'd been taking notes to stand beside her.

They became real to me in that moment, the two women: The one whose clothes lay carefully spread over the meager mattress, the one I was already thinking of as the dead girl. And the other, who crouched on the hard floor to embrace somehow the spirit that had inhabited those clothes and stroked its hair with that brush. The second woman, whose breathing had slowed, whose tears seemed to have ceased, that woman was thrillingly alive to me, taut with emotion.

I leaned over to stroke her back, seeking to comfort Miss Lucy Paul. She seemed to grow in stillness as I rubbed rhythmically at the knotted muscles between her shoulders. She relaxed as a cat does in your lap when you pet it slowly and quietly. After a moment, I let my hand rest at the base of her neck, just below the loose bun of her hair. Rest there, and then began to knead the lean muscles of her neck as they, too, slowly loosened.

When I started to kneel beside her, she pushed herself up slowly and turned to sit on the hard cot, moving Ciara McManaway's things aside. "Don't touch me unless you mean it," she said.

I froze, halfway to sitting, half standing. "Mean it how?"

"Meaning that since I've come here, seeing all of these people stranded in the middle of their lives, I've started to feel lost myself. And I'm hungry, starved even, for human touch. Some hand that will reach out and pull me out of the frame of my life. Sometimes I cry at night from loneliness, and I never, never cry."

I all but collapsed on the cot beside her, very careful not to touch her. "I'm not . . ."

"Let me finish. Whatever you're *not*, let me finish. I couldn't stand it if you pitied me. Or if you overlooked me, ignored me like I was a child. Put your hand on me and then walked away."

"You're not a child, God knows."

"Are you . . . ?" She started one question and then broke off into another. "I only meant can you care about someone? Do you have any feelings inside you at all, other than that constant poking and peering into things, searching for the lost?"

I considered before I replied, my mouth half open, my tongue wet with words. "You have no idea," I finally whispered. "I am cursed with a ragged heart."

Now it was she who reached out to touch me, her nurse's fingers gentle against my face. "Do you cry at night?" she asked.

"No, but I feel like I might be a candidate for the psychopathic ward."

We both smiled at the thought, at the irony of where we were.

"Cursed are you?"

"Dry, harsh, and yet somehow . . ."

"Flooded at the same time?"

I nodded. "Don't show it, but . . ."

"Now you can touch me," she said.

"I'm not sure I should, Lucy. I think . . . I'm in love with someone else."

"Maybe you are." She shrugged. "Maybe I am too. Maybe I don't want you to love me. . . . Just hold me together so that I don't fall to pieces while we're on this damn island."

CHAPTER FOURTEEN

We lay down on my thin cot on top of the covers, and I held her while she lay on her side with her back to me, curled against my stomach and chest. At first all we removed was our shoes, and we shared my thin pillow. My right arm was folded under her head and my left wrapped loosely around her waist.

It was coming on dusk, and the gloaming seemed to gather in the room as if it flowed in through the windows and pooled around the scant furniture—the scarred wooden table and chair, the two cots. In some way that I'm not sure I can explain, the moment seemed to slip out of the gears of time, to suspend itself without motion except for our breathing, and without fear or worry for the coming night.

The top of her head was just under my chin, and wisps of her hair tickled my lips and nose. Her hair didn't have the strong chemical smell that filled the wards but rather something cool and citrus. Orange, I thought, or lemon, with maybe a hint of vanilla. She'd been wearing her nurse's whites at supper, so she must have washed her hair along with the rest of her when she changed her clothes.

As we lay there, light seemed to ebb and flow with the same tidal motion as the waves I could hear pulsating against the breakwater. Lucy's breathing slowed and deepened as the length of her body relaxed into the mattress and sagged against me. There was a peace in the rhythm of her breath, in the waves, in the flickering light. I thought of an ancient word that I had learned long ago from a rich family's library down in those Southern mountains: *crepuscule*. It was precisely the word for this particular night fall. This quiet place in which—

She jerked suddenly, the top of her head hitting my chin softly. She moaned. She had dived so deeply and so quickly that she was dreaming. She clutched at my arm around her waist and muttered something under her breath.

"I've got you," I whispered into her hair. "I've got you." Almost cooing to her. And after a moment her head nodded against my neck.

She sat up on the edge of the cot. "Thank you," she said. And then, "I'll be right back." She stood and went out through the door and down the hall, her bare feet whispering on the wooden floor. I stood and took off my jacket and unbuttoned my shirt. From the lavatory down the hall, I could hear a toilet flush and water running.

In a moment, she walked back in carrying, of all things, a candle in a brass holder. "We use these when we lose power," she said. "And the light is so much . . ." She gestured with her other hand as if to say *softer, kinder, sweeter.*

"There are matches in my jacket pocket," I said. "Hanging over the chair."

"I can't go back out there," she said, "to the dormitory. Not tonight. Can I sleep here with you if I promise not to attack you in your sleep?"

I nodded, not sure what else I could say or do.

She sat the candle down on the desk and fished in my jacket pocket for the matches. "Go on and wash then," she said. "I'll be under the blanket when you get back so you won't have to shut your eyes when you come in."

And I did just as she suggested. Spent at least ten minutes in the lavatory, thinking about Anna, wondering if I was betraying her just by lying down beside this woman. Knowing deep in the pit of my stomach that Anna had all but broken it off between us, even though she was afraid to say the final words. Where is comfort in this dreary world? I thought as I finally turned back down the hallway. Comfort for Ciara McManaway, though it might be too late for her? Comfort for Lucy Paul, stranded on this island? Comfort for me, once again a prisoner behind bars?

I could feel my heart begin to pulse in my neck as I neared the room. From the doorway, I could see her shoes and socks side by side under the other cot and her brown slacks neatly folded on the mattress beside Ciara's bag. "Close your eyes," I whispered to her, "and I'll take . . ."

I could see her smile in the flickering light and her eyes close. They were all but black, those eyes, in the pale, yellow light.

I unbuttoned my shirt and pulled down the suit pants and placed everything—shoes, pants, shirt—in the tiny wardrobe that stood in the corner of the room. Wearing only shorts, what I normally slept in, I got under the meager covers beside her. She rolled onto her side facing the wall, making room for me, and after a bit of awkward maneuvering, we fit together comfortably as before, when we were fully dressed. She still wore the yellow blouse, made of some soft fabric, and her briefs, but the rest was all skin.

Again we seemed cut from the same piece of cloth—so naturally did her curves settle against mine. One thin pillow and two tired heads.

My right arm was around her waist, as there was no place else it would fit, and she pulled it against her stomach. "This is what I need," she whispered dreamily. And then after a bit, "All I need . . . just this."

And we slept. She first, again plunging beneath the surface, and I following after some minutes of wonder.

At one point, when my arm under our shared pillow was stiff from lying cramped for so long, I began to turn over. She turned with me, almost as if in response to some silent command. Then she was nestled against my back and the backs of my legs. The fabric of her blouse soft against my skin. The sheets, the thin blankets, the pillow—everything about the bed—smelled like some strong antiseptic. But Lucy Paul did not smell like antiseptic. Just the opposite . . .

I didn't fall asleep after that, at least not for a long time. My always restless mind recalled Ciara McManaway's meager possessions only a few feet away, and I reached out toward them in my imagination. The underthings stiff with salt, the two homemade and threadbare dresses, the small Bible, the almost empty purse.

Where was her money, the mandatory fifty dollars or its equivalent she had to have in her possession in order to enter the country? Where were her immigration papers from her port of departure in Ireland, her steamship passage documents, her identification card? The pieces of paper that said who and what she was?

Although Lucy had held up the Testament, she hadn't opened it, and I imagined reaching out to the other cot and picking up the small, worn book to search through it. For what? For scraps of paper . . . a name or an address for someone other than the congressman. Her family or friends in the gigantic, teeming world to which she'd come. A photograph perhaps, or a letter. Where was she going when she spun off the face of the earth? When I'd asked Lucy earlier what was missing, I hadn't meant clothes or shoes or other possessions. I had meant the small things that named the girl, that placed her. I was asking the question that a man would ask, and Lucy had responded as a woman might, wishing comfort for the ghost of Ciara McManaway.

Lucy stirred against my back and, in her sleep, thrust her hips gently against me—as if to interrupt my thoughts with just how real *she* was. Her warm breath against my neck, her arm lying along my side with her hand cupped over my shoulder. One foot nestled between my calves. *She* was not a ghost. Again, I could hear the stirring of the harbor waves against the rocks that rimmed the island, and even the waves seemed to flow and abate with the warmth of blood. I wondered if the two of us were drifting out to sea, leaving the rule-bound world behind.

In another chamber of my mind, I was saying a long, silent prayer for Anna and for me with Anna, though she seemed far away and receding from me by the day and the hour.

I was glad that Lucy Paul lay against my back in all her solid, delicious reality. I could sense the tide of her pulse as her breasts stirred against me, the restless pressure of her hips. I was glad that with my back to her, she couldn't feel how all the hard front of me was tumescent with need.

CHAPTER FIFTEEN

She was gone when I woke the next morning. Had slipped off the narrow cot, dressed, and made her way without waking me, though I was most always restless in sleep.

When I walked down the hall to the lavatory, I saw how she had removed the bucket and chair—our primitive alarm system—to open the door to the ward but then pulled it back almost into place when she closed the door behind her. Something made her fear what might come through that door while one or both of us was asleep, and I felt the same way.

When I got back to my room, I found a note she had left on the other bunk beside Ciara McManaway's carpetbag.

> *Thank you, Stephen.*
> *I slept better last night than I have in months.*
> *You kept me from the nightmares.*
> *My shift starts at eight, and I have to be on time*
> *or Nurse Adams will eat me for her breakfast.*
> *　　　　　　　　　　　　　　　　—L.*

I had to smile, imagining the giant Adams munching on lesser mortals.

Self-conscious now in the pink morning light, I reached into the wardrobe and pulled my pants on before I began again on Ciara's possessions. Her purse was empty except for one small, nondescript coin, something Irish I assumed and quite old. The Testament had the girl's name carefully traced in ink on the first page: *Ciara Deirdre McManaway*, along with a date: *April 1909*. And nothing else till the very last page, where inside the cover was penciled in careful block letters a name and address. The name was *Samuel Kennedy*, and the address was *411 West 33rd Street, City of New York, United States*. And just below that in a hasty scrawl with the same pencil: *and Angela*.

Samuel Kennedy, whoever he was, certainly wasn't our interested congressman; his name was Brendan McCarthy. I turned the pages of the Testament again, from back to front this time so that I wouldn't be distracted by the text, looking for anything unusual or out of place. Nothing.

I dumped the contents of the bag out onto the mattress and sorted through the clothes again, carefully comparing them to the list I had written from Lucy's descriptions. Again nothing.

Where were her papers? Letters? Photographs?

Then, with one hand inside and one out, I began slowly to feel my way over every inch of the thick wool plaid that made up the body of the bag itself. If I were Ciara McManaway or her loving mother or her doting father, I would have sewn the things that mattered most into the lining of the bag, where they wouldn't be stolen on shipboard.

Maybe it was the Celtic in my veins, because the instinct was right. I didn't find what I was looking for, but I found where someone had gone before me, cutting and then ripping the lining of the bag, searching for anything of value. I wondered if it was the same person who had emptied her purse. And I wondered if it had anything to do with her disappearance.

It was my third day on the island, and I was due to report back to the Honorable Augustus F. Sherman in the main building. But first I had to figure out where to hide the McManaway girl's bag so it wouldn't end up back in the hands of whoever was in the process of removing it from the storage lockup. When I had dressed, I slipped her small Testament into my suit coat pocket, put everything else, including her shawl, back into the bag, and then carried it down to the nurses' station at the front of the ward. There, I emptied a low cabinet of medical supplies, stuffed the carpetbag to the back, and replaced the bandages and towels in front to cover it. It would be safe there, I thought, at least for the day.

This time I had to wait to see Sherman. His assistant—the secretary to the secretary—let me know that Sherman was tied up in a formal appeal, acting as witness and recorder in a meeting wherein two German men who had arrived as stowaways had been summarily rejected but then begged asylum. He—Sherman's assistant—wasn't sure how long it would take but predicted probably less than an hour. He drew his pen across his throat to signify that the Germans had no chance. Not as Germans and not as stowaways . . .

I wandered back out onto the balcony that rings the walls two stories up above the giant registry room, the balcony that provides a view down over the long rows of benches that funnel the masses of immigrants into lines before examiners' desks. A ferry had arrived a quarter hour before, releasing a surge of bodies, pressing forward to be first into the lines. Some of the crowd of immigrants had now made their way up the stairs, past the point of the initial examination, where men in uniforms were chalking strange hieroglyphics directly onto their chests and directing them into the various lines delineated by the benches.

For a moment, I had the weird sense that I was some sort of minor god, floating in the sky above the sorting ground that is human experience. And below me, struggling and clawing and striving, was the mass of humankind, being funneled into the tracks that would determine not just who they might become—as if potential mattered—but who they were all along. Who they were fated to be from the beginning of the journey? From birth?

"They tell me it used to be cages down there, not benches." The voice was flat, curt almost, and it brought me back from my musings. It was Ludmila Kuchar, my tour guide from the first day. Only now she wasn't dressed as a European peasant but in the less showy, more practical guise of a New York working woman. She was leading two impossibly pale, impossibly blond children by the hand. Both stared up at me in naked terror until she leaned over and whispered to them in what must have been their native tongue because after a moment, they visibly relaxed.

"You're not serious," I said. "Cages?"

She nodded grimly. "I didn't see it, for it was previous to the war-time. But where the benches go now, there were long rows of metal fences, and everyone had to stand packed into the spaces with no sit-ting except on the floors. When the inspectors needed to put someone aside without losing track of them, they had cages for that part so they wouldn't go away . . ." She paused to think of the right word.

"Wander off?" I suggested.

She nodded. "Wander off. Go looking for their family or someone who was planning to . . . meet them at the gate. Sometimes women in one cage and men in another. Children like these"—she lifted the hands of the two she had in tow in case I somehow hadn't noticed them—"in another cage in another place." She shook her head fero-ciously, her blue eyes suddenly icy and her cheekbones sharp enough to cut. In that moment, she was not a woman to be trifled with.

"This has to be better." I gestured to the floor below, where the space between several of the benched-off sectors was already flooded with human bodies, and the chatter of at least a dozen languages drifted up to where we stood. Though it was supposed to be quiet and orderly, the whole mass seemed to quiver with energy, and mysterious tides of emotion passed visibly through the crowd.

"It is better." She shrugged her thin shoulders. "At least they can sit. The mothers with children. The old ones who will probably get sent back. They sit."

"Are they afraid?"

She nodded. "Of course they are, Stephen Robbins. That is why they cluster together by the language. The people they can talk to. Who can share the fear."

"What are the white marks on the shoulders and chests of so many?"

She shook her head and bent to speak again to the two children. Telling them, no doubt, to be patient.

"No, it happens on the grand staircase. It is the first test the new-comer must pass. The guards make them into lines as they get off the ferry, and the medical inspectors watch them as they approach the stairs and begin to climb. The medicals pass judgment like this . . ." She tugged one hand free and snapped her fingers. "Like this, no?" She snapped them again, and I nodded. "They make the snap judgments and label you with chalk. If you stoop over, they mark you with a B for back. If you limp, with an L for lame."

The sharp flicker of a smile came and went on her face without changing its contours. "You would be marked with an F." She shook one hand free to trace some letters with a stiff finger on my chest. "For that scar on your face, and with an X for suspected mental defect."

"Why the mental defect?"

"Because the scar rises up into that white place in your hair, so your brains must be . . ."

"Deranged?"

She nodded once vigorously. "Beyond the repair. It's the psychotic ward for you." Now her eyes might be smiling, though her mouth was a strong, straight line.

"What is the mark for pregnant?" I said it in a joking way, match-ing her mood, never imagining there was such a symbol.

"PG," she said matter-of-factly. "PG and you go to the isolation."

"And is there a mark for hope?"

She smiled. Finally, I had gotten her to truly smile, so that the hard angles of her face softened. "No chalk mark for that, Stephen Robbins," she said. "They all hope."

CHAPTER SIXTEEN

The secretary to the secretary—a very busy, very officious young man—finally let me into Augustus Sherman's office to wait for him. Which gave me time to look further at the photographs he had displayed at eye level around the walls of the room. The images were fascinating; the labels even more so . . .

Montenegrin men

Romanian shepherds

Turkish bank guard John Postantzis

Italian woman

Group of Borana people from southern Ethiopia

Sikh from India

Greek woman

One portrait of a plain, dogged-looking woman wearing an elaborate hat was described in one word: *Holland.*

Something stirred inside me that I hadn't noticed before. Except for the bank guard, John Postantzis, the people who were frozen inside these prints had no names but were described only as types. I made a quick circuit of the room, and the impression became a conviction. These were portraits of nationalities or even something beyond nationality . . . racial identity. There was a name here and there—Antonio Piestineola, Eleazar Kaminetzko, Peter Meyer—but even these were described by their nationality and propensity: Antonio was an *Italian Piper*, Eleazar a *Russian Hebrew* and a *Vegetarian*, Peter a *Wealthy Dane in search of pleasure.* Peter, I thought, had a frightening intensity in his pleasure-seeking eyes.

I paused before one portrait of a *Ruthenian woman from the former kingdom of Ruthenia,* who wore a fantastic costume consisting of an embroidered blouse tucked into a high, elaborately stitched waistband, an animal skin vest of some sort, and a layered rope of beads. Her hair was covered by a white scarf decorated with some dark figure, the scarf pulled back and tied behind her head. Her face was burnished by the sun; she must have worked outside in her native Ruthenia. Her mouth was a solid horizontal line that gave away nothing of emotion or expression. She gazed into Sherman's camera with a direct, anxious gaze out of what must have been startlingly blue eyes.

I was sure now that what Sherman saw when he gazed through the lens of his camera box was the costume and the headdress, and if he examined this woman's face at all, it was to determine her racial type. What was the shape of the head, what the size of the features, the slope of the eyes? Was she Teutonic or Alpine or Mediterranean?

What I saw was that she was hauntingly beautiful.

"They are remarkable specimens, are they not?"

So consumed was I by Sherman's photographs that the man himself walked in on me unexpectedly. I turned and shrugged. "Pardon me for looking," I said. "I couldn't help myself."

"Of course, of course. I'm pleased that you find them interesting. Too many people see only the elaborate costumes and miss the hair, the skin, the eyes."

"The shape of the head?" I suggested helpfully.

With his hands behind his back, the portly gentleman rocked forward on his toes in delight. "Yes, yes. And the face. The head and face reveal all, do they not?"

"All of the personality?"

"If by personality you mean that of the individual, then no. The individual personality is nothing compared to the features that survive through generations. The flesh perishes, but the pattern remains. If you look closely, the faces in my photographs reveal the family, and by family, I mean the parents and grandparents and the grandparents beyond the grandparents." He walked around his desk and lowered himself stiffly into his office chair.

"Are you dissecting these people when you take their portraits?" I sat as well, once again having found a topic that he relished talking about.

He chuckled. "I would never say dissection precisely, for that suggests their mortality, but I see your meaning. . . . You might say that I'm dissecting their origin, their racial features, which is the key to their true natures. I am not an artist with the camera, Mr. Robbins, but rather a scientist."

For a brief moment, I wondered what Anna Ulmann, my Anna, would say about this conversation. She was an artist with the camera.

"Is portraiture a form of analysis then?" I asked.

"Here on this island, it is," he replied. And after a moment, "Most certainly."

"Is that why you've stayed here so long, because of the opportunity it affords you?" I was afraid it was a question too far, too personal perhaps, and that he would recoil. But no . . .

"I came here in 1892, Mr. Robbins, twenty-eight years ago. Worked my way up through the ranks to the post I hold today. I didn't start taking photographs until almost the turn of the century, but once I began, I was . . ."

"Addicted?"

He smiled. "Again, too strong a word. But certainly, I was taken with the process, and I discovered that this island, this little speck of land in the middle of the world's busiest harbor, is the best place on earth to view all the races of the world. I may not see every human type that exists, but most of the types pass through this building where we sit sooner or later. I don't have to go in search of them. They come to me. Right out there on the children's playground, in the men's and women's dormitories. Sometimes I have to ask them to unpack their native costumes in order to be photographed, like the Cossacks I showed you a few days ago, but most often they are happy to pose in their native garb."

"Is a group photo better than an individual portrait?"

"For revealing the type?"

I nodded.

After a considered pause, "Yes, it is. Especially for the uninitiated viewer such as yourself. You can see how the faces of a mother and her children are essentially the same face in successive generations, and so the individual significance fades away."

I wanted to ask him about fathers and children, but I also didn't want to interrupt his flow.

"Look at the first photo beside that bookshelf, Mr. Robbins. What do you see?"

The image he pointed me to was labeled *Johanna Dykhoff, 40– Holland– with 11 chln. "Noordam" May 12–'08. To Loretta, Minn.*

"They're all wearing a card with the number five on it, and the mother's name is Johanna Dykhoff?"

"Yes, that's the one, but those details don't matter. They are ephemeral. Do you know what—?"

"Yes, I know what *ephemeral* means." I nodded to reassure him that he hadn't hurt my feelings.

"The cards are to show the inspectors which ship they arrived on fifteen years ago. The woman's name is already lost to history except, perhaps, in Minnesota. What matters is that the same face, give or take a few insignificant details, appears on each of those twelve human beings, even the baby if we could see it."

I nodded. The half dozen faces from the family group that peered directly into the camera did bear a marked resemblance.

"Look at the photo directly beside it, the Wallachian group."

There was a mother, again holding a baby, and two children, all dressed in elaborate native garb. The older girl, standing in the middle, was smiling broadly and holding what might have been a giant milk can. The youngest child was either yawning widely or in the middle of a sneeze, impossible to say. The mother wore a card with the number twenty displayed, presumably keyed to the manifest of ship number twenty.

"Can you see the resemblance? Can you see the family features?"

I nodded. "Three different expressions—scowling, smiling, sneezing—but the skin tone and the noses, the eyes . . ."

"I know. One of my better efforts, don't you think?"

"By family features, do you mean racial features?"

"Of course. The names come and go here. There are millions of names. But the races remain the same over the generations . . . unless there is interbreeding through successive generations once they have arrived here."

"The world is a very large and strange place, isn't it, Mr. Sherman."

"Indeed. And its largesse comes here to me and to my camera. In many ways, I am extraordinarily fortunate." And then after a pause, "What have you found out about our Miss McManaway? Discovered her hiding in a cupboard?"

I'd been waiting for the question, assuming he'd exhausted the topic of his photographic gallery. "I've found the last person who apparently saw her alive," I said. "I've heard about the bed she was sleeping in when she disappeared. I've talked with a dozen doctors and nurses." On instinct, I left out the discovery of her luggage. I didn't yet know who was aligned with whom in this place nor how much I could trust Sherman.

"Do you think she's alive?"

I paused. I knew the answer but wasn't ready to give it up. "She's gone from Island 3. Perhaps she's in the hospital wards somewhere on 2. Or perhaps she's made her way back here, to Island 1, and managed to mingle with the immigrants going ashore. What is the likelihood of that?"

"Very slim," he said, inserting his monocle into his eye to study my face. "Since the war, we haven't yet gotten up to speed in terms of our ability to handle a true influx of foreigners, but the one thing we do have is an excess of security. More guards than we ever had prior to 1916. I'm not saying it couldn't happen, but it's unlikely. . . . Even more unlikely given her condition."

I nodded. "Does your personal authority extend to Island 3?"

He pursed his lips and shook his head. "I have to admit it does not. I know very little about the isolation wards. Have you talked to Dr. Knox?"

I smiled. "Yes, but so far, he doesn't have much to say."

CHAPTER SEVENTEEN

I had another delightful conversation with Dr. Knox's secretary while waiting for him to return to his office from the wards.

"What is your name?" I asked her once again as I sat across from her.

"Stephen Robbins," she replied.

"No, *your* name," I said with the slightest emphasis.

"Who?"

I tried pointing at her.

"Melissa."

I was making progress.

"So, Melissa—that's a lovely name, by the way—when will Dr. Knox be back?"

She studied a delicate gold watch on her wrist and then looked back up helpfully. "In about ten minutes," she said. "That's what he told me when he left."

"Who is he with?"

"Nurse Taylor."

Now we were at a pause, for it would take two or three questions to elicit even one more answer.

"What time is it now?"

Her brow wrinkled, as if only an idiot would ask such a question.

"Nurse Taylor, I told you."

"I was asking about the time . . ."

"Oh." She smiled and looked at her watch again. "It's a quarter past ten."

"You're a fascinating individual," I told her.

She didn't stop smiling, though God only knows what she was thinking.

When Knox came in a few minutes later, he was grinning—the leftover sunshine, I imagined, from his ten minutes with Taylor. But then he saw me, and the grin faded.

"Robbins." He nodded to me as he went past and into his office.

I followed on his heels, not wanting to leave him the option of closing the door.

He circled his desk, still impressively piled with papers, and sat. "You know, Robbins, I'm a—"

"Very busy man." I finished his sentence for him. "I won't take but a minute or two of your time. And I think I can help you in return."

He did look up at this, even making eye contact for a brief moment. I sat down opposite him without being invited.

"How can you help me?" he asked.

"Me first. I have two questions. First item, one of the nurses told me that when the McManaway girl disappeared, he found her paperwork on the standard clipboard by her bed the next morning but no girl, no clothes, no shoes, and so on. Where would that paperwork have gone?" I nodded at his desk. "I'm wondering if it made its way into all that deluge of documents you have to deal with."

He seemed intrigued by the thought. "Something should have," he said. "Since this became such a . . . high-profile case, I've looked, and I've had Melissa look as well. So far we've found one sheet of paper, a referral form filled out by an inspector on Island 1."

"That's it?"

He nodded morosely. "Yes." He reached into a metal desk drawer just at his right hand and actually leaned across the desk to hand me the form. "Take a look for yourself."

It was a blurred copy of an original form that had been filled out in blue ink by someone with a clear hand given to a flourish or two. Name. Date. Port of origin: *Dublin*. Age: *23*. Ship / Manifest: *Relentless, 14*. And so on. Under Reason for Referral, the clerk had clearly written *PG*. Action: *Referred to isolation for examination and processing.* Quick, efficient, and on to the next in line.

"So where do you think her medical records and such went to, the papers that were on that clipboard?"

"It's an open case. When there are disappearances like this, the actual medical notes compiled by the doctors and nurses stay in active circulation on the wards. You said you had two questions . . ."

I made a mental note—he'd said *disappearances*, plural. "When someone dies on the island, either in the hospital or here in isolation, where do they go?"

"Oh, that's easy enough. The body is transferred to the morgue. First floor of the office building at the base of the island."

"Is there an autopsy?"

"If there is any mystery as to the death, yes. Or if it is a particularly interesting case. There is an autopsy theater adjacent to the morgue, where one of the senior staff performs the actual process for the young doctors and nurses while they take notes and ask questions. It's standard procedure."

I nodded and stood. "Thank you. I'll ask one of the staff to show me if that's okay."

"Certainly. We're especially proud of that morgue." He raised his eyebrows. "I believe you were also going to help me with something?"

I shrugged. "You have a killer in your midst," I said. "I imagine you'd like him caught sooner or later."

CHAPTER EIGHTEEN

I wanted to interview Nurse Taylor before Knox had a chance to warn her. I was haunted by my initial reaction to her personality, that soft, beneficent smile and those glowing eyes. I didn't think I was susceptible to sainthood, but she'd had me going the first time around, and I wanted to see the show again.

I walked straight down the spine of Island 3 at a good clip, intending to corner Taylor in her own office to quiz her about McManaway's medical records. The giantess Ethel Adams showed me in, clapping me happily—and painfully—on the back as she did so.

Adams pulled the door closed behind her as she slipped back out to the more officious outer office, leaving me with Taylor. The head nurse patted the cushion beside her, clearly meaning for me to join her on the couch, but I deliberately chose the chair opposite, where I could see her face.

"I think I'm getting a cold," I explained, "and I would hate to pass it along."

She opened up the throttle on her smile another notch or two. "Thank you for your thoughtfulness," she said. And the words bore out my memory from several days before. Her voice had a purring quality, almost like bees buzzing in flowers. Even with all my hard edges, I couldn't help smiling back at the woman.

"I'm so thankful I've made tea," she said. "And you must take it with lemon for your throat. When you're coming down with a cold, the throat is everything." Husky—that was the word I kept searching for. Her voice had a *husky* quality, as if there was more emotion behind every word than the words alone could possibly convey.

"Thank you," I replied hoarsely, and I wondered if I really was coming down with something. "I've come to ask you about Ciara McManaway's medical records."

"First your tea," she said and got up to fetch a plate of sliced lemon from a small refrigerator under her worktable. "We have to take care of your health while you're with us." She came back to the couch and busied herself with the cup, saucer, and teapot, giving me a chance to study her hands. They were large and competent, homely almost. No rings but with carefully groomed, surprisingly feminine nails. Again the sweet aunt you never really had.

"Now then." She looked up. "Here's your cup. What was it you wanted again, Stephen?"

"Ciara McManaway's medical records. Nurse Thompson told me that on the morning she disappeared, the only thing left behind was her standard medical papers on the clipboard, hanging on the hook beside her bed. I asked Dr. Knox, and he said that since hers was an open case, the records would still be on the wards. Or perhaps in your office."

I added the last bit just to prod her. I was getting tired of constantly being pointed elsewhere by everyone I met.

She frowned. "I'm afraid I don't know where they are, but I'll send Nurse Adams with you once our interview has concluded, and I'm sure she can ferret them out for you." The idea of a six-foot, four-inch ferret, weighing in at 250 plus, struck me as ludicrous, but I didn't let it show. "It was Nurse Thompson who told you of them?" she asked.

I nodded.

"Has he been helpful in your search?"

Another nod.

"Good. He's such a kind person and a surprisingly gifted nurse for a man." Behind her on her desk, a telephone receiver jangled. She excused herself to answer it.

73

I studied her profile as she talked on the phone, and it gave me something interesting, something unexpected. She answered the phone with the same beneficent smile she seemed to give every human encounter. It was almost as if she couldn't speak any other way. After the sweet preliminaries, however, the smile faded. It didn't suddenly disappear as it would have from your face or mine, it slowly expired, as if the light went out inside her thoughts, leaving the smile to die on its own. "He's here right now," she said, "and we're sharing a cup of tea with lemon." She turned away from me then, so that I was staring at her clean, starched back.

I assumed she was talking to Knox and that his words had extinguished the smile.

When she hung up the receiver and returned to the couch, however, the light was already back, her face once again the picture of grace. "What were we saying . . . ?" she asked.

"That Nurse Thompson was a good man," I suggested, "for helping me. And that you were about to share the McManaway girl's records . . ."

"Oh, that's right. Or rather, that I'd have our friend, Miss Adams, help you find them." She paused to sip from her cup. "But I am concerned to hear from Director Knox that you think . . . oh, I can barely say it . . . that foul play was involved."

I smiled at her, fascinated. "Why does that seem so outrageous? So far as I can tell, your little oasis is fully staffed by human beings—and after all, we are the world's most vicious species."

"Not here," she said firmly, and I was reminded that she could adopt the tone of an adult admonishing a child. "*This* is a hospital. Staffed by people who are dedicated to the healing arts. Doctors and nurses whose lives are devoted to the care of others. If we were talking about the streets of New York, which I confess I find terrifying, I might agree with you. But here . . . no."

"What do you think happened to Ciara McManaway?"

"I think that once she came to understand that we intended to

74

keep her isolated until she delivered her baby, she very quietly slipped away. I think she somehow made her way ashore . . . stowed away on a ferry. I like to think that she's found her family and will live happily ever after."

I found myself nodding at her, even found myself believing her. Not that it had happened that way, but that she might think so.

"So there's nothing dangerous here?"

"Oh no. There are no monsters here. But even so, Stephen . . . even so, please be careful in your searching. I've grown fond of you during your short time with us, and I would feel terrible if anything happened to you."

Later, when I repeated the conversation in my head, it seemed to me that those words were the first false note she played.

CHAPTER NINETEEN

Once more I was sent out into the hallway with Nurse Adams, who seemed genuinely happy to see me. Taylor had said the same thing to her that she'd mentioned to me—that Adams should "ferret out" the McManaway girl's records if she could.

Twenty feet, thirty feet down the hall, and I reached out—up actually—to grasp her elbow to slow her down. "Do you have any clue where Ciara McManaway's paperwork would even be?" I asked her.

"No, no, I don't have much to do with any of the files. That's not my job." She looked vaguely troubled by this.

"So you don't have any notion where to start looking?"

"Not really."

"Then why are we tearing off down the hall like we're going to a fire?"

She knew the answer to this question. "'Cause Nurse Taylor asked me to look."

"Do you always do what she tells you to do?"

"Oh yes."

"Why?"

"Well . . . because she is who she is."

I nodded. "She is that. Tell me something. I was thinking about what you said the other day about the Gypsies."

She nodded vigorously, her trim little nurse's hat shaking in her hair.

"Is there such a thing as a true American?" I asked.

She put one giant hand on my shoulder. "Well, Stephen . . . Mr. Robbins . . . of course there is. Everybody knows that."

I nodded to encourage her. "Help me understand then. Who is it?"

"It's you and me and people like us," she said and then paused to look around. Then, with almost no effort whatsoever, she pulled me through an open doorway into the anteroom to one of the wards, apparently seeking a more private spot to enlighten me. She leaned down to conspire. "Me and you," she whispered. "And the English and French and German people. Well, used to be German people before the kaiser came along and started that war. And . . . Scandinavians. Do you know about Scandinavia?"

"Sure. You mean Norway, Sweden, Denmark."

"Switzerland. We like Switzerland."

She would have made a good teacher for grade school children. She was that sincere.

"What about Spain?"

"Yes." She beamed at me. "You're starting to get it, Stephen."

"And Italy?"

"Italy is alright. Although, Stephen, neither them Spanish nor them Italians speak English. Did you know that?"

I nodded. "But they can learn it once they get here," I suggested.

"That's right. And then they'll be Americans."

"Real Americans?"

"Are you making fun of me, Stephen?"

"Not at all. Don't you have to speak English to be American?"

She nodded enthusiastically. "Yes, you do. But if you can learn to speak it—like you and me are speaking now—then yes."

"What about the rest of the world? Can they become American?"

"The rest of the world?"

"Asia, Africa, South America?" I shrugged. "Lithuania?"

She gazed down at me, her face filled with pity for my ignorance. "That ain't so easy," she said. "Those people are different."

"How different?"

She regarded me somberly for a moment. "Stephen, are you a Christian?"

I nodded. "When it's called for."

"Well, Stephen. Those people are decidedly *not* Christians. And the ones from the hot parts of the world . . . they breed like rabbits."

I found Lucy at lunch in the doctors' and nurses' mess sitting at a table with one of the young doctors, who was trying desperately to flirt with her over sandwiches and bowls of watery soup. I carried my tray—same sandwiches, same soup—to their table and sat down directly across from her.

"Do you know where Americans come from?" I asked her, pointedly ignoring the doctor.

"Is this a joke?"

"No. Deadly serious. Do you know . . ."

"From their mama's bellies, I suppose, most of them."

"Before that. Where do they come from to get here to this country?"

She'd already pivoted ever so slightly away from her young pup of a doctor and was leaning toward me. He took the hint—finally—and after staring at his watch for a long moment, cleared his throat and told us that he had to get back to the wards. We all smiled and nodded and did the customary things so he could leave.

"Where did you find him? At the orphanage?"

"He's what we call a baby doc," she said. "Barely out of medical school, all brilliant and accomplished. All nurses know not to get caught alone in a room with a baby doc because they are horny little devils."

"All of them?"

"All of them. But where do Americans come from if not their mama's bellies?"

"I have it on good authority that they only come from England.

Or some other clean, Christian, European country where people keep their clothes on and respect . . ."

"Respect what?"

"Hell if I know. The church steeple and the clock tower, I guess. But mostly, they are good Christians from a cold climate, because . . ."

"They have to keep their clothes on."

"Something like that. Because people from hot countries breed like hamsters . . . or rabbits. I can't remember."

She stifled a laugh. "And your authority on this bit of scientific insight is . . ."

"Nurse Ethel Adams."

She gave up and guffawed. Laughed so loud that half the nurses and doctors in the mess turned smiling to look at her.

"Fe-fi-fo-fum."

"Who?"

"Adams. The nurses call her Fe-fi-fo-fum." Lucy was whispering. "Just think of her with her clothes off . . ." She was still chuckling.

"Hell no. Too frightening."

"Well, just be thankful that *she* is from a cold climate." She wiped her eyes with her napkin. "What are you doing this afternoon?" she asked. "I'm off duty, and I'm desperate for a nap."

"You don't need me to take a nap."

"Actually, I think I do."

"No."

"No?"

"Well, at least not first. First, I need you to show me the morgue. I need to know what happens when someone dies on this anthill."

CHAPTER TWENTY

Instead of turning yet one more time down the long central hallway, Lucy led me out through the kitchen adjacent to the nurses' mess. The women working there, mostly black and brown skinned, didn't cease their easy chatter except to nod in a friendly way, and one even winked at Lucy when she saw her with a man in tow.

Once outside, we skirted the buildings along the edge of the lagoon that was being filled in by barges full of earth from Manhattan. It was quiet in the sunshine, the men on the one barge moored close to the bank lounging and smoking over the remains from their lunch pails.

We paused to sit easily for a moment on the stone steps where we had sat and talked a few days before. Now, just after noon, there was no shade from the long row of pavilions behind us. I loosened my tie and unbuttoned the top button of my shirt. After a quiet moment, she went me one better and loosened her stiff collar down to the top of her slip, letting herself breathe in the salt air. She leaned back on the step behind us and closed her eyes, and I could sense the morning's work tension draining out of her.

That simple motion, a few buttons undone, seeing the faint pulse in hollow of her tanned throat, spoke to my body, reminded me viscerally that I hadn't seen her since she'd slipped out of bed early that morning. Ages had passed since then, or so it seemed, and yet no time at all.

"Why are you so interested in the morgue?" she said lazily. "You think Ciara McManaway . . . ?" She let the rest of the question ask itself, lazy like a cat in the humid air.

"No," I said honestly. "I doubt she was ever in the morgue. But this morning Knox let slip without meaning to that there's been more than one disappearance. Maybe a lot more. And you, my dear, implied that along with the disappearances, there have been too many unexplained deaths."

I, too, had leaned back but only on one elbow, so that I could study her face as she basked in the sun with her eyes closed.

"*My dear* is it?" she said, her lips twitching, flirting with a smile. "Just because you sleep with a woman, you think you get to call her dear?"

"Hope so."

She opened one brown eye to glance lazily at me and then closed it again. A reverse wink, I thought. "I like *dear*," she said. And then, "Why did you come to me for your tour of the morgue? You could have asked anyone if Knox gave his permission."

I must have been more relaxed than I knew myself, there in the midday heat . . . because I let slip the truth. "Maybe it was because I wanted to see you," I said, and then after a pause, "see if you were real."

There was more than a flicker of a smile then. A quiet snort of humor. "Real enough," she said. "Not a dream."

She blinked, first slowly and then rapidly, almost as if waking out of a doze. I could feel her gathering herself to sit up even before she did it, rubbing her hands together to scrape the dirt off. "What I actually told you," she said, "was that I was sent here because of the unusual number of deaths."

"By the American Medical Association," I added. "Is that true?"

She nodded but didn't smile. Her eyes were almost black now, in the dazzling light. "Unfortunately, it is true. And you came to the right place. I've spent more time in that morgue than anyone except one of the attendants."

The morgue itself was one half of a two-room suite, the other half being the autopsy theater that Knox was so proud of. Both rooms were painted an institutional gray, including the cement tiers that rose five rows high like giant steps on two sides of the theater. The tiers were three feet deep, space enough for folding chairs if the demonstration lasted long enough to make chairs for the audience a necessity. At the front of the room was a metal gurney on wheels, which could be used, Lucy explained, to roll a corpse in from the adjacent morgue, prepped and ready to dissect.

Before taking me into the morgue proper, Lucy stopped to speak to a wizened little man who was mopping down the floor of the theater. He wore the uniform gray that I had seen on all the custodial staff, still clean and starched like the nurses' uniforms but obviously of a different class. Lucy called him Ezra and asked him how he did. He didn't speak but bobbed up and down from the waist, obviously pleased to be recognized.

Ezra's black hair was cut short and oiled tightly to his scalp. His face was a strange, dark gray-brown, the skin of his hands where they clutched the mop handle almost black but dry and cracked from what I imagined as gallons of soapy water, laced with antiseptic. When Lucy smiled at him, his expression didn't change but his eyes gleamed in response. And when she asked him if his back still hurt, he didn't stop the bobbing up and down, a kind of bowing to her, even while shaking his head. He was better, thank you, he seemed to say.

When we passed through to the morgue itself, I raised my eyebrows at Lucy in question, and she explained that Ezra had strained his back helping the morgue attendants lift a corpulent woman from slab to gurney, and she had given him enough pain killers for three days— three days only, she emphasized—so he wouldn't have to miss work.

"Does he speak?" I asked.

"Never," she said. "Or at least I've never heard him. I saw him hurt himself and then later trying to stretch his lower back when he thought no one was watching." And then after a moment. "He's Indian."

"From a local tribe?" I was teasing.

"From India, idiot!" she whispered, for the morgue attendant had stood up from his desk to greet us. "Or at least that's what the nurses say."

The morgue was a narrower room by ten feet than the theater, and it soon became obvious why. The back wall, opposite the hallway entrance, held a bank of eight doors, each of which was perhaps three feet square. There were two columns, each of four doors. Lucy explained the facility as the attendant took his own sweet time in reading through my letter of introduction and examining my ID.

"Dr. Knox should be proud of this place," she said. "It's the most modern I've ever seen, much better than the city hospitals. Behind each door is a refrigerated chamber, insulated from the others, so that you can slide out the tray that an individual body rests on and examine it for symptoms of disease or decay without disturbing the other—"

"It says here that I'm supposed to show you every . . . courtesy," the attendant interrupted her. He was staring at me, ignoring Lucy. I assumed that, unlike Ezra, she didn't know him.

"It does say that," I agreed. "Will you show me one of the bodies?"

He looked uncertain.

"So that I can see how the system works. Miss Paul says it's one of the finest she's ever seen."

"I don't know about—"

"It's alright," Lucy assured him. "Dr. Knox himself sent Mr. Robbins to examine the morgue. He's here on government business." It was the first time I'd seen her use that particular smile with that particular voice, and it had just the desired effect.

"Well, I suppose it's . . . My name is Paul," he said helplessly.

"Isn't that fascinating," she purred. "My name is Paul too."

When he glanced down in confusion, she winked at me and then nodded at the wall of doors.

I slipped behind Paul and his desk while she held him hypnotized. I heard her say, "It's my family name." And then I pulled the handle on the first compartment I came to. The door opened with a quiet whoosh, just like the fancy walk-in cooler in the Algonquin kitchen. I pulled out the metal drawer within, and a long tray slid silently out on hidden rollers.

A sheet-covered form lay on the metal tray with its cold, gray feet exposed. The feet were small, well-formed, and clean. There was an official looking tag attached to the right big toe with twisted wire. The tag read *Hebrew Girl, perhaps 14* and then, almost as an afterthought, her name: *Anne Korhonen.* I thought immediately of the labels on Sherman's photographs, where the type took precedence over the individual.

I pulled the tray on out of its cubicle and reached to fold the top of the sheet back from her head. It seemed in that cold moment that it was vital to see her face, give her back something of her personality in that bleak place. But my hand froze when it touched the sheet itself. Had I any right to see who this girl was, to look into . . . ?

At that moment, Lucy stepped up on the other side of the tray and, sensing my hesitation, made the decision for me. She carefully folded back the top of the sheet so that it exposed the girl's head and shoulders. Thin . . . Except for her small, round head, everything about her was thin to emaciation—her neck, her shoulders, her arms. Even her dark-brown hair, now shorn close to her scalp, was thin.

"I ain't sure you two should . . ." Somewhere behind us the attendant's voice droned on, which we both ignored.

"What killed her?" I whispered to Lucy.

She only shook her head and folded the sheet on down to the girl's waist, which revealed the only thing about her that was not gaunt ... her belly below her barely developed breasts was vaguely rounded, swollen perhaps.

"Is she?" I whispered.

"Either pregnant or malnourished," Lucy said, her nurse's voice hard in response. "More likely both."

"At fourteen?"

She nodded grimly.

"What killed her?"

The tray on which the girl lay began to slide back into the wall, seemingly of its own accord. Lucy and I looked up simultaneously and realized that the clerk was pushing it back in. "I said I ain't so sure that you two should be looking . . ." He nodded at the open maw of the cubicle as the tray slid in.

I made eye contact with Lucy, and she nodded almost imperceptibly at the door to the hallway. "Let's take a walk, Mr. Robbins, and I'll explain what I know of morbidity on Ellis Island." And then as we both turned away, she smiled grimly at the attendant. "Thank you, Paul," she said. "You've been most helpful." This last in her officious voice, with her nurse's formality, and I could sense the strain beneath it.

CHAPTER TWENTY-ONE

W hat the hell?" I asked.

But she didn't speak. Rather she pulled me almost roughly by the arm down the hall toward our sanctuary in the psych ward.

I could feel and even see the emotion blowing up inside Lucy as she hurried me along. Her jaw was clenching from strong words being choked back.

The one person we passed in the hallway—a male orderly carrying a cardboard box full of files—smiled nervously at us, aware that something was wrong. Lucy ignored him.

When we turned into Building E, which housed our retreat on the second floor, I shut the door behind us till the latch clicked, and only then did she start to spit up the words that had been almost gagging her.

"Damn it . . . damn it . . ." Her usually warm brown face was hot with it, her eyes blinking rapidly.

"Come on," I whispered. "Not here." And now I led her up the stairs till we were on the second floor, both of us a little breathless from the climb and her with the litany of *damn it*. Me with the sudden, unexpected urge to help her, calm her.

She went straight down the hall toward my room while I set up the chair and bucket that served as a wedge and warning against the outer door.

"What is it, Lucy?"

She had kicked her shoes off and was standing in her stocking feet, staring out the barred window of our room toward the Statue of Liberty and the ocean beyond.

"Talk sense, what is it?"

"It's what happens here. Over and over, goddamn it. I hate it."

"Hate what?" I stifled the urge to walk up behind her and rub her shoulders to help her relax, help her form the words.

"People die who have no business dying. Did you see a wound on that girl? Any sign of disease? Anything that would carry off someone who had barely reached puberty?"

"No, but then I don't know enough to—"

"I do. I'm a professional, Stephen, and there was nothing except maybe, maybe malnutrition."

"She was awfully thin."

She turned from the window, seemingly to see my face. "Not really," she said. "No thinner than ninety percent of the people who come through here." She was a dark silhouette against the brazen light from the window, and I couldn't see the expression on her face. "Stephen, you're an American. Compared to us, most of the world's people are stick thin."

"So it was her belly that bothered you?"

The silhouette nodded. "Her belly."

"Pregnant?"

"Maybe." And then after a moment. "I have to go back. I have to examine her."

"For the American Medical Association?"

"Yes. That . . . but also for me."

"Why for you?"

"Because I can't get pregnant. Because I can't have a life like the one she was going to have. Because I can't figure out what's going on here, on this goddamn Island 3, and I can't stop it." The catch was back in her voice, a rising sob. She was talking herself back into a frantic state.

And now I did step forward and wrap my arms around her. Held her against me as well as I could with her folded arms between us. And after a moment, her head bent forward against my chest, vibrating with emotion at first and then, ever so slowly, easing.

"Do you want to have a child then?" I whispered.

"I used to, more than anything in this wide world," she muttered against the collar of my shirt. And I thought that was it, all she would say. But after a moment there was more. "But I was . . . wounded. When the doctor took my baby, the fetus out of me, he said I'd never have another. . . . My own life lost, and I can't even save the lives of the people on this goddamn island."

Our plan unfolded as late afternoon unspooled into evening. Turns out that Lucy was on friendly terms with the night shift attendant at the morgue, a younger nurse who admired Lucy and who would sit and talk, sharing a smoke while Lucy casually examined the corpses, seemingly at random. All of which, of course, was expressly against regulations.

Lucy's friend didn't come on duty till midnight, so we had some hours before us. I swallowed the dozen questions I wanted to ask her. Did she really think she was barren? Had she lost a child? With a twinge, I thought of Anna and our own child that was born dead. Who was the father of Lucy's child that never was? Where is he now?

I let those questions go unasked. Too intimate, too close, too warm for now. Questions that, if she answered them, might open up a bloody vein of truth between Lucy Paul and me. Truth that bound us, perhaps, or flung us further apart.

For now, I needed her to solve this place. Which was also what she needed me for—quite probably all she needed me for. The mystery of Ciara McManaway, whose ghost was slipping through the shadows with that of the *Hebrew girl* on the slab, two shades holding hands in swirling motes of dust. One leading the other away, perhaps into light.

When I looked up from these thoughts, Lucy was putting on

her shoes, double tying the laces with her swift nurse's efficiency. "I'm going to bathe," she said, "and find something edible in the canteen. . . . Are you going to eat?"

I shook my head. "No, I'm going to go spend a little time on Island 1. Send a telegram to . . . to the man who sent me here."

"Make your report?"

"Something like that. Ask him what the hell he's dropped me into. What the hell we're both into."

"Meet you back here then . . ." It was half a question, half suggestion. "I'll bring you something to eat."

"And the gin?"

That brought a smile and some shadowy light back into her eyes. "The gin or something else to answer the day."

William Smith . . . DEPARTMENT OF JUSTICE
Missing girl may be one of many[.] Unusual situation[.]
Need direction[.] Please advise[.]

Needless to say, William Smith was still my only official name for Will, the Nameless Man. The alias that would land my telegram in his pocket as opposed to that of a dozen others like him . . . if indeed, there were a dozen others in the world like him.

I wanted to walk and think before making my way back down to Island 3, which had begun to feel claustrophobic. I'd been there only a few days, and I was swimming in a dark, deep current, or so it seemed to me. I needed Anna, or at least the idea of Anna, to hold me upright, keep my head above water, and yet I couldn't find her with any certainty in my mind.

I stopped and bought three cigars from a vendor outside the Great Hall, slipped two into my jacket pocket and trimmed the third as I stood there. He tossed me a book of matches without our ever exchanging a word, and I walked on.

I had faith that the smoke would help me think, penetrate the maze of my mind and help me say to myself what I knew so far . . . and name the legion of things I didn't know.

I wandered down to the end of Island 1, through an open, parklike green, to the point at the edge of the breakwater. As so often happened in the harbor, the sky had changed radically during the afternoon, new weather sweeping in off the Atlantic. It wasn't raining, but the noonday sun was gone, and banks of fog were rolling in with the waves, obscuring the tip of the island from the Great Hall behind me.

I climbed over the iron railing and sat down below on one of the breakwater rocks. The tide was out, so my seat was dry, and the salt spray didn't reach me. It felt like a private place for my thoughts. Beneath, below, secreted from the human race.

I took several matches to set fire to the cigar, finally pulling strong puffs of smoke despite the fog-damp air. And after a few moments, fog and smoke and brine seemed to be all there was of the world.

I let my thoughts drift back to the south, toward Island 3. And in the drift, I knew that Ciara McManaway was dead. Nothing else made sense. The only real questions that I was faced with were what happened to her body, how had she died, and why had she died.

She easily could have ended up in the morgue like the *Hebrew girl*, with a misleading tag wired to her toe and her records destroyed or misplaced. She could have left the island in a pauper's pine box, labeled as anything, as a *German woman* or a *Spanish matron*.

Deeper. Another set of questions that lay further down. Who was Lucy Paul? Even if she wasn't a fiction, even if she was exactly who she said she was, there was still more mystery to her than reality. Her voice, her laughter seemed to swirl around me. The heat of the cigar smoke on my tongue brought more of her—the pressure of her body sleeping against me, her arms, her shoulders, the plaintive light in those eyes that shone like a raven's wing.

Who the hell was she? Where did that light come from? Why was she really here? The fog swept in around me, laced with the harsh, wild smell of the sea.

Out of the fog, another vision. Deeper yet. Beyond the one girl dead and the one living. I closed my own eyes, let my senses lapse except for tongue and lips, the tip of the clenched cigar that always reminded me of my father. Of my father and the high, plaintive fiddle tunes of home. In the memories, by the music, through the smoke, I drifted into a far distant time and place.

The farm in Anderson Cove, high in Madison County, the steep, green walls of North Carolina mountains. Morning now, and luminous fog drifts over the fields from the creek as dawn warms the cool fall air. My father coming from the barn, where he's already seen to the livestock. Walking toward me out of the sun-drenched mist with a grin on his face. Overjoyed in the bright, diffused light to be alive . . .

And to see me, his son.

He gestures toward me with one work-worn hand but doesn't speak— or rather speaks as one mind might directly to another. He tells me clearly to be careful.

He tells me to finish up my job and come home.

This was not so remarkable, this waking dream. I often meet up with him there. Talk with him. This was only remarkable because my father died of pneumonia when I was ten years old.

CHAPTER TWENTY-TWO

Returning home was not what the Nameless Man's reply instructed me to do:

Stephen Robbins . . . ELLIS ISLAND
Not surprised [.] Am in NY[.]
Meet tomorrow 2 pm[.] Brady's Saloon by the ferry docks[.]

I reread the telegram outside the Great Hall and then folded it carefully and slipped it into my jacket pocket. What did he mean by "not surprised"? Multiple disappearances and he's not surprised. Had the game changed from his perspective as well as mine . . . in the few days since I'd come to the island?

My walk back to Island 3 was shrouded in fog, rolling off the harbor in billows so thick at times that the Statue of Liberty a half mile away was invisible behind white walls. It was the middle of an August afternoon, but I was chilled inside my thin shirt and suit coat.

All the more reason that I was glad to see Lucy Paul, who had beaten me back to the psych ward. She had bathed and changed in the few hours since I'd seen her. She wore the same brown slacks from the night we'd broken into the baggage room, the same flat, practical shoes. But her blouse was a light tan, the color of sand perhaps. The skin of her neck and face were a darker umber that stood out against the soft cloth, and I caught again the faint scent of citrus when we sat together at the rickety table.

She'd brought sandwiches made from slabs of wheat bread, cut rough from the loaf, and hard cheddar cheese, sharp to the tongue and slathered with mustard. The sandwiches were thick and crusty and needed the dark-red wine she'd foraged from somewhere.

When I asked where, she just winked and said that it was better I not know.

"What did your boss say?" she asked as she chewed.

"You didn't ask who my boss is." This around my own mouthful of cheese and bread.

She nodded. "Who is he then?"

"Hell if I know." I paused before taking the next bite. Enjoyed a swallow of wine that tasted of sun and old barrels. "Works for the Justice Department, Bureau of Investigation. Hires me when there's something he can't find."

"Or someone."

I nodded.

"So you're a finder then?"

Again I nodded. "That's what I think. When he loses track of something . . . someone . . . then he sends me."

"So what did he say?"

I handed her the telegram and watched her as she unfolded it deftly with her left hand, balancing the crockery cup of wine in her right. For some reason, I was trusting her despite all my questions. Treating her as if I knew her.

"What does he mean, 'not surprised'?"

"Not surprised that Ciara McManaway is one of many. Not surprised that there are more to be found."

"Mmmm." She laid down the telegram on the table between us and took another bite. She seemed to enjoy the rough pleasure of biting and chewing the hard bread and thick cheese. After she swallowed, she said, "So you're leaving me . . . for Brady's Saloon."

"Twenty-four hours ashore, I imagine. Overnight anyway, depending on what the Nameless Man says. There was a name written in the back of Ciara McManaway's Testament. Something *Kennedy*. And an address. I'll try to find him to see if there's a connection."

She sipped her wine. "And you'll see her, I imagine."

"Her?"

"The woman. The one you can't shake out of your system. The one who keeps standing . . ." She motioned to me with her mug. "Standing between you and the rest of the world like . . ."

"Like a shield?" The wine, dark and strong, had already had its effect, and the words slipped out before much thought.

She nodded and smiled, her lips twitching. "Armor," she said. "It's like you're wearing armor, and I say it's because of her, if she's even real."

"Oh, she's real," I admitted. "I just don't know . . . how . . ."

"What's her name?"

I stared, unsure.

"No harm in my knowing." Lucy's smiling lips were stained with the wine. "I'll never meet her."

"Anna Ulmann," I said. "She's a photographer." I corrected myself. "A *documentary* photographer."

"An artist then. New Yorker?"

I paused. I'd never really thought to name her as such, but there it was. Anna was a woman bred and born in the city. Grew up on soot and concrete with only the living patch of Central Park for anything green. "She is," I admitted to Lucy, "a New Yorker."

"Different from you then," she replied with an impish grin. "With your Southern accent and your antique ways."

She had ruffled me, but only slightly. "Why the hell is this all about me? Who's the man that stands in your light? Who is he?" I'm not sure that what I said made any particular sense, but she caught my meaning.

It was her turn to pause. To consider. There was still a rose of wine on her brown lips, but now those lips were frowning.

"There have been several . . . men, I mean. But the one I loved, the one I thought to make a life with was the one who stabbed me in England."

I could feel my face tightening, and I leaned toward her, my whole body asking the next question.

"His name is Brantley McCallister, a Brit, a doctor. I served with him in an army hospital in London. Tall, blond, beautiful skin. Long, thin surgeon's fingers that he used to play the piano . . . and me."

"What happened?"

"A lot happened." She said it quickly, almost harshly. "I got pregnant, and he aborted the fetus. Do you know what that means?"

"Of course I understand. He—"

"Do you understand what that means to me as a woman! That he killed my baby? Do you? Took it from me because he didn't want the inconvenience of a child . . . or a marriage. Do you get that part?"

"No," I admitted. "I don't understand. But I can tell from your voice that it's the most important part, the scar that lasted."

"It is that."

"Where is he now?"

"In England, I think. He was discharged from the army and lost his medical license. But his family is very old and very wealthy, so I doubt if he's starving on a street corner."

"Did you want the abortion?"

She shook her head, not roughly, not riven with emotion, but firmly, out of long reflection. "I did not, your honor. I begged him to let me keep it and come back to America, but he was determined, and I was so under his spell that I let him talk me into it."

"And later you caught him stealing?"

"Morphine. I was a trained nurse, and the Army Medical Corps stationed me at that hospital to investigate why so many drugs went missing." She shrugged. "And after several months, I was too much in

95

love to see what was right in front of my face. My Brant, my beautiful, beautiful Brant, who played the piano like an angel, was an addict. Used it and sold it on the black market." She shrugged again, as if to shake off how much it all still haunted her. "He was probably high when he performed the abortion, but I was too stupid and too scared to see the signs."

"And when you found out, he stabbed you?"

She nodded, slowly then, reflecting. "I caught him red-handed, transferring vials of morphine from a supposedly locked cabinet into a padded case. I screamed like a banshee. Screamed so hard that I was hoarse for days. And he picked up the first thing to hand, a scalpel, and stabbed me to shut me up."

She stood and stepped around the corner of the table and then pulled up the bottom of her blouse. Without asking, she reached for my hand and lifted it up to her bare skin. Placed my fingers against the ribs beneath her left breast, which was still covered by her shirt.

I could feel in the slight indentation between ribs the puckered skin of the scar. An inch long perhaps.

For a long moment I let my fingers and then my hand rest against her. I could feel her breathing beneath the lift and play of her rib cage, beneath her warm, copper-colored skin. And in that moment, she was once again as real as anything in this shadowed world could be.

"He was enough of a doctor," she said, "that he was trying to puncture the lung and shut me up for good. But he missed somehow, probably because he was doped up."

"Thank God he missed." My voice was hoarse.

She gently lowered my hand to the table and let her shirt fall.

Still standing beside me, she put her own hand on my shoulder and let it rest there. "I suppose," she said. "At the time, I was sorry he didn't just kill me."

"Don't say that," I whispered.

"I'm not sorry now," she said softly.

Dusk had crept into the room while we were talking. She was

standing, I sitting, in the dark—a tableau of sorrow. I rose and lit the candles she had brought in previously, and by silent accord, we refilled our cups and carried them over to the matching bunks to sit across from each other—she on the bed where I slept, me on the bed where we'd gone through Ciara McManaway's bag.

"Enough about Dr. McCallister," she said after a sip. "And enough about me. What I want to know is the history of you and your Anna Ulmann."

And so I told her. All that I had words for.

CHAPTER TWENTY-THREE

Lucy's friend who worked the graveyard shift in the morgue was named Mabel, a medium-height, freckle-faced girl from Pennsylvania, whose broad, blue eyes always seemed wide with wonder at what she was seeing or hearing.

When Lucy introduced me, Mabel looked back and forth from Lucy to me with her wide-eyed stare and then winked dramatically at Lucy, which caused them both to laugh out loud.

Lucy had brought a half packet of cigarettes, the Chesterfields that Mabel favored. They both walked into the autopsy theater next door, where there was an open window, so they could blow smoke out into the midnight air.

I was left alone in the morgue. The hallway door was locked, and Mabel preoccupied.

I started at the top left-hand drawer and pulled open the door. Nothing. Worked my way down the first column, all four drawers, and still nothing. So I skipped to the middle of the second column and opened the drawer where earlier in the day we'd seen the Hebrew girl.

And there she was. Just as we'd left her, with the sheet pulled up to her chin and draped loosely over her face. I folded it down gently to her shoulders, as if she were sleeping and I might disturb her. I was still not as familiar with the dead as Lucy seemed to be.

I studied her face as if to memorize it, photograph it. There was a sprinkle of freckles over her nose and her cheeks just under her eyes, tiny dots of brown against the sallow gray skin. Her eyes were half-open, and I had again the uneasy sensation of disturbing her while she slept. I could just make out the bottom half of the iris of each eye. They were now a faded brown, the surrounding whites a cloudy gray like the skin of her face. No light, I thought.

It was then that I noticed a faint blush of blue-green on her left temple, just at the front edge of her ear. I reached out with both hands and tried to turn her head so that I could better see. But her neck was as stiff as a board, and I had to crouch a bit and lean in so that my eyes were only inches from the side of her head. I combed her hair back with my fingers, and there it was, what Lucy and I had both missed earlier in the day. A dark-blue bruise that went up into the hair above her ear, and the top of the ear itself blue and abraded.

Perhaps she had fallen and struck her head, or much more likely, someone had struck her hard enough to knock her out if not kill her. I called out to Lucy, and when she came back in, chatting easily with Mabel, I showed her the bruise.

She eased me out of the way and took my place, her face inches away from the corpse's head. Only she was much less gentle, pulling the girl's hair this way and that, peering into and behind her ear. Fingering her scalp, feeling for any depression in her skull. I know all of this because she described what she was doing as she worked, almost as if she was dictating, though neither Mabel nor I took notes.

"Someone hit her hard enough to render her unconscious," she concluded. "Probably with an open hand or a fist. Hit her hard enough so that there's blood in her ear. If it had been a club or other blunt object, there would be more swelling and you'd feel it in her skull. The blow didn't kill her but likely left her helpless."

She then pulled the sheet all the way down to the Hebrew girl's knees and began to go over her body almost inch by inch, searching for what might have killed her once she was unconscious. I turned to her friend Mabel, intending to distract her while Lucy worked.

"Where do the bodies go when they leave here?" I asked. "Surely not back across the ocean."

"Oh, Lord no," she said. "They go out one of two ways. If the deceased has a family or someone to claim 'em, then they is shipped to a funeral home in the city . . . at the family's expense. If they is no one to claim them, then they get boxed up in that cheap yellow pine and go straight to the potter's field on Hart Island." She leaned in closer, as if telling a secret. "I hear tell they ain't no individual graves out there but just one big hole where they get covered over by them inmates they use to bury 'em."

"How soon after someone dies do they get shipped out?"

"Why as soon as the family sends for them, or if there is no family, they go out to Hart Island ever Thursday, like clockwork. Unless the doctors want to cut . . . I mean dissect them for a lesson, and then we might keep 'em an extra week till they can schedule the theater." She nodded with her head to indicate the room next door. She was proud of all this knowledge, and I smiled to encourage her. "I help get 'em ready for the lesson study before my shift ends."

"Stephen?" Lucy's voice interrupted Mabel's happy explanation. When I turned back to her, she pointed to what looked like a pinprick on the inside of the Hebrew girl's arm. A small spot of blood on the inside of her elbow surrounded by bruises under the skin. "Hypodermic needle," she whispered to me when I leaned close. "That has to be it."

She covered the corpse back up, pulling the sheet neatly over the dead girl's quiet face. "Anybody else in here?" she asked Mabel after pushing the tray back into the wall and closing the cubicle.

Mabel pointed. "Supposed to be somebody in that last drawer on the bottom," she said, "though I ain't looked at the paperwork."

I leaned over to open the door to which she'd pointed and pulled out the slight, sheet-covered form on the tray. With Lucy standing across from me, I pulled down the sheet as far as the body's waist. The corpse was recognizably that of a thin white man, but the body was weirdly pink and gray, boiled almost, and every inch of skin was swollen tight as if from within.

"Oh my God," I muttered.

"What is it?" Lucy whispered.

"Not what—who! It's that nurse who told me all about the McManaway girl. His name is Thompson."

"What in God's name happened to him?" she asked, reaching out gingerly to touch the skin on his chest.

"I don't know. But whatever it was, whoever did it, this changes everything."

She straightened up to stare closely into my face. "Why?" she whispered.

I leaned over close to her. "Don't you see?" I muttered into her ear. "He's dead because he talked to me."

In Print

The present law excludes idiots, insane persons, epileptics, persons who have been insane within five years previous and persons who have had two or more attacks of insanity at any time previously. In 1904, under these provisions, 49 persons were debarred out of 812,870. Of these 49 persons, 16 were idiots and 33 were insane persons. While the law no doubt tends to exclude some who are obviously insane, there is reason to believe that many escape detection, and that some come in through Canada who would be debarred by inspectors at Atlantic ports. Probably there is a much larger class who have been out of insane hospitals in Europe only a few months when they enter the United States. These persons are sane enough to pass the ordinary inspection; but, failing to find employment and having spent their money, they become ill-fed and soon go to pieces; after which they are recommitted here.

The act of 1891 added to the excluded classes persons suffering from loathsome or dangerous contagious diseases. In 1903, 1773 persons were debarred for these causes. These diseases include two practically unknown in America until the beginning of immigration from southeastern Europe and Asia, favus and trachoma. The former is an affection of the scalp; the latter a disease of the eyes and eyelids, which if not cured results in blindness. Other diseases causing exclusion are small-pox, cholera, tuberculosis, and venereal diseases. Favus and trachoma have attracted most attention because of the difficulty of their detection and the serious results of their domestication. In 1904, out of 812,870 immigrants, 1560 were rejected because suffering from loathsome or dangerous diseases, and 6440 were treated in the hospitals for various ailments.

While a few immigrants are thus debarred because of diseases, large numbers are allowed to land who are poor in physique and destined shortly to develop acute troubles. In the majority of cases it is impossible to detect incipient cases of tuberculosis among the steerage passengers in the time available for observation; and there are many immigrants, not actually tuberculous when they land, who quickly become infected through living in unsanitary conditions and in close contact with those already affected.

from *Immigration and its Effects upon the United States*
by Prescott F. Hall, A.B., LL.B
Henry Holt and Company (1906)

PART TWO

CHAPTER TWENTY-FOUR

Brady's Saloon at two in the afternoon was almost empty. Dark and cool inside as if the dusty heat and glare outside couldn't penetrate a building that old. The Nameless Man was one of only a handful of people in the place, and he had claimed a booth along the back wall near the kitchen door. Since the Volstead Act, places like Brady's couldn't serve beer out in the open, which in this case meant that it had to be brought in from the kitchen in a crockery pitcher rather than poured straight from the tap at the bar.

When I walked in a few minutes before two, the Nameless Man had a pitcher and what looked like two coffee mugs already on the table. He tossed me a menu when I sat down. "Corned beef," he said.

"What?"

"You're going to ask me what's the best thing they serve. It's corned beef. Get it on rye."

"Sure. You?"

He was pouring out of the pitcher into my mug. "I ate hours ago. And as soon as we're done here, I'm headed back."

"To Washington?"

He smiled but didn't so much as acknowledge the question.

I sipped from my own cup. It was dark and cold and surprisingly good.

"Tell me," he said, "what you've found so far. And try not to—"

"Leave anything out. I know the drill. You'll hear something in what I say that I didn't know was there."

He nodded.

And so I told him, even referring to some notes I'd taken to be certain I got all the names right. He had me describe Thompson's body twice when I was done. "What would do that to a man?" I asked him, sensing his interest pointing there.

He shrugged. "Very high heat maybe. An oven of some kind. It's a hospital. Do they wash dishes or sanitize instruments?"

I made a mental note. He was right. He'd heard something in my own telling that I hadn't had time to think of.

"Describe the woman again," he said.

"Which?"

"Lucy Paul, the nurse."

I described, keeping to the surfaces and leaving out the night she'd stayed in my room and some of our more private conversations. But I did throw in most of her story about England and the doctor who'd stabbed her.

"What was the doctor's name?" he asked.

I told him, assuming he'd use it to check her story.

And then suddenly, he changed directions entirely. "Do you know who Prescott Hall is?"

I shook my head.

He's a little pissant college man. Lives in Boston and wears a very stiff collar. Some kind of lawyer, but mostly what he does is advocate for the purity of the American people.

"Whatever that is."

"Exactly. Whatever that is. He's the founder of something called the Immigration Restriction League, and he's especially perturbed about the decline of the Nordic race in America due to interbreeding with foreigners. Here, take this with you." He reached into his jacket pocket and handed me a thin, formal-looking pamphlet.

"What does he have to do with . . . ?" I nodded out toward Ellis Island, which sat in the harbor not a mile away.

"Hall himself? Probably nothing. But his ideas might have everything to do with it." He had been restlessly looking around the bar and out into the street but turned at that point to stare into my face. "I'm thinking of pulling you out of there," he said quietly. "I think you're right that there's a killer or killers at work, and I'd rather not have you disappear on my watch."

He caught me off guard with that, but I could feel myself shaking my head even as the answer was forming in my mind. "You forget where I come from," I said to him. "Don't you remember watching me stand trial for murder?"

He smiled grimly but then seemed to relax. "I recall visiting you in the sinkhole of a jail they have down there in . . . what? Bunk County?"

"Buncombe. Close enough."

"You saying you're up to this? If you are, you should know that there's a lot of attention being paid to that island and everything it represents. The war stirred up all the anti-immigration feeling in this sorry old country of ours, and there's a lot of hatred in the air. That New Jersey congressman who first pulled us into this . . ."

"Ciara McManaway's uncle?"

"Yeah, the Irish leprechaun. He's a staunch anti-immigration boy. Says we're all going to be replaced by hordes of Eastern European Gypsies and red Russian rabble. And Jews. He's especially terrified of Jews."

"I thought it was the Irish that were going to destroy us?"

"You're late to the dance," he said with an ironic grin. "That was last century. Now it's Polacks and Jews from Russia. Anybody who's not white as paper and English speaking."

"So what does all this have to do with . . . ?"

The smile faded from his pale, nondescript face. "We think it likely that there's a conspiracy of some kind going on at Ellis Island. Has been since the war. And if we looked hard enough, we'd find out that there are forces there who are doing their own brand of immigration restriction. Keeping out the unwashed and unwanted."

"Why didn't you tell me this before?"

"We didn't connect the dots. The McManaway girl didn't seem like she fit the profile. Irish girl with contacts didn't seem like the kind of victim that they would keep out."

"So these mysterious forces are more dangerous than you thought?" He nodded. "Probably."

"I'm your man," I said.

"I thought you'd say that." He paused to gesture with his cup, and we clinked our crockery mugs together.

"Here's to survival," I said, and we both drank.

"In the interest of survival," he replied after a moment, "I'm sending you a present."

"Which is?"

"See the man seated at the far end of the bar?"

"Looks like he could eat the bar if he wanted?"

"That's him." The Nameless Man shrugged. "Don't let his size fool you. It's not all fat. He's sitting there so you can get a good look at him. In a minute, he's going to finish eating and walk out."

"What's his name?"

"Doesn't matter. Call him Santa next time you see him."

"'Cause he brings Christmas?"

"Sure. Next time you see him will be the four o'clock ferry tomorrow at the main dock out there on Ellis Island. He's going to disembark just long enough to give you a package."

I raised my eyebrows, let my face ask the question.

"As I recall, you're not afraid of guns." It wasn't a question, and he went on. "What could you use in this case?"

I thought for a moment. "Something that looks dangerous. A shotgun, double-barrel. And something that will more or less hide in a pocket but still pack a wallop."

"Thirty-eight enough of a wallop?"

"Sure," I said. "Though I hope not to use it."

"You use it if you need to." He slid to his end of the booth but then paused. "Almost forgot. When you get back to the island, make an appointment and go by to see Wallis."

"The new commissioner?"

"Yeah. We've warned him you're there and that he's to let you go about your business, but it wouldn't hurt for him to put a face with the name."

"What kind of man is he?" I asked.

This brought a flicker of a smile to that pale face. "Oh, he's a Christian gentleman," he replied. "And he's likely to keep you in his prayers."

CHAPTER TWENTY-FIVE

T he address in Ciara McManaway's Testament, 411 West 33rd
Street, was a tenement building in several long blocks of the same.
Two cliffs of concrete facing each other across the avenue, the avenue
itself crowded with horse-drawn wagons and carts as well as gangs of
children playing every game imaginable, including stickball with a
homemade ball and bat.

It was a warm, sunny afternoon, and the wash lines overhead,
strung from one side of the street to the other, were festooned with
two or three stories of laundry flapping lazily in the breeze. There was
the smell of manure from the horses below and cooking food from
several of the windows.

The front steps of 411 were made of rough planks scrounged no
doubt from some job site elsewhere in the city. The once ornate doorway stood wide open into a hallway lined by doors on either side,
leading to a broad stairwell. Most of the doors along the hallway stood
open to let the air circulate, and while it was quieter than the street,
the interior of the building still had the busy daytime clatter of pots
on stoves, children crying or yelling, women calling out to each other
from room to room. I knocked politely on the frame of the first open
door I came to—so politely that no one heard me. I leaned in and
rapped on the door itself to make more noise, and a woman emerged
from an inner room, most likely the kitchen.

"And who are you, then?" she said pleasantly, wiping her hands on her apron. "And what is it you be wantin', with your knockin' and callin' out?" It was, as best I could tell, broad Munster, and I was half guessing at her words.

"I'm looking for a family named Kennedy, perhaps a Samuel or Angela."

"And why would you be lookin' for the Kennedys?"

"I'm from Ellis Island, the Immigration Services, and I'm trying to find someone who may be related to them—a young woman named Ciara McManaway."

"Why do you want to find her? To send her back, is it?"

"No, no. Just to return this . . ." I showed the woman the girl's Testament, including the words written in the back. "And to make sure she's alright."

"I canna read that," she said pleasantly. "But you have an honest face, and I take you at your word."

"Do you know the Kennedys? Can I talk to them?"

"You could talk if they was here, and a pleasant talk it would be. But Angela and her Sam are gone. Long gone."

A haunting thought flitted across my mind. "Surely not dead?"

"Oh no. Mary, Joseph, and Patrick preserve us." She paused to cross herself. "Gone on to Boston this spring in search of a livin'. What did you say the girl's name was, the girl you're lookin' for?"

"McManaway."

"There's a McManaway on the third floor up, a cranky old man from Dublin that works mornins cleanin' the streets. You might ask him about your girl. But, mister . . ." She paused.

"Yes, ma'am."

"Don't go tellin' the people you're from that island if you want them to talk to you. They'll think you come to take 'em back."

I gave the entire building two hours of that increasingly hot, increasingly muggy day. On the second floor, I said I was from the police department and got nothing but blank stares and sullen looks. On the third floor, I found old man McManaway, who was no help at all except to say that Sam Kennedy owed him money and where the hell was he anyway. On the fourth floor, I tried a different approach altogether and said I was from the Catholic charity uptown and was blessed by three different women, one of whom kept calling me Father. And so on to the top floor.

Nothing that said anything about Ciara McManaway except what her life would have been like had she made it ashore. The building held twenty apartments and at least one hundred people of all shapes, sizes, and ages. All Irish. Many who spoke little or no English. Hot, sweaty, crowded.

And happy.

I was offered three tots of whiskey and a pint of cream. I was asked to judge the relative beauty of two pale-as-milk babies with identical carrot hair and startling blue eyes. I was given a charm against the devil and forced to taste a mysterious but delicious stew.

I was sure that had Ciara McManaway survived and somehow made her way to 411 West 33rd Street, she would have slipped seamlessly into this teeming, bustling life, blessed hourly by St. Patrick, her and her baby both.

But she had not survived, nor had her baby found a safe passage into this life.

I got a different sort of welcome at 1000 Fifth Avenue; although, the accent that greeted me was much the same. This was the address I had shared for several years with Anna Ulmann, and the some-time servant who kept house for us while Anna worked was Maitlen "Mattie" McCall, a tall, thin Irish woman who had trained my ear over those mostly happy months. Trained my ear such that I had understood most of what was said to me in the tenement on West 33rd Street.

It was early evening by the time I arrived there, across the street from the lush trees and sun-flecked greenery of Central Park. After

Mattie brought me a cup of tea into the front parlor room, I asked after Anna, who wasn't at home, and for once in my long and happy relation with Mattie, she hesitated in reply. Started at least three sentences but broke each off in turn, and this from someone for whom talking was as natural as breathing.

"Is she at the gallery?" I finally asked. "Working up the exhibit?"

She nodded emphatically, relieved, I thought, not to have to say where her mistress was.

"Working late, is she?"

"Sometimes she works late and late, most of the night."

I should have caught the tone in her voice, but it was so soft and so lilting that I missed it. "I think I'll go surprise her there," I said. "I long to see her."

"Oh, sir . . . why not . . . just spend the evening here at home? Rest you from your labors."

But I didn't listen to Mattie, didn't hear the subtle plea in her voice. I was distracted by the room in which I sat, a room that held so much of her, of Anna. Her camera itself stood to one side on its new wooden tripod, for it was in this room that she took the portraits of famous artists that generated much of her income. The walls were lined with bookshelves, which contained many of her father's books, with a dozen or so of mine now, books on the Southern mountains that we had once enjoyed reading together. How long ago? A year perhaps, when we were glad simply to be alive and together.

So yes, I was distracted both by the haunting thoughts of Ellis Island and the mysteries that swirled there, lingering in my mind from the previous hours and days, and also by the ambiance of this room where I sat drinking my tea. It was a room that less than a year before I would have called home, easy and relaxed. A room which still had the power to move my heart within my chest.

" . . . make up the spare bedroom for you," Mattie was saying, interrupting my drifting thoughts.

"Why the spare bedroom?" I asked. "Why not . . . ?" And I realized that she was assuming Anna and I no longer slept together.

"No . . . thank you, Mattie. But I will take my old valise, the one I brought from North Carolina, and several changes of clothes."

She looked so sad, did our Mattie, that I sought to reassure her, and in so doing, myself as well. "I'm not leaving for good," I told her. "But this job I have now may keep me away for another few weeks."

"And what is it you are about, Mr. Stephen, in this job of yours?" But she was out of the room even as she asked, bustling to find my old, scarred leather valise.

"I'm trying to find someone," I replied softly to the empty room.

In 1920, the Anderson Art Galleries were at Madison Avenue and 40th Street in what Anna liked to call the old Grant residence, one of the finest private homes in the upper Murray Hill section. I had little sense of what the Grant residence or Murray Hill meant in her world, but I knew how to locate Madison and Fortieth, and I knew a mansion when I saw one.

The ornate front doors to the place were standing open into a vestibule lined with oak paneling and lit by gaslights to either side. I knocked at the inner door, for it was nearly seven o'clock by then, and even the long summer afternoon had begun to wane. I had no idea if the gallery was open to the public.

A young male attendant, impeccably dressed in what looked like livery, came to let me in and took the valise along with my hat into what must have been the mansion's cloakroom once upon a time. He was quite friendly and asked me if I was from the press and would I like a tour of the paintings on the first floor.

I inquired about Anna and her photographs, the exhibit scheduled for the end of the month, and he nodded crisply. "'Portraits of Famous Artists and Writers,'" he replied, "is being installed on the second floor, just to the left at the head of the stairs. If I'm not mistaken,

Miss Ulmann is up there now with the show's sponsor, Ezekiel Grant, giving him a private tour."

I glanced into the bland, friendly face. "*Grant* as in the former owner of this house?"

"Well, yes . . . I mean no." He leaned closer and whispered, "The former owner of the Grant Mansion is Ezekiel II. The gentleman with Miss Ulmann is Ezekiel III."

"Who made the money?"

"Ezekiel the First, or so I'm told."

"Shipping?"

Slight shake of the head. "Railroads."

I walked slowly up the wide marble stairway to the second floor, leaving my young acquaintance at his post by the front door. Halfway up, I could hear voices above. Voices and laughter, from which I could pick out Anna's, dear to me as always, but with a slightly exaggerated tone as it echoed through these high ceilings and wide halls.

Not sure if I would be interrupting an important conference, I was quiet as I climbed, even more so when I reached the landing above, sliding my feet noiselessly along the polished marble. The wide doors to the room on the left were barely ajar, leaving just enough room for one or perhaps two people to slip through. The voices had stilled. But from just outside the door, I could hear someone gasping.

I stepped quietly through the doorway into the gaslit gallery. I suppose I noticed that Anna's photographs lined the walls, because later, when I recalled that moment, I could sense them there, faces famous in New York and as large as life. Those black-and-white faces surrounding us and seeing the same thing I saw . . . Anna holding and being held. Locked inside a hungry, consuming kiss with a tall, beautiful man dressed in evening clothes. Their sighs—even, God help me, her moan—were audible through the thin, frozen air. Audible though their mouths were busy tasting and devouring.

I don't remember the stairs going down or the young doorman. I can't recall anything till I was back on the sidewalk, my hat crushed in one fist, the worn, cracked handles of my valise clutched in the other.

CHAPTER TWENTY-SIX

Alcoholics.
Anarchists.
Contract laborers.
Criminals.
Convicts.
Epileptics.
Feebleminded.
Idiots.
Illiterates.
Imbeciles.
Insane persons.
Paupers.
Persons afflicted with contagious diseases.
Persons being mentally or physically defective.
Persons with constitutional psychopathic inferiority.
Political radicals.
Polygamists.
Prostitutes.
Vagrants.

All of these persons—from alcoholics to vagrants—were forbidden entry to the country by the Immigration Act of 1917. Locked out

119

of the U S of A by congressional action, during a wartime spasm of righteousness so convulsive that it overrode Wilson's presidential veto.

The bitter as gall irony is that on that night in August 1920—I qualified. I was most of the people on that list: *alcoholic, contract laborer, criminal, convict, idiot, imbecile, insane, afflicted, defective, inferior, vagrant.*

I walked the echoing streets of Manhattan that night, lost in a buzzing nightmare of despair. I had already been tried for murder twice before, and if I could have gotten my laborer's hands around the handsome neck of Ezekiel Grant III, I would have gladly qualified for a third time.

Alcoholic? I'd walked that stony path as well. And on that dreary night, I was consumed with thirst for something wicked.

Idiot, imbecile, insane, afflicted. Take your pick . . . I was all of those to believe that a scarred and battered man from the mountains of Western North Carolina, a childhood runaway who all but taught himself to read, could earn and keep the love of a New York sophisticate. Anna Ulmann, an artist with the camera, who spoke three languages and had traveled in first-class luxury to Europe, probably to some of the same countries we now forbade entry. A woman whose ex-husband had roped her with pearls and dropped diamonds down the front of her frocks.

Defective, inferior? Oh, *hell* yes. In her eyes—obviously. If she thought I was worthless, then I was worthless.

In the eyes of Ezekiel Grant III and his Princeton or Yale or Harvard classmates, I was less than worthless. In the eyes of the art critics who would attend the opening night of her extraordinary "Portraits of Famous Artists and Writers" and praise her in the *New York Times*, I didn't exist at all.

I only stopped walking once that long and ugly night, when I went into a dingy café down near the docks. A hobo had told me I could get a drink there, and he was right. I ate ham and eggs washed down with what the brawny waitress promised me was rye whiskey. Thirty minutes later, I heaved up the whole mess into a trash can in an alley, leaving my gut empty and my head spinning from liquor fumes.

Walking. And on that night, the city stank. With unwashed human bodies, with sacks of garbage left too long on the sidewalk, with the tons of horse manure dropped daily onto cracked and broken pavement. The street sweepers were out in force that night, fighting their epic losing battle, but what could they do in the heat of the summer night to take the stench of wealth and humanity out of the air?

At some point, it began to rain. So that the air was made of sweat and grease and soapy water flung from a tenement window, while rainwater stained yellow with horse piss foamed in the gutters.

Was I a famous artist? I asked myself over and over in the slap-footed rhythm of endless walking. "Hell no," I whispered or spoke or yelled to no one in particular. I was the soaking wet garbageman who came at night to clean up after foolish, stupid, lonely humanity. The ignorant country boy whose mouth was stuffed with corn bread and his brain with banjo twang.

Did *my* portrait hang on the ornate walls of the Anderson Galleries, framed by her loving eyes? Would it ever hang there? Not now, I realized as I stumbled along those drenched and lonely streets. Not ever.

Oh, I might hang. Especially if I kept working for the Nameless Man. But my portrait?

Never in the gallery of the living.

Unless there was an exhibit of the Idiot, the Imbecile, and the Afflicted.

CHAPTER TWENTY-SEVEN

I was on the first ferry back to the island the next morning—wet, bedraggled, exhausted from walking. I was so tired, my eyelids were sore. My arms ached from carrying the old, scarred valise in first one hand and then the other. Somewhere along the way, my hat had disappeared, left in an alley or flung into a trash heap.

When I stepped off the ferry at the dock in front of the main processing hall, I didn't stop to rest or speak to anyone, rather kept walking the quarter mile farther I had to go. My mind was fixated on the shabby little haven in the psychopathic ward on Island 3. If I could just keep moving, shuffling one foot in front of the other, to there, then I could barricade the door and sleep. Just sleep with—please, God—no dreams.

The stairs were the worst. Climbing up to the second floor of Building E, it was all I could do, using the handrail, to pull my tired legs up, thighs burning, one step at a time. I made it to the second floor on my own, climbing slowly, all but blank with despair and fatigue. I'm not sure that I would have made it all the way down the hall if she hadn't found me there, stranded on the landing.

At first, I thought she was a dream, an apparition. Dressed all in white, from her toes right up to the white cap in her hair. It was only with touch that the specter became slightly more real. She—for it was a woman—pried the valise out of my right hand, set it on the floor, and began to massage the clutching fingers.

"Stephen?" The white form was saying something. A name . . . perhaps my name. "Stephen, are you alright?"

I nodded, though it was probably more like a shiver.

"Do you want to go to your room?"

Shiver again.

"I just came off my shift. I'm going to take you to your room."

Which seemed like a wonderful idea to me, that she would help me get home to that cot, with the morning breeze blowing sunlight in through open windows.

Lucy Paul carried the valise in one hand and used the other to haul me along. Pulled me from the landing into the hallway and then barricaded the door behind us. She didn't take me straight to my cell, however, but led me unexpectedly into a larger room halfway down where there was a tub in the center of the room.

She sat me down on a bench that ran along one wall, told me to stay put, and fiddled with the handles that fed hot and cold water into the tub until she was satisfied with the temperature. While the tub began to fill, she unpinned the hat from her hair, removed her white shoes, and sat beside me on the bench to unbutton her white stockings from their garters and peel them from her legs.

Demure, I thought vaguely as I watched her. She seemed to me ever so demure, even as she was stripping white hose down over her bronze thighs. I was vaguely aware of wanting to touch her; my hand twitched where it lay between us on the bench.

As the thought of touching drifted through my mind like smoke, she knelt beside me and began to pull my wet shoes and socks off my aching feet. When she was done, she stood me up and began to undress me.

"What in the world happened to you?" she said conversationally as she peeled first the soaking wet jacket off my shoulders and then moved on to the shirt beneath.

"Should you . . ." I finally managed to say as she worked at the buttons. ". . . be doing . . . ?"

"Be doing this?" she said, stripping the shirt over my shoulders and down my arms. "Probably not, but I am a nurse. Trained to treat the weak and infirm."

She paused only long enough to turn and check the water temperature in the tub by lifting one leg over the side and dipping in her toes. "Not warm enough," she muttered and gave the hot water knob a twist.

She turned back to me and, without hesitating, reached out to my belt buckle. With her hands on my belt, the fingers tantalizingly against my skin, she stopped to stare questioningly into my face. "What did happen to you, Stephen?" And then after a moment. "She happened to you, didn't she?"

"Anna . . ." I managed to say.

"Yeah . . . her. Your Anna Whatever. She said something, didn't she? Or did something?"

"Rich man," I said. "Patron of the arts."

"She's screwing a rich man? And he's mounting her . . . what did you call it? Her exhibition?"

I nodded. "Mounting her . . ."

"City bitch," Lucy said decisively and began to unbuckle my belt.

She held my arm as I climbed over the edge of the deep tub. Tears seeped out of my eyes as I sunk down into the delicious heat of the water. She leaned over me then and licked the tears away, almost as a cat might.

After undoing the top button or two of her uniform and rolling up her sleeves, she began to wash me. She used a bar of soap she'd found in a drawer, and with strong, professional hands scrubbed first my back and then my chest and stomach.

"You get in too," I think I said to her at one point. Though the water was so hot and what it did to me so fine that my memories are hazy.

"Tonight maybe," she said. "When you're rested."

Then she stood me up and began to soap and rinse everything

from the waist down. Her hands, with the bar of soap and washcloth, were sure and professional. But even so, when she came finally to my penis, I was as hard as kingdom come, stiff with need.

"Is that for her?" she asked, soaping my balls with just such a gentle squeeze.

"You," was all I said. And then, "All you."

She stroked the shaft with a soapy hand. Once. Twice. Almost pulling me out of my skin. "If it is for me, then it'll keep," she said.

Then she must have put me to bed on the cot in my room because that's where I woke around noon. Drifted up out of the depths of sleep slowly, ever so pleasantly, trying lazily to recall a dream. Not the nightmare that came first the night before, but the later dream of hot water and soft hands.

Eventually, a splinter of reality needled its way into my consciousness as I sat up and began to pull fresh clothes out of my valise. There was something I was supposed to do. Or several things . . . from talking to the Nameless Man. It seemed like the conversation had taken place weeks ago rather than just hours, and it took a walk down to the bathing room to find my shoes to bring back my memory.

I was supposed to meet the large man that I'd seen in Brady's Saloon on the main dock. Watch for him on the four o'clock ferry.

I needed to make an appointment to see Frederick Wallis, warn him what we were up to and ask him some questions. Was there a mechanism somewhere in the hospital wards that would cook an entire human being . . . what was left of Thompson?

But first, I had to go meet Santa.

CHAPTER TWENTY-EIGHT

When he got off the ferry, the man from Brady's was carrying a large black duffel bag with a strap over his shoulder. It looked innocent enough but heavy.

"You Robbins?" he said jovially after picking me out of the crowd milling on the dock.

"If you're Santa, I am."

As he transferred the bag to me, he leaned in to speak more privately. "There's more Christmas in here than was originally discussed," he said quietly but clearly. "Also, he said to tell you that she is who she says she is."

"Who . . . ?"

"There's a woman nurse. She checks out. Is who she says she is. Make sense?"

I nodded. "Best news I've had all day."

He grinned. "See you around, Cap. Good luck with that." He nodded at the bag and slipped easily back into the crowd. A moment later, I saw him skip nimbly back onto the ferry.

By the time I marched the duffel bag back down to Island 3 and up the stairs to the psych ward, the canvas strap was cutting into my shoulder. When I had reset the barricade on the outer door and lugged the duffel down to the end of the hall, Lucy Paul was there, having bathed and changed. Maybe I hadn't dreamed what happened that morning after all.

She laid what she had been reading down on the rickety table and watched while I unpacked the duffel. Weirdly, the very first thing in the sack was a book. I handed it to Lucy, and she read the title aloud: "*The Passing of the Great Race: Or, the Racial Basis of European History* by"—she held it up to the light from the window—"somebody named Madison Grant."

After I dug under the blanket that came next, I pulled out a small, heavy object wrapped in a chamois cloth. I handed this to Lucy as well, who, once she felt the weight, was careful in unwrapping it. "Smith & Wesson .38," she said immediately, and I glanced up in surprise. "I was issued one like it in England," she said. "Even learned to fire it at a melon one Sunday afternoon."

"Did you hit the melon?"

She smiled. "Eventually."

Beneath it was an Ithaca 12-gauge with the double-barrel disassembled from the wooden stock. I snapped it together and was surprised to see that the barrel was sawed off short just an inch beyond the end of the stock.

"Good Lord," Lucy said. "Do you . . . ?"

I nodded. "This is from my world," I said. "Some call it a scatter-gun . . . for negotiating with recalcitrant drovers and such down South."

"I can only imagine."

"It's not a precision instrument, but it will blow a hole in a wall."

"Or a person."

"That too."

And then beneath it was something neither one of us had ever seen . . . something I hope never to see again. It was a machine pistol. Brand new with Thompson stamped on the side and a round magazine that was apparently designed to snap into the mechanism and feed .45 caliber bullets into the chamber more or less constantly. The magazine was heavy enough that it was obviously full, but it wasn't attached to the gun. I laid both on the spare cot, so that Lucy and I could examine them.

"What in God's name does your boss think you need that for?"

I smiled grimly. "He said that things here . . . said there was a conspiracy on the island to prevent unwanted people from entering the country. Leftover from the war. Apparently, he thinks it's bigger or nastier than even you and I thought."

She nodded at the table. "That pamphlet was in your jacket pocket. Prescott somebody or other says we're about to be replaced by the immoral rabble of Eastern Europe and Northern Africa. They will outbreed us, and soon there won't be any Americans left in America."

"He gave that to me. Said that brand of horseshit was likely behind all this."

"You think he's right?"

I shrugged. "As stupid as it sounds, think about what our friend Nurse Adams preaches."

"The Gypsies?"

"And the Romanians and the Slovakians and the Russians. Although she does seem to think the Gypsies smell worse and make more babies with more, different fathers than anybody in the history of the species."

"That thing"—Lucy nodded at the Thompson with its oily gleam—"scares me. Not much scares me, but that does."

We put the machine gun back in the duffel and hid the whole behind a stack of blankets in a cabinet in the adjoining room, the shotgun with its box of shells under the mattress of the spare cot, and then folded the .38 inside my shirts in the corner chifforobe. Then, and only then, did we break into the bottle of honest-to-God, illegal scotch—bonded and sealed—that was also in the sack. Books, guns, and Prohibition booze . . . Christmas come early.

By that summer, whiskey of any kind was a rare thing. The scotch we'd slipped into the Nameless Man's coffee mug at the Algonquin was from a secret and dwindling supply that we'd saved back, mostly for our friends from the Round Table.

The bottle that was buried in that black duffel bag was better than anything I'd seen since the summer of '19, before the Volstead Act actually took effect. It had enough of a bite at the end of a long sip so that both Lucy and I added a splash of water along with some of the ice she'd brought with her from the nurses' canteen. It was dark and smoky, which fit the mood of that haunted evening.

The fog was back outside, ghosting in from the harbor, and what had been midafternoon an hour before suddenly felt like early evening. We lit one candle for our rickety table, and Lucy laid out the dark, crusty bread and sharp cheese she liked.

I'd already thrown off my jacket and unbuttoned my collar. She was wearing a black skirt that night, along with one of the loose linen blouses she favored when she was off duty. She must have kicked off her shoes when she first came into the room because they lay haphazard under the table.

Dusk heightened by a sense of fog and smoke, the room drifting off from the rest of the hectic world. We nibbled at the bread and cheese but mostly sipped from our glasses. Conversation, always so playful between us, always so vibrant, died slowly away, and since my glass was somehow going dry, I got up and built us both another scotch with ice and a splash. While I was pouring, I kicked my own shoes off as well.

When I sat back down, I let one full dollop of the scotch sit in my mouth, swirling it and warming it with my tongue. And while the chill, smoky numbness spread into my face, I watched her tear off a bite of bread with her teeth and chew it slowly, a smile tickling the corners of her lips as she moistened the hard bread with her own sip of the whiskey.

As I watched those berry-brown lips sip and chew, the tip of her tongue moistening her lips, the harsh strain that had riveted my head to my neck since the night before slowly began to flow out of me, down my spine and out of my body.

She must have sensed that she was having an effect on me because she stood and whispered that she had a present. She reached into the pocket of her skirt and brought out, of all things, a key. Held it over the candle so that I could see the light reflected along its side. She walked over to the hallway door and slipped the key into the dead bolt, and after toying with it for a moment, locked our door from the inside.

"Locking me in?"

She smiled and shook her head. "Locking the world out," she said in her husky contralto. "All the murderers and faithless lovers, all the pretty doctors and fancy artists. All the rich bastards in the world, mounting their exhibitions and playing pianos."

The breeze was blowing freely across the corner of our darkening room, billowing the curtains in our two windows and winkling the candle flame. As the human world retreated, it felt quieter in the room. She slipped from the door back to the table only a few feet away. I lifted and turned my chair to face her, not sure what was to come but feeling that the most natural thing in the world was to turn fully toward her.

She was standing with her bare feet spread on the scuffed wooden floor. Slowly, languorously, she crossed her arms in front of her and lifted the linen shirt over her head and dropped it on the floor.

I could feel the pulse in my throat.

"What is that?" I whispered hoarsely.

"It's a corselette," she said. And then by way of explanation, "French. I made it to Paris for a week after the war."

"You're the last woman on earth who needs a corset."

"It's not for me, silly. It's for you. . . . Besides, it hides my ugly scar."

"Does *it* come with a key?"

Her lips pursed in an ironic smile. "No, it doesn't. But I figure a bright boy like you can manage it. Do you like it?"

She stood there in that dusky, breezy room with her hands on her hips. Black skirt, lacy black corset and not much bra, and everywhere else her skin. Creamy in the pale quiver of candlelight. The evening tide was rising outside, and the air was salty.

"I like it," I confessed. "All of it."

She reached behind her back, unzipped her skirt and let it fall. More black lace and not much of it.

I stood, lightheaded with whiskey and need. And when she stepped forward into my arms, she felt, for the first time since I'd met her, small. Small and perhaps fragile.

"You're trembling," she said. "Are you cold?"

"No," I said into the tangled mass of her hair. And then into her open mouth, teeth and tongue, "No . . . not cold . . . warm . . . yes."

We managed the corselette and a belt buckle, a sock, some buttons here and there, cotton and lace, all without a key. We found our way inside the sheets on that small cot, and later as the candle flared, found our way inside each other.

There was moaning and whimpering within the Ellis Island psych ward that night. My own and hers. Mingled in the wind.

And later, just as we were falling into a tangled, dreamy sleep, I whispered into the seashell whorl of her ear, "You are far more than just your scars."

She only had to turn her head slightly on the pillow in response, so that her tongue could flick out to lick my own battered face.

CHAPTER TWENTY-NINE

She left me before midnight after slowly untangling her legs from mine, slipping her arm from under my neck.

"Don't," I said. A whisper in the ambient dark. "Stay."

"My shift starts at twelve," she said quietly. "I have to go, or I'll end up on report."

She was sitting on the side of the cot to pull on her underthings. I rolled toward her and slipped my arm around her waist, not helping at all. "Tomorrow," I said, not at all sure what I meant.

She nodded. "Tomorrow." And then after a moment, she added, "You have to get up, Stephen, and lock the door behind me. I want you safe."

"You," I said quietly. Meaning *you too*.

"I'll be careful."

I sensed her finish dressing more than watched her; it was that dark in the room. When I heard her slip her shoes on, I pulled myself to my feet, found my own shorts with my bare foot, and pulled them on. "I'll walk with you to the end of the hall," I said, not wanting to let her go quite yet.

As I went along with her, carrying the key and holding her hand, it struck me how like children in the dark we were. Blindly brave.

"As soon as I'm gone, go back to sleep," she whispered when we reached the outer door. "I'll enjoy thinking of you asleep and dreaming."

The funny thing is I did dream. Something in what we'd done on that moondrift night, the flare and detonation between our bodies, loosed my imagination. What had been frozen within me flowed again, and as I swam into sleep, *I visited a high rock cliff along a mountain river. Paint Rock, it's called, after ancient Cherokee hieroglyphics. I was standing alone at the top of the cliff, watching the river flow far beneath me, the water rippling and running north into the wilds of Tennessee. . . . Somewhere in the rushing air, a voice made all of wind was singing the old ballad song about pretty Saro, the lost lover never to be found. . . .* If I was a poet and could write a fine hand,

> I'd write my love a letter that she'd understand . . .

. . . the river gray-green and singing. The mountains surging up on either side, wild with the colors of old fall. Maples orange, red oak and dogwood, the chestnut yellow stirred by the wind into a choir of color. Ranks upon ranks of trees rich in fluid light . . . I'd write it by the river

> where the waters overflow . . .

. . . there, just there, I belonged, and in the sky below me, over the river, broad wings beat, and I could hear the hawk's strident call to its mate and the answering call from the sky above. Flexing feathered wing and screaming flight painted in the freshening air . . . I'd dream of pretty Saro

> wherever I go . . .

. . . in my dream, the mountains were dancing, singing as I rode with them into the fierce light of dawn.

I had to wait to see Frederick A. Wallis, the new commissioner of Ellis Island. He was a political appointee at the end of Woodrow Wilson's second term and unlikely to last more than a year, but for now, he ran the show.

I wasn't waiting long. After only a quarter hour cooling my heels in the anteroom to his office, I was ushered into the great man's presence by his harried assistant. A meeting in the inner sanctum was just breaking up, and I saw Dr. Howard Knox from Island 3 leaving with the group as I was waiting for my interview. He was surprised to see me there, and his face showed it.

The Honorable Augustus F. Sherman was also in the group, and he, on the other hand, seemed glad to see me. Favored me with a wide smile and leaned over to me as he passed. "Come by my office when you're done," he said quietly. "I've got something to show you."

Wallis himself was the very picture of a confident, well-heeled politician. He had all the solid bulk of a successful man in his fifties, with a round head and slightly fleshy face. His skin was unblemished and his haircut immaculate, both testaments to the talents of his barber. He wore a fawn-colored linen suit that might have been stitched by a busy angel, topped off with a burgundy bow tie.

On the corner of his desk was a straw boater with a pair of white gloves tossed casually inside, both of which would accentuate the effect of the suit. There was also an ashtray with a live cigar, half smoked, and an open Bible.

Wallis maneuvered easily around the desk with his hand extended. "Mr. Robbins, sir," he intoned. "I was told to expect you, and I look forward to hearing your report." His grip was as dry and strong as a churchwarden, which was mostly what he was.

He settled me into a chair before circling back. I noticed a slight limp as he went and how he braced himself ever so slightly against the edge of the desk.

"Were you wounded in the war, sir?" I asked as he settled into his chair. It was a common enough question in those days.

"Oh no," he said with a genuine smile. "Nothing so romantic as that. Gout in my ankle." He gestured to his own face and nodded at me. "I might ask the same of you. War wound?"

"Nothing so romantic as that," I echoed him and smiled, leaving off any further explanation.

There were other pleasantries, two men getting to know each other, each probing for the other's personality but in an easy and relaxed sort of way. His cigar still smoldered, untouched, and air in the closed room was pungent with smoke. Then, as we were on his turf, he began. "Mr. Robbins, I was told by the BOI that you were working on the island and that I should expect you to stop by, but other than that . . ."

I smiled. "I was sent here to find a missing woman, a girl really. An immigrant from Ireland who disappeared shortly after she'd arrived. I traced her as far as the isolation wards on Island 3, where she vanished."

"Is it a bookkeeping problem?" he asked. "Sloppy record-keeping?"

"No, she's gone, and I have to assume dead."

He leaned back in his chair, and his habitually pleasant face clouded over. "I'm not surprised," he said. "I've been here a little over two months, and I've seen overcrowding, locked doors, hunger and boredom, poor people lured here and then sent back. I've seen—"

"It's not that," I interrupted him, for the righteousness in him was getting wound up. "It's something else."

He leaned forward again, resting his elbows on the desk. "Go on."

"I think immigrants are being murdered on Island 3. I've seen a second body, also female, also pregnant. Also a male nurse, who was helpful to me when I first started asking questions."

"My God," he said. "Here of all places." He sounded more resigned than shocked, and I recalled that he ran prisons before coming to New York.

I nodded. "At this point, it looks to me like there are several people involved, not just one deranged individual. It may have something to do with the extreme anti-immigration feeling in the country. I can't tie the two things together yet, but it's there, under the surface."

Wallis stared at me for a long moment, obviously thinking. He reached out, perhaps unconsciously, and touched the Bible on his desk. "What do you need from me?" he asked. "Or from the people I supervise."

I shrugged. "To stay out of my way," I suggested. "And if things get rough, to call off any guards who might be tempted to arrest me."

"Or shoot you?"

I smiled at his irony. "That too. . . . Oh, and one other thing. If I should suddenly disappear, let the BOI know."

He nodded, his face pristine again. Thoughtful. "I will also pray for you," he intoned. "For your safety and for the progress of your Godly work."

CHAPTER THIRTY

As I was leaving Wallis's office, I paused on the balcony overlooking the Great Hall. Ten o'clock in the morning, and the floor below was already packed—long lines of immigrants, organized into groups before the examiners' tables, translators chattering away in a dozen languages. Heat was radiating up from below as hundreds of men, women, and children in all sorts of native garb were restlessly urging forward toward a destiny they couldn't imagine. Near the steps leading up from the ferry docks, I could see Ludmila Kuchar, dressed again in the peasant's clothes she used to greet new families, comforting what appeared to be a weeping mother surrounded by a mob of nervous children. Ludmila was simultaneously gesturing, translating, and pulling children out of harm's way, all with one arm around the mother's shoulders.

Two guards walked by behind me, talking together in a Brooklyn accent so strong that I could pick only a few words out of the *dese* and *dose*, but the few words I did recognize were *goddamn* and *animals* and . . .*Wallis don't know what the hell he's talkin' about.*

I had only just begun to translate what that might mean when Augustus Sherman called out to me. I had to swallow a rising tide of nausea when I entered his private office because of the photographs displayed on the walls. They took me momentarily back to the Anderson Gallery and the "Portraits of Famous Artists and Writers," Anna throwing herself at that bastard Grant. I shook my head roughly and forced myself to focus on Sherman, who was saying something to me. Who was pointing down and at his desk and asking me what I thought.

The secretary had spread out four new photographs for me to examine. And for once, he'd actually placed his monocle carefully in his right eye so he could focus more closely on the pictures. For some reason, he had decided that I was as consumed with seeing his images as he was with making them. And I have to admit, they were interesting, and the people captured there were not famous artists and writers.

"They're all families," I said to Sherman after a moment.

"Precisely," he all but crowed. "I knew you'd see it."

There was a *German-Jewish family from Eastern Europe*, a group portrait labeled simply *English-Jews*, one noted simply as *Syrian*, and one interesting one named *Rome family*.

"Two of the groups have fathers, and two don't." The Eastern European portrait showed an old man with a bushy white beard who had apparently fathered a baby not long before on a dark-skinned, weathered woman.

"Fathers! Bah . . . fathers are expendable, except that they give us a clue to type."

"Type? You mean race?"

"Of course. What else do you see?"

"Both the Jewish families have six children, but the English version is all dressed in white and wearing sweet little straw hats. The children look curious and happy and dressed for the occasion. The Eastern European children look terrified. . . . So do the Syrians."

"True, true. Part of it is they don't speak the language. But terrified or not, do you see the family face in each of the photos? The eyes, the hair, the skin? The shape of the head!"

It was obvious, as though he had chosen the families expressly to illustrate his conviction that we were all just painted by our genes. "What about the Gypsies?" I asked. "They're not terrified." Indeed, the mother in the photo had a broad grin on her face, and the father had what looked like an ironic smile hidden behind his whiskers. The children appeared ready to leap out of the photo and run around the room.

"Who cares! Look at their skin. . . ."

They were all dark of skin and eye. "They've spent their lives outdoors," I said to Sherman. "You ever consider that? The English children are made of milk 'cause they've never seen the sun."

"Exactly! And over time, that becomes part of their family feature too." He was incorrigible. "The clothing, of course, is indicative of their origin, and it is interesting. But as our Miss Kuchar is proving every day, clothing can be changed. These people can learn to dress like Americans, but you can't change their bodies into Americans."

"So what? Isn't America supposed to be the great melting pot?"

He still stared down at the photos, fascinated by what he thought he'd captured. "Oh, it's a pot alright," he said after a moment. "But you can forget about the melting."

I went to the nurses' canteen at noon for something to eat. Sat by myself in the corner with my back to the wall and spooned up some stew, lamb perhaps. With a fistful of crackers broken into the bowl, it wasn't bad, and it quieted my stomach. I drank two cups of hot black tea that also seemed to ease the twitching inside my gut. I had given up on seeing Lucy when she came in with two other nurses, chattering away about something. She winked at me behind their backs and sat with them in the middle of the room to eat. When I got up to leave, she held her hand down on the bench beside her hip where they couldn't see it and showed three fingers. O'clock, I assumed she meant. And I was strangely glad—both for the rendezvous and for the hours alone in between.

I wanted to think. So much had happened in the previous two days that I could feel myself drifting, cut loose inside my head, wondering who I might be or become. Anna Ulmann had been the love of my life. A mainspring that would continue ticking inside my chest. I had intended to stay with her forever, until I died, or she did.

Apparently, *forever* in our case meant three years and change.

I must have needed air, outside air, because a few minutes later I was standing on the inner side of the isolation wards, facing the lagoon. There were a half dozen picnic tables knocked together out of lumber, and I claimed one for my meditations, facing out into the lagoon, where I could watch the barges being emptied by the steam shovel.

If Anna wasn't forever, an eternal marker in my life, then who was I? Where was the north? The south, the east, or west?

Where was the family photo that showed our teeth, our hair, our skin? My parents were both dead and buried in Anderson Cove, high in the North Carolina mountains. My two sisters were there as well—alive but far, far away from where I sat in the middle of New York Harbor. I had fathered no children except for the boy from my failed marriage who had died of infant cholera and the baby that Anna had lost in the eighth month. There was nothing alive before me or after me. There was no camera that could reach through time and capture those who had disappeared and place them around me in one frame, one moment, one place.

I thought of Sherman's "Rome family," two boys ready to run and yell, the glint in the father's eye, the baby relaxed in the mother's arms, and her confidence as she stared straight into the camera. No wonder she had that wild grin on her face. They might be dirty and poor and hungry, but she was alive, and her family alive with her, all in a huge, new world they intended to conquer.

My own shabby world felt old at that moment. Worn thin. I was a moving shadow in the back of one of Sherman's photographs, my body blurred by motion and my face turned away from the lens. Was I recognizable to anyone other than myself? And if I did disappear, suddenly, the victim of whatever was killing people here, what then? If I was scrubbed out of the photograph of this place, would anyone remember to mourn the loss?

Did Lucy Paul have the eyes to see what I was? Did she even care? Or was she just nursing an invalid?

After some time with these lonely ruminations, I began to watch the men working on the barge, perhaps fifty feet out. They were shouting at the steam shovel operator. He had shut down operations, the mechanical arm and bucket poised in the air. They were pointing down into the water. I got up and walked out to what had been the breakwater and then farther out onto the fill dirt that was slowly sprouting weeds. One man began to yell something at me as well, apparently thinking that I was some sort of official from the island. "What do we do?" he called out, pointing and gesturing.

It was only then that I realized they had suspended work because there was a body floating in the water.

It took most of the afternoon and a half dozen guards from Island 1 with a rowboat, but the end result was that Nurse James Thompson returned to the morgue. Returned, in fact, to the same drawer where Lucy and I had seen him originally. Knox emerged from his office long enough to express outrage that Thompson's body had been "misplaced." His counterpart, the saintly Nurse Taylor, came down the long hallway and burst into tears when she heard the news, for little Jimmy Thompson had been such a sweet and caring man. Nurse Adams wrung her huge hands, whether over Thompson or Taylor, it was impossible to tell.

Turns out, there was no internal authority on the island to review how Thompson's body had ended up in the lagoon, and since he was already dead, there was no murder to investigate. I listened as Knox harangued the guards from Island 1, all of whom were muddy with salt water and fill dirt. They just shrugged their shoulders and talked some sense about how the Island 3 authorities should be more careful with their corpses from now on.

Taylor had been led ever so gently back to her quarters by Adams. Knox had shaken his head in disgust and dismay till his neck must have hurt and then had gone off to fill out some obscure paperwork. And the whole event was over.

Except that it wasn't over for me. They had reminded me why I was there.

CHAPTER THIRTY-ONE

There's something about his body they want to hide, something about the way he died . . ."

"Before he went into the water," Lucy replied, "he looked like he'd been boiled."

We were back outside not long after the small crowd surrounding Thompson's resurrection from the lagoon had broken up. She had wanted to see where Thompson's body had been found, and I'd led her back to the same picnic table where I'd been sitting when the steam shovel suddenly ceased work and the shouting began.

"Boiled," I agreed. "Or baked. Cooked at any rate . . . like he'd been in . . . hell, I don't know. An oven."

"It would be hard to tell much at all now, after he's been immersed in salt water," she said finally.

I nodded.

"But we should look, shouldn't we . . . at his body, I mean."

"Better look tonight before he disappears again."

"I might have plans for tonight," she said, with no inflection.

I turned to study her profile. "Do they involve me . . . these plans?"

Her lips twitched. "Couldn't do what I had in mind without you."

"Morgue first?"

She nodded. "Goddamn morgue first. Vegetables before dessert."

"Scotch?"

She smiled outright. "Morgue before scotch . . . and dessert."

We basked in the sun for a few minutes more. I knew she wanted to bathe and change, and the afternoon had already burned down to evening.

"Oh!" she said suddenly. "I almost forgot. We've been invited to a prayer meeting."

"You're joking."

Her eyes were closed against the slant evening sun, but even so, she was grinning at the irony. "Hell no. Adams came to tell me. Tomorrow evening in Taylor's quarters. It's your standard Sunday evening prayer meeting, you know, the kind of thing they have down South where you're from. Taylor sent Adams specifically to invite you and me."

"How did Adams know that all she had to do was invite you in order to snag both of us?"

That brought her up short. "I don't know. Maybe they think we're . . ."

"In cahoots." I finished the sentence for her.

"Sleeping together?"

"Maybe. Or maybe that we're spying on them together. Maybe that we were sent here as a team."

"Can't we just be screwing?"

"Maybe. And if that's what they suspect, then maybe they're just trying to save our sinful souls. But if that's not what they're thinking, then we need to pay attention to whoever else is there."

"Why?" She leaned forward and shaded her eyes with one hand so she could see my face.

"Because what they may be doing is fingering us, both of us, for who the hell ever is involved."

"Whoever is there is part of the conspiracy—is that what you're saying?"

"Maybe. If Taylor or Adams is involved, then chances are that at least some of the people who are there will be accomplices."

"Should we even go?" she asked.

"Oh yes. They show themselves to us at the same time we show ourselves to them."

"Should we carry a gun?"

"Probably. In fact, I want you to start carrying that thirty-eight with you everywhere. Practice shooting some more melons on your day off."

"Stephen." She scooted a little closer on the table and slipped a hand under my jacket to burrow into my pants pocket.

"Hmmm?"

"I'd rather just be screwing."

The second time we saw James Thompson's corpse up close, there was almost nothing to see. The flesh was slack from having been cooked and then soaked for hours. It hung off his bones so that his skeleton seemed to be rising up out of a puddle of skin. The skin itself was mottled in odd red and gray patches, and fish or crabs had been chewing on him, even on his face. The smell was nightmarish despite the refrigeration, and even Lucy, with her years of nursing, gagged slightly and then turned away after only a minute.

The strangest thing of all, however, was a long indentation that ran across the body in its softest part, in the stomach below the navel. It was a welt of some sort or even something like a burn imprinted into the flesh, as if a belt had been brutally tightened around the body just above the hips. I pointed it out to Lucy, and she covered her mouth and nose with her hand while she bent over to study it.

We stopped in the long hallway a few minutes later by an open window, just to swallow the fresh air that ghosted in from the ocean. "God, that was awful," she muttered after a moment. "Something had been chewing on his eyelid."

"Fish maybe," I whispered. My stomach was still roiling too.

"What was that around his waist? It wasn't there before."

At that moment, Lucy's friend Ezra came slowly by, using a mop to push a rolling metal bucket half full of steaming, soapy water. He was headed in the direction of the morgue, sent there, no doubt, to clean up. Lucy spoke to him, calling him kindly by name. He bobbed in return, nodding and smiling up at us. Even reached out shyly to touch Lucy's arm.

When I spoke to him, he also smiled at me but more thoughtfully, as if he had something to say but no words to say it with. Finally, he reached up to his own face with one gnarled finger and pointed to the side of his face, tapped his cheek just below his eye. Smiled again and went on slowly down the hall, pushing his bucket before him.

"What was that about?" I asked Lucy quietly.

She shrugged. "I'm not sure. Maybe he was pointing to your scar."

"Maybe. . . . Lucy, are you sure that the welt wasn't on Thompson's body when we saw it before? It's important."

"I'm sure. Ever since England, I remember corpses too well. Have nightmares about them. That mark wasn't there."

"Then it's a rope burn," I said quietly and took another deep gulp or two of air. "Or wire. Somebody tied him to something heavy enough to take him down. Concrete block maybe . . . from the construction site. Something heavy anyway."

"Good God."

I nodded. "They don't have to get the bodies off the island. They just drop them into the lagoon and let the construction fill bury them under tons of dirt and rocks. . . . It's pretty much the perfect graveyard."

CHAPTER THIRTY-TWO

I think we both felt squalid after that visit to the morgue. As if our clothes and even our skin smelled just from having pulled that drawer open. I say that because we went by silent agreement straight to the bathing room in the psych ward—the room where Lucy had resurrected me the morning before. I started a tub of hot water while she rummaged through several cabinets for clean towels that weren't threadbare.

While the water ran, I walked down the hallway to our cell, wrestled the 12-gauge out from under its mattress, loaded both barrels, and brought it back down to the bathing room. Even though the outside door was jammed shut with a stout chair, I still wanted protection after what we'd seen that day.

When I returned, all Lucy had on was her white underthings. They were like those that must have lived under her nurse's uniforms for years, only these were satin rather than cotton, and the bra cups were pointed in a way that made it hard for me to breathe.

"You should quit staring and get undressed," she said dreamily as she sat on the edge of the tub, "unless you're going to wash your clothes along with the rest of you."

I leaned the shotgun carefully in the corner of the room, where it wouldn't get wet, and stripped down to my boxers. When I stepped over the edge of the tub, the water was up to my knees and at least 100 degrees. It brought back memories of how she had washed me the day before, which all but brought tears to my eyes and tightened the front of my shorts.

I knelt in front of her in the water, in part to hide the fact that I was aroused just by the thought of her. Moved forward on my knees and put my open palms on her thighs.

Her black eyes were closed, her brown lips barely parted. Steam was rising off the water in the cool evening air. I slid my hands up under her panties till my thumbs rested in the soft hollow inside her hip bones and my hands cupped each side where her body swelled below her waist.

"Tonight, you should let me wash you," I said, my voice hoarse in my throat. "Turnabout for yesterday."

"You be the nurse then," she whispered. "I'll be the patient."

I never knew till that night the true meaning of soap. Never before washed a woman so slowly and closely—so deeply or so well. Never put my fingers and hands and mouth to such good medicinal use.

Even so, when we were drying each other off from our bath, she would say that she was having dirty thoughts.

Once again, she got up from what I had come to think of as *our* bed during the darkest part of the night. Again, I got up to walk to the end of the hallway with her before returning to lock the door.

But that evening took on a poignancy that the night before had lacked. We were beginning to know each other physically. Sure, we were screwing, as she had put it so delicately that afternoon sitting in the sun. Twice in twenty-four hours.

But there was more than that. The sex itself felt like two people wolfing down a meal who hadn't eaten in days, weeks even. Two dying people who suddenly found sustenance and tore into it without stopping to ask who or what. That part was luscious and mindless and exhausting.

But again, there was more than that. We had also begun to know each other in those ways that are deeper and more disturbing to the psyche. We had begun to caress each other when we were close by. We had begun to seek out each other's scars, visible and invisible, to nurse them. We had begun to lie awake when by all rights we should have been asleep, whispering to each other like children, questioning and answering, shining a light deep into the past. Telling long and intricate stories, we began to develop a secret language of our own.

In short, we were becoming friends—not just lovers.

Which, if real, is always more satisfying and more sustaining. More transforming of some inner landscape where the sun and moon, rising and falling, are more personal and more real than the dusty outer world, which is haunted by the voices of others.

So it was all the more unexpected and more upsetting that she was crying when she got up that night to leave. The midnight before she had been confident and sure. But that night, the second night, she was sniffing as she sat on the side of the bed to dress, and when I reached up from where I lay to caress her face, her cheek was damp.

"What in the world?" I asked. "Are you scared?"

"No." There was a tremble in her voice, so unlike her brazen nature.

"What then? Is it that you have to leave?"

"Yes . . . that." But she didn't sound certain as she stood to finish dressing, and I sat up to pull my shorts on so that I could walk with her to the end of the hallway. "Partly that."

"And what's the rest then?" I asked.

"It's that you make me so sad."

"How do I do that?"

She only shook her head as we lit a candle to carry with us down the dark hallway. When we came to the final door at the head of the stairwell, she turned and kissed me quickly, on the neck beneath my ear. And then she whispered the rest of it.

"You make me want a child again, damn you," she said. "You make me want more than I can have."

CHAPTER THIRTY-THREE

We read the verses while sitting in a loose circle in Nurse Blanche Taylor's homey quarters.

"'Ye have heard that it was said by them of old time, thou shalt not commit adultery.'" This by Taylor herself, whose milk and honey tone made even the word *adultery* sound like a minor misstep rather than a hellfire sin.

"'But I say unto you, that whosoever looketh on a woman to lust after her hath committed adultery with her already in his heart.'" This in the voice of a young nurse named Scottie Phillips, who struggled to say *looketh*.

"'If thy right eye offend thee, pluck it out, and cast it from thee, for it is profitable for thee that one of thy members should perish, and not that thy whole body should be cast into hell.'" An old orderly who introduced himself as Jimmy Cain, who had gravel in his throat. He made *hell* sound like it was supposed to sound, with the rumble of eternal damnation. He handed Taylor's Bible to Lucy, who was next in the circle, and pointed with one thick finger to the following verse.

"'And if thy right hand offend thee, cut it off, and cast it from thee, for it is profitable for thee that one of thy members should perish, and not that thy whole body should be cast into hell.'" Lucy's voice was firm but neutral, and she read her bit of the Sermon on the Mount like a nurse describing an operation.

"The word of our Lord," Taylor intoned softly, which elicited from everybody but Lucy and me, "Thanks be to God."

Taylor's ornate white Bible—of course it was white, like her clothes—had come clockwise around our little circle, stopping just short of me. I sat beside Lucy, and on my left were two other orderlies. One was named Ross and the other Ray; it seems like Ray's last name was Chandler. Then beside Taylor in a large chair was Ethel Adams, dressed for once in civilian clothes, a floral print dress that would have made any one of us a tent.

"Dear Mr. Robbins and Miss Paul, we meet once a week on Sunday evening to refuel our inner fires with the sanctified word of the Lord." This from Taylor, our host. "Dear Miss Adams first suggested our Bible study." She reached over and patted Ethel's massive knee, and Ethel visibly simpered. "Our little band takes such sustenance from our Sunday evenings that it's become something we all look forward to during our hectic lives here on the island."

"It's like a meal for the hungry," I offered helpfully.

"Yes, yes," Taylor replied, thankful that I was getting her point. "It's a kind of communion, if it's not sacrilegious to say so. We have tea, and often cookies or cake, and we delve into the scripture for guidance. And just as we take turns to read the night's verses, we also are careful to take turns in our discussion as well. Each among us gets to say what he or she"—she paused to smile radiantly at Lucy—"thinks the verses have to teach us."

"Miss Paul," said Adams breathlessly, "you're holding the Bible. Why don't you begin?"

Lucy might have blushed, hard to tell with her skin. She handed the Bible straightaway to me and suggested that since she'd had an opportunity to read, maybe I'd crank up the commentary. Or words to that effect.

What Taylor and Adams, along with their little circle of Holy Rollers, didn't know was that I'd cut my teeth on the King James Bible back in the mountains, and I'd been listening to this sort of critical exegesis since I could walk and talk.

Lucy had closed the white Bible before she handed it to me, but I knew exactly what ground we stood on. "This is part of the Sermon on the Mount," I said with a grin, looking first directly at Taylor and then letting my eyes roam around the circle. "Gospel of Matthew. It's a much longer sermon than most people realize, and this comes along in the middle.

"The part about sinning with your eyes just by looking at a woman seems plain enough. Or by looking at a man." I grinned at the young nurse, Scottie Something or Other, and she smiled ruefully. "Means that you can sin in your heart or in your mind without acting on it. But then things get a little less certain after that. Does that old Jesus mean that you should literally blind yourself or cripple yourself to keep from sin? Or is it a figure for something else, some other action we're supposed to take?"

"What the hell you mean, old Jesus? Don't be sacrilegious in this room, boy!" It was the orderly named Ray, and he wasn't joking.

"I wasn't. It's how one of the holiest preachers back home referred to him . . . a term of affection," I replied. "So the question, which I've heard debated by old granny women sitting in their porch rockers and by a famous preacher or two, is what to make of *pluck out your eye* or *chop off your hand* . . ."

At that moment, Ethel Adams did the most extraordinary thing; she slapped herself.

She suddenly swung up from where her hands had been folded in her lap and with her open palm, hit herself over her right eye so hard that the sound was like a pistol shot. Beside me, Lucy gasped, but the rest of the men and women in the circle didn't even flinch.

"I'd pluck the eye right out of my head," Ethel cried, "if Jesus asked me to." One half of the woman's face was already turning bright red, and I knew she'd have a black eye by morning. I suddenly thought of the custodian Ezra, who'd looked straight at me and pointed to his eye when Lucy and I had passed him in the corridor.

"I believe," Nurse Taylor said soothingly, "that our Lord might have meant something metaphorical, or as Mr. Robbins put it, something figurative."

"For sure, he meant that you'll go to hell if you commit that awful . . . adultery." This from Nurse Scottie, looking at Taylor the way a dog looks at its master.

"Of course he did, my dear. You are exactly right, and I'm sure no one here would even think of such nasty things."

Nurse Scottie nodded enthusiastically.

Beside me, Lucy muttered, "Silly bitch," under her breath, only for my benefit.

"I know what it means." This from Jimmy Cain, the orderly with the froggy voice sitting to Lucy's right. "Means that whatever part of your life is sinful, you have to cut it out like a cancer. Take for your example, liquor. Cut it out. It's why we got Inhibition."

Taylor must have seen my blank look. "I believe Jimmy means Prohibition."

"Yeah," Jimmy echoed. "Prohibition."

"We do have that," I admitted, "and it's plucked out the liquor from a lot of people's lives. But what else do you think it means? Chop off your hand if it offends you?"

Just then, Nurse Taylor picked up the thread of the conversation and began to preach her own little sermon. In the gentlest, most dulcet tones you can imagine, as if she were talking to children who might be frightened otherwise. "Why, we know what it means if we'll only think about it. Our Lord and Savior was telling us that when there are nefarious elements in our society, groups of people that are given over to sin—whether that sin be in the mind or in the deed—then it is our responsibility to remove that part of society so that it doesn't sicken and destroy the rest of us. America, the home of God's chosen people, is like a large and healthy body, a body that sustains us all with its churches and its traditions."

"Amen," muttered one of the two orderlies to my left. And when I glanced around the circle, it was obvious that except for Lucy and me, the rest of those present were fully mesmerized by her words.

"If a cancer invades the body of America . . . if a disease comes into the body, why then the body is corrupted and must sicken and die."

I couldn't help myself; I had to ask a question, to throw her off her stride if nothing else. "Can't Jesus cure the body . . . work one of his miracles?"

"Why, of course he can, Mr. Robbins, but the book you hold in your hands says that there are times when the good Lord helps those who help themselves, and we believe that this is one of those times."

"Bad times," from Nurse Scottie, and echoes of the same in male voices.

"This is one of those times when the body of America, the holy body of God's chosen people, is being invaded by the cancer of dangerous people. By the disease of those who rape and steal, those who take our land and our jobs, make and peddle that vile liquor, those who seduce our daughters and our sons into unholy unions . . . They are the eye that must be plucked out, the filthy hand that must be cut off."

There was a hypnotized silence around the circle. We were into the real deal now. You could almost smell the passion in the room. "Who are the invaders?" I asked. "How will we recognize them when we see them?"

"Not long ago, the invaders were the slant-eyed hordes from the East, with their heathen religions and dirty ways, but we have shut that door, praise the Lord!" Taylor managed to say this in a tone so kind and mellifluous that it sounded like we were passing out chocolates. "But now, there is a new disease, a new malaise that comes at us from the West."

"Jews from Russia?" I suggested. "Eastern and Southern Europeans?"

"Oh yes," she said, obviously proud of me for catching on, and in thrall to her own voice. "The Jews and the Muslims. The Catholics from Southern Italy. All lost souls spreading the disease of their beliefs. The illiterate, the violent, the drunken, and what must follow from it all, the sexually deviant."

"Deviant?"

"The fornicator, the adulterer, the prostitute, all the immorality that is coming into our decent, God-fearing country from the lands beyond." She was staring straight at Lucy and me now, and her eyes were infinitely sad and loving. "We are on the front lines," she stage-whispered, "in a war to protect our way of life and our physical purity. And we want the two of you, good people that you are, to understand us, and perhaps to join us. Join us here where it matters most. That blessed lady across the harbor . . ."

It struck me that she meant the Statue of Liberty.

". . . that blessed lady is a Christian. She holds the scripture in her arms and raises high the torch of purity."

"Amen," almost in unison and from all sides of the circle.

I admit I was stunned, and I wished we'd brought the pistol.

CHAPTER THIRTY-FOUR

After the closing prayer, Nurse Taylor asked me to stay for a few minutes so she could ask my advice about something. Ethel Adams and Scottie Phillips offered to walk with Lucy back to the nurses' quarters, which felt to me for a brief moment like a setup, as if someone was in danger.

But Lucy leaned toward me as everyone stood. "I'll be fine," she whispered. "See you later." And then she was gone, chatting and giggling with the girls as the three of them left together.

As soon as we were alone, Taylor came to stand beside me. She reached out to grasp my elbow and told me how upset she was by what had happened to Thompson. "You are a man of the world, Mr. Robbins, an investigator from the government. Can you shed any light on how poor James Thompson . . . ?"

"Ended up floating in the lagoon?"

She nodded sorrowfully.

"Somebody put him there, of course. Stole his body out of the morgue, presumably at night, attached him to something heavy, and dumped him in the water where it would be covered by the fill. Brilliant, really, if you want to get rid of a corpse."

"But why?" Her tone was sad and plaintive.

It struck me again that either this woman really was a Christian saint or she was a brilliant actress, almost as if there were a half dozen personalities swimming around behind that benevolent mask. She could go from plucking out Jews and cutting off Gypsies to this troubled state of mourning for a fellow human being . . . all without blinking an eye.

I shrugged my shoulders. If she was involved, I'd only told her what she already thought I knew. And if she wasn't, then it didn't hurt to deliver just a few volts of electricity to her saintly self-assurance. Either way, I didn't need to tell her anything more. "I don't know," I muttered. "The salt water will have erased anything the body might have told us." And then—since she seemed wound up by her little prayer meeting—I decided to ask a few questions of my own. "Did James Thompson have a family?"

She shook her head sadly, and an honest-to-God tear crept out from under one eyelid. "Yes, but they were way out west. Idaho, I believe. He hadn't been in touch with them for years. It seems that he was alienated from them in some way."

"So they won't send for the body?"

Again, the sad shake of the head, and she reached up to wipe the tear away, in case I'd missed it.

"And he'll end up in the potter's field on Hart Island?"

"I don't know. I suppose so."

She had to be lying. Of course she knew. "It's sad, isn't it," I said, "to think that a boy from Idaho, the heartland of America, will end up in the same grave with all the human refuse that washes up here. End up with all those nasty people you were talking about. There ought to be something we can do about it."

If I expected a trace of guilt or even irony from the woman, I didn't get it. I'd touched a nerve, and the Old Testament prophet from the prayer meeting rose up in her again. "James Thompson would probably like being buried with the ignorant, shiftless people who attempt to come through these gates. He was entirely too sympathetic to some of the people he nursed. He gave himself to those who were least worthy. He—"

"Are you saying he was the good Samaritan?"

She wasn't used to being interrupted, and her forehead creased in irritation. I had used the Bible on her, so she fired back with the same ammunition. "'While they promise them liberty, they themselves are the servants of corruption.' Second Peter, Mr. Robbins. Perhaps it was Thompson's own deviance that made him . . ." She paused, maybe sensing she'd gone too far.

"His own deviance?"

"His family rejected him because he was . . . he preferred men."

"I'll be damned." What the poor guy must have gone through, I thought, all his life! And then to end up here, at the knife edge of the continent, in the godforsaken isolation ward . . . "The Medical Association should pay for his funeral," I said to Blanche Taylor, "and you know it."

When I got back to Building E that night, I had the sudden uncomfortable feeling that I was being followed. Even though the long corridor that served as the spine to Island 3 was well lit and empty, something felt wrong.

Building E, like most of the isolation pavilions, consisted of two floors, with the psychopathic ward on the top floor. The first floor had been vacant since I'd arrived on the scene, the doors from the stairwell locked. That night, the door that led to the first floor was unlocked, and it creaked open when I pulled the handle. The ward beyond was completely dark and, when I stood silent for a long moment waiting on what might be lurking there, the space beyond the door stayed empty. The air that stirred within was dusty and stale, as if it hadn't been breathed for a long time. I stood on, stock-still, just like I was deer hunting down home in the mountains, barely breathing myself.

Nothing.

I eased the door shut again, and this time the creak in the unused hinges was less. Less but still enough to make your skin pucker.

I eased on up the stairs to the second floor, where Lucy and I had created our little haven. The stairwell was lit, but the hallway beyond dark. I paused under the sign—**Psychopathic Care Unit**—and listened.

Again nothing.

When I reached out to push the door to our floor open, the chair we normally used to wedge it shut was missing and the door swung easily.

For the second time that night, I cursed myself for not carrying the .38. I slipped through the doorway as noiselessly as possible and edged down the left side of the hallway, out of the cast of light from the stairwell, so I wouldn't make a target.

When I came opposite the doorway to the bathing room, that door was open, and there was the faintest specter of light from its windows. The door at my shoulder, opposite the bathing room, was also slightly open. It shouldn't have been; we never left the hallway doors open.

I felt more than heard a presence in the room. Sensed something breathing in the darkness. Sweat prickled my neck, and I knew I wouldn't be able to hold my own breath much longer.

Time and tide, I thought, and swung my right leg violently around to kick the door open. There was a hoarse grunt as someone staggered back. I dove through and tackled the figure that been set to ambush me. Drove forward pulling his legs out from under him, and we crashed together to the floor. Something heavy clattered across the floor, something that had to be a gun. I fought to get my hands around his neck.

And if the figure hadn't been so familiar, if I hadn't known its very pulse and breath, I wouldn't have realized it was Lucy before I began choking her.

CHAPTER THIRTY-FIVE

We lay there together for a long moment, our breath coming in ragged gasps, our bodies locked together in what was almost a death struggle. I rolled onto my side and pulled her to me, cradling her then rather than trying to crush her with my weight.

Neither of us spoke for the longest time, our bodies slowly adjusting, slowly uncoiling one ragged inhalation at a time. The top of her head was against my neck, and I could feel my own pulse thumping against her hair.

"It's like after sex," she whispered eventually. "When you come crashing back to earth."

I nodded, my chin scratching her scalp. "Dying for a while and then coming back . . ."

"I was going to shoot you," she whispered.

"Good." I shifted slightly so that my lips could reach her ear. Freed one hand to sweep her hair back so that I could murmur directly into the depths of her mind. "I want you that ready, that certain. When they come for you or come for us, I want you to pull the trigger. . . . If it's not me, shoot it."

"Are they coming for us?"

I paused as I thought about how much to tell her.

"That means yes," she muttered. "If you have to stop and think what to say, it means yes."

"You already knew," I said and helped her sit up on the hard linoleum floor. "Or you wouldn't have been waiting in the dark with a pistol."

She stood up easily for someone who had been thrown down hard not ten minutes before. She reached down to help me. "I think we should go to bed," she said, "before we accidentally kill each other."

We turned on the electric light in each room down the psych ward hallway, searched the room briefly with the .38 in hand, and then clicked the light off again. That, and almost dying, must have made a kind of foreplay. By the time we reached our cell and I pulled the door shut behind us, we were both breathless, both on tiptoe with something that was no longer fear.

When I turned with the key to lock the door behind us, she pressed her body against my back, slid her hands up under my loose shirt and began to caress my stomach and chest as if starving for it.

We tore at each other's clothes as we half-staggered toward the bed, each wanting the other naked, each ripping at leather, linen, cotton, any vestiges of civilization that stifled the electricity crackling between us.

We landed on the bed almost exactly as we had landed on the cold floor of the room where she'd almost shot me. Only this time we didn't pause. We bore into each other, both with our eyes open, staring with frightening intensity into each other's irises. Diving in . . . searching the deeper sanctuaries as our bodies arched and rocked, making a little death between us.

Later as we lay cupped together in a sweat-soaked daze, she giggled and then asked, "Stephen, are we adulterers?"

"No." I had to smile. "We're fornicators."

During our previous nights together—few and intense—I had lapsed into dreaming during the early morning hours after Lucy left me to go on shift. That night, I dove deep immediately, in a sort of postcoital coma. And as often happened during the time on Ellis Island, I returned home in my dreams.

There is a place along Spring Creek above my hometown in the mountains that I loved to go to when I was a boy working at the old Mountain Park Hotel. I first discovered the place fishing on my day off from the hotel and ended up spending hours in the spot that day and often over the years.

. . . a sandy, sun-drenched beach below some large boulders, and though only thirty feet wide, the creek just above splits around a small island with a few trees and races down on either side in a fast, sparkling run over a fall of rocks into a pool that washes past the beach. In the steep, green bowl formed by the ridges on either side of the creek, the sound of rushing water reverberates above and below and through your hearing.

. . . where you sit on the beach, the creek seems to spring out of the trees to your right and rush into your world around the little island, flow past you in its own intricate brown logic, rippling over ledges into a fast, deep pool, and then, no more than twenty yards farther along, curve again out of sight.

. . . complete unto itself, bathing all your known senses in light and sound, replete in sensation and entire . . . time does not pass in that place.

That night, as I lay curled with Lucy Paul a thousand miles away, *I stand on that beach with my own fly rod in hand, casting into the still water beside the downstream furrow below one of the ledges, a place trout like to rest as the buffet of stream life flows by their noses . . . casting lazily, arm rising and falling through long habit.*

. . . as though a splinter of light shoots from the tip of the rod, the glistening line sings taut and begins to move of its own accord. The rod tip bends all the way to the surface of the pool as I lift it to set the hook. There is something ancient made out of gill and fin that is running deep. Something so strong that it pulls me one step ankle-in and then another step knee-deep into the rock-slick edge of the creek.

What monster swims so?

. . . wading deeper on straining legs with back bent and arms to

play that fish—all the world above the surface of the water rinsed in red light . . .

What is on the other end of that line?

I woke from the dream without answering, with Lucy's concerned hand on my face, for in my sleep, I had been both laughing and groaning, calling out.

We slept on into the remainder of the night. Lucy was off the next day before beginning a weeklong stint working the day shift in the TB ward. She was going into the city to shop for things she needed and to supply our own little domestic arrangement. Coffee, fruit, bread, the cheese she loved. Cigarettes, though I had only ever seen her smoking once, and that was in the morgue at night with her friend.

I planned to walk with her down to the ferry dock on the main island, just to see her off and then watch the sorting process that took place when immigrants got off the boat. It felt like I'd been on Island 3 for a year, so intense had been the previous days, and I needed to disappear myself for a few hours—let my mind go blank and see what emerged when I wasn't chasing the truth like a bear dog running in the shadows.

As Lucy bathed and dressed, I waited in the empty office that served as the anteroom to the psych ward. On a side table in the office were a half dozen oddly shaped pieces of wood left over from some repair project. I was staring idly at them when Lucy found me.

She laughed when she saw me examining the scraps of wood. "Sit down at this table with your back to the window," she said. "And I will administer an intelligence test to see if you will be allowed to enter the country or not."

I sat, amused at the pretend serious tone of her voice. She was playing doctor, and I was to be the poor, unfortunate immigrant whose fate was in her hands. Then she did the oddest thing; she picked up the pieces of wood from the side table and brought them to me in the center of the room. "You will have exactly one minute," she intoned, "to assemble this puzzle. I cannot tell you what it is a picture of, only that when properly placed, these pieces create an image common to all the people of the earth. Are you ready to begin?"

I nodded, and she placed the pieces of wood on the table in front of me one at a time, obviously laying them down in a completely random way. There were five of them, not six, as I had supposed before. One large and four smaller pieces.

"Very well then," Lucy said, "you may begin." She referred to an imaginary stopwatch in her hand.

I stared at the scraps of wood, and they stared back at me. One of the smaller pieces was a rectangle that obviously fit into a similar hole in the larger piece. I picked up the rectangle and slipped it into place.

"Forty-five seconds," Lucy said in her doctor voice.

The other pieces were . . . I can't quite describe the shape of the other three pieces except to say that they were an odd collection of angles and curves.

"Thirty seconds," Lucy said.

I began to push the three smaller pieces against the larger mass at random, trying first this placement and that, searching for any sort of visual clue, letting go of any preconceptions and trying not to think about what image might be common to people of all—

"Fifteen seconds."

I finally thought I saw an answer and clumsily shoved the pieces together to approximate my vision.

"Time's up," she said. "What is that you have created there, Mr. Robbins?"

"A whale?" I said. "It is most definitely a whale."

She couldn't help herself; she laughed out loud. "And is a whale a common image for all people?"

"No," I admitted. "But . . ."

"You have failed the Feature Profile Test," she intoned. She paused just long enough, perhaps ten seconds, to place the other three pieces so that they resembled the profile of a rather unpleasant looking person, with a tiny mouth and a bulbous nose.

"It still looks like a whale to me," I lied.

"I must mark you down as feebleminded, Mr. Robbins. You are quite likely to become a burden to the state or may produce offspring that will require care in prisons, asylums, or other institutions. You will have to return to your place of origin."

"Are you serious that this is a test?"

"Of course it is. An intelligence test, designed by our good Dr. Knox, and you failed it gloriously—just like half the people who take it."

"And I have to go back to that damn potato patch in Slovakia?"

She nodded happily.

But then the grin on her face visibly faded into a sad smile. "But I'm half glad you failed. Maybe it will help you understand."

"Understand what, Lucy?"

But she wouldn't say anything more until she was just about to board the ferry. Then, just as she stepped onto the gangplank, she paused to ask me, "Do you know what a mulatto is, Stephen?"

CHAPTER THIRTY-SIX

I suppose all of us are composed of at least two minds. Or more like three or four minds, dancing to some music inside our heads that we can't really hear with our external senses. That day I spent finding out what it was really like to step off the ferry as a newcomer to the United States—scared, anxious, staring wide-eyed and listening for any clue. I did all of that with one mind. But another mind, a deeper, more visceral mind, was thinking during all that long day of Lucy Paul and what she had said. Two minds at least, questioning the ways of the world, seeking for any clue to the rhythms that shape the lives of our kind.

When Lucy Paul first turned away from me to walk up the gangplank to the ferry, I stood as if stuck to the spot. Not because what she had said outraged me. Everything about the way she had asked the question—the expression on her face, the flicker in her eyes, how she almost reached out to touch my arm but stopped herself—everything said that she was referring to herself when she asked the question. But even so, I didn't feel betrayed or lied to. I was too fond of the whimsical light in those coal black eyes, too taken with the smudge of coffee in the milk of her skin to feel any hurt or dismay. She was who she was, her own creature, unremarked and only now discovered.

But everything about her question echoed in the empty reception hall of my mind, blending into the whispered, blurted, shouted questions about racial features, ethnic proclivities, the family face in

Augustus Sherman's photographs. Language, origin, passage, reception, examination. The shape of this head, the curious slant of those brows. The pursed white lips or berry-stained grin . . .

I was so lost in thought—my two minds or three twisting into odd patterns and symbols like smoke in the breeze—that I hardly noticed that I was swept up into the wave of immigrants pouring off the ferry that had replaced Lucy's departing boat at the dock. I was stumbling up the slight incline toward the Great Hall, jostled more or less innocently on all sides by the mass of humanity determined to navigate the maze that confronted them at the end of the walkway, at the top of the stairs.

I let myself go with them, my own disoriented feelings so in tune with theirs that I must be one of them, as far away from home and as anxious to survive as they. I didn't stand out. With my worn, tanned face cracked in half by the jagged scar that ran from my broken nose between my eyes up into my hairline. The missing tooth that showed when I grinned back at life. The pure white patch in my hair at the temple where the scar disappeared. My eyes a tired blue that could look almost reptilian when I was insulted or angry. I imagined that I fit right in, with my battle scars and anarchist glance.

When I did bother to look out and around me at the people I was forming into line with, I saw that many had changed into their best clothes for this occasion, dug into bags and boxes for their native garb, which only served to make them stand out like strange birds of an exotic plume. But many could offer only the stained and dirty clothes they'd traveled in to the New World. And though they had dusted and scrubbed, their best was still worn hard and smelled of shipboard cooking, too many days and nights with little more than a basin of cold water to wash in. I glanced down at my own suit of clothes, and though it was clean and smelled faintly of detergent, I could boast the same shabby attempt to look presentable as they.

The only difference was that most had a numbered tag tied to a buttonhole—the number of the ship manifest their names had better appear on—and were clutching their identification and travel papers. I had no tag, but I pulled a clutch of notes I'd been writing out of my pants pocket and my Bureau of Investigation badge from inside my jacket. Now I look the part, I remember thinking. Now I can pass up the stairs with the rest.

So I did. At the bottom of the fabled stairs that led up from the great doorway to the second-floor main hall, we were divided into two swarms, one with women and children and the other with just men. The swarm of men were shoved into one line at the foot of the stairs by guards from the Immigration Service who barely bothered to even look at us. I was pushed in between what must have been a father and son, both of whom seemed desperate to stay together, so I surreptitiously pulled the son in front of me and returned their grateful smiles.

Then we were on the stairs, mounting slowly up one step at a time as the doctors who stood at each landing regarded us each in turn, quickly and efficiently, almost like meat inspectors, I thought. The father who I had reunited with his son had a weak leg, and he was careful to take each step up with his left foot to hide the lameness in his right. But the doctor on the first landing wasn't fooled for a second. He brought out his piece of chalk and marked the lapel of the man's suit, perhaps his only suit in the world.

Who were we? Those who stood in line from this one ship. European certainly. A half dozen vaguely familiar languages were being whispered around me, including a rough Scots burr. And what? Austrian, Italian, not African or at least no skin darker than Lucy's. Jewish. Nothing of the pure Nordic strain that the anti-immigration forces seemed to think populated the American heartland.

Then the son was on the landing in front of the first doctor, who glanced up and down at him quickly and nodded him on past. I stepped up and suddenly felt thin and shopworn before the physician in his uniform. With barely a glance, he brought out his chalk to work on my jacket. I could feel the letter F being scribed against my chest over my heart. He paused then, still grasping my lapel, and regarded my face closely, impassively. Stared into my eyes ever so briefly. And then the chalk again; I could feel the label X for deranged. Ludmila Kuchar was right, I thought. It's the psychotic ward for me.

The doctor nodded, and I stepped up to the next stair.

Mulatto. What did the word even mean? That there was in the beaker from which an individual life was poured a stronger, more exotic liquor? That some strong man and some strong woman forgot for a moment that they were supposed to keep to their assigned places in the long line and stepped out? At night, in the dark?

I stepped up to another stair.

Did it mean that there was violence in her past? Rape? The flickering, godforsaken scene of a vile white master and abused slave girl thrown down again and again? Or something different, something from a foreign shore where white was less white and Black less Black? Where a woman chose the one she wanted and drew him in . . . ?

Another stair.

Care. In this shabby world, who cared for whom? Who took care? Who cared what you did in the allied darkness when the door was closed and locked and the ocean breeze coursed in through an open window?

Where did she come from, Lucy Paul? From what blood? Who had made her this creature that she was, her mind so strong and her fingers curious? That she was sometimes afraid of sleeping alone and sometimes embraced the night? What lineage had produced that throaty laugh? What family had made the curious way she almost dozed while soaking up the sun and then suddenly said the thing that brought me wholly inside her mind? Wholly into the world . . . ?

Another stair, another landing. Across from me, in the line of women and children, a young mother was weeping from the tension, clutching her two, no three children against her skirts as she waited. She had even more letters chalked on her chest than I did.

Then the doctor who was checking the men on my side of the stairwell nodded, and I stepped toward him. He was swarthy with a full black mustache. "Turn," he said brusquely, and I shuffled a full 360 degrees. After glancing at my F and my X, he too looked critically at my ravaged face, shrugged, and nodded me on.

The next stair.

The thing that mattered most to me was not *what* she was but *who* she was. *What* I was had not been enough for Anna Ulmann. Had not held onto her, heart and soul. Had not bred out of our lovemaking a further generation of love. *What* had trumped *who*, and I was left to rush down the marble staircase of the Anderson Gallery, fleeing the vision of her inside the wealthy arms of her patron. On that searing night she was made all of silk and lace, but her dress was already unbuttoned down to her waist and his pale, blunt hands at work on her willing body.

The next stair.

Creole . . . half-breed . . . mongrel . . . what did any of these words even mean in the long wash of the human striving? I was a mongrel if ever such a thing existed. Scots and Irish, Welsh and German. I once heard my uncle curse his son for *messing with a high-yaller gal.* "You stupid bastard," I said aloud to Uncle Foster as I stood there on the stairs at Ellis Island—growled at him across thirty years and a thousand miles. People in line turned to look at me, alarmed by the tone of my voice even if they didn't understand the words.

Another stair . . . and another.

Then we were at the top. Our line moving slightly faster now as it was divided up into the several long chutes made of wooden benches leading to the examiners' stations. But first, the eye test. Each man, woman, and child in turn had first one and then the other eyelid turned inside out as the doctor searched for any sign of the dreaded trachoma. I was still in line—still thinking about Foster Robbins and his fury over his son's dalliance with a maid at the Mountain Park Hotel—when I stepped up to the eye doctor. He reached for my face, and I exploded. "Keep your hands off me, you son of a bitch."

It took some time and more than a little palaver to make the guards understand what I was doing in line and why I had barked at the eye examiner. But eventually they had to let me go on about my business when three stowaway Italians—tattooed and battle-scarred—showed up in line behind me with no ship's manifest tag and no documentation.

My business? To circulate for the first time through the entire maze of Island 1: dormitories, piles of luggage, lunchrooms, restrooms—all built to industrial scale and all sadly outdated. Cold water when it ran at all. Torn carpet if not bare wood. Detained children playing on what the sign called a yard but was nothing but dusty dirt. The place was a gorgeous façade, but in those bone-tired postwar years, it was seedy and threadbare behind the scenes.

I ate my lunch from a soup wagon set up to feed detained immigrants, only to discover that the hard roll and thin, watery soup was actually worse than what was served in the nurses' canteen on Island 3. Much worse. But the men and women in line with me accepted it without complaint. Late that afternoon, feeling that I'd spent most of the day as a detained and frightened immigrant might, I shook off that persona and circled back to buy a bouquet of fresh flowers from an enterprising vendor.

Pink and red and white tulips with full and open throats, these were the flowers that I handed to Lucy Paul at a quarter to five that afternoon when she walked down the ferry gangplank. When she saw them, she set her packages on the ground and buried her face in the blossoms.

In Print

It must be borne in mind that the specializations that character-ize the higher races are of relatively recent development, are highly unstable and when mixed with generalized or primitive characters tend to disappear. Whether we like to admit it or not, the result of the mixture of two races, in the long run, gives us a race reverting to the more ancient, generalized and lower type. The cross between a white man and an Indian is an Indian; the cross between a white man and a Negro is a Negro; the cross between a white man and a Hindu is a Hindu; and the cross between any of the three European races and a Jew is a Jew.

In the crossing of the blond and brunet elements of a population, the more deeply rooted and ancient dark traits are prepotent or domi-nant. This is matter of every-day observation and the working of this law of nature is not influenced or affected by democratic institutions or by religious beliefs. Nature cares not for the individual nor how he may be modified by environment. She is concerned only with the perpetuation of the species or type and heredity alone is the medium through which she acts.

from The Passing of the Great Race: Or,

The Racial Basis of European History

by Madison Grant

Second Edition (1918)

CHAPTER THIRTY-SEVEN

T ell me the story."

We were sitting out at one of the few picnic tables on the ocean side of Island 3, facing out across the harbor but tucked back between two of the pavilions. Lady Liberty was out there but hidden from view by the two stories of Building C, which rose up just beside us. There were a few open windows to the Island 3 breezeway behind us, but mostly we felt alone, with the aquamarine waves before us and the sound of laughing gulls all around.

"Which?" she asked around a bite of bread and meat. She had brought a loaf of bread and a beef roast back with her from the city, along with a smuggled gallon jug of wine, wrapped up in an old carpetbag stuffed with clothes.

"Mulatto," I said.

"Hmmm." She nodded and paused to wash down a bite of her sandwich with a sip of wine. Strong, red, homemade by some Italian. We drank it from coffee mugs since we were outside where we could be seen. "My grandfather was the son of a freed slave who lived his whole life in upstate New York. After the war, the Civil War, he worked for a group of white religious fanatics who followed the Apostle Abraham, a self-proclaimed man of God who talked to Jesus in his sleep."

"Worked for them?"

"All I know is what my mother has told me over the years. In particular what she told me right before I left for Europe as a nurse. My

173

grandfather was paid—God knows what—to work the farm where this Apostle Abraham lived with his family and to take him around to the various places where his followers would meet. Mostly in barns in the winter, outside in the summer. The apostle had a long white beard and several wives at various times. I don't know how many, but several. Any number of children. My grandmother was one of his daughters, from one of the wives. And given the crazy ways of their little church and family, she thought she could marry my grandfather."

"Even though he was . . ."

"He could read and write. He ran the farm and kept the accounts. According to my mother, who remembered him well, he kept the whole concern going until the apostle died in his sleep while talking to Jesus, and the family—various wives and children—scattered to the wind." She paused to take another healthy bite of beef and bread.

"It seems impossible," I said. It did seem impossible. Not that there was love but that nobody died because of it. The summer before, 1919, white mobs had attacked Negro communities all over the country, including New York City, and they had fought back. Black soldiers returning from the war in Europe who knew how to fight and were willing to do it.

She nodded. Another sip of wine. "I know, but apparently, my grandfather, a man named James Harrison, kept a low profile even on the farm and among the crazy, mixed-up family. According to my mother, he and my grandmother had a kind of secret marriage. At any rate, my mother swore they loved each other. He taught her and her brothers and sisters to read. When the apostle died and things fell apart, no one knew who was to inherit or what was to become of all of them, and my grandfather disappeared . . . or at least my mother, who was only a child when the family fell apart, never knew what happened to him."

"Where were you born?"

She smiled her mischievous smile. "Are you asking me how old I am?"

I reached out and quietly brushed some crumbs of bread off her chin. "I didn't ask when. I asked where."

She laughed. "September 6, 1883. Almost thirty-seven."

I could feel my own mouth lifting into a grin despite myself. "I didn't ask . . ."

"New Jersey. In the western part that nobody's ever heard of, mostly farms. Almost mountains, though you wouldn't call them that. My mother was just light-skinned enough to almost pass for white, and she married a farm boy who was too besotted with her to care." She shrugged.

"Does it bother you?"

"What? Being mixed? No, it doesn't bother me, but I've had to lie about it for so long, that when the time came to tell you, I choked on the words. I was terrified."

"Why do you have to lie about it?"

"They didn't allow Negro nurses in the Army Medical Corp, or at least not overseas. Not half Black, not even a quarter. Nothing but pasty-skinned girls with freckles."

"Did that damn British doctor know?"

"Why do you think he aborted my baby?"

After we ate, we threw our trash into a barrel and carried the mugs back inside. As we climbed up the stairs to the second floor of Building E, I took her elbow, and she glanced up at me in surprise. "When did you turn into a gentleman?" she asked.

"Today . . . maybe," I muttered.

She looked down, perhaps embarrassed.

"I don't . . ." But she didn't finish the thought. Not while we climbed the stairs and not while we carefully barricaded the stairwell door behind us and systematically searched the second floor, just as we'd done the night before when she'd almost shot me and I'd tackled her to the floor.

It was coming on dusk, but there was enough light through our open windows that when I undressed her I could savor her burnished skin, especially that part of her skin that never saw the sun. Could find tucked away places of that skin to cherish with my fingertips or the tip of my tongue.

The sun seemed to stand still in its track across the top of that ancient harbor, and those last delicious moments before it sank behind the land stretched out languorously. And where we touched each other was deeper than before and how we touched was slower. Much slower.

After, when we had released the sun to his duty beyond the horizon and darkness had flowed in from over the ocean, as we lay not sleeping, she whispered the real question, the one that mattered. "Who are you, that you could be so gentle?"

"I am your very own mixed-blood mongrel," I said.

CHAPTER THIRTY-EIGHT

We slipped along the edge of sleep that night, dozing but not falling. Lucy hadn't been back to her quarters in the nurses' dormitory since her day ashore, and she wanted to spend most of the night there to unpack, sleep, and ease back into her work routine. She went on shift at eight the next morning in the tuberculosis ward.

At midnight or thereabouts, we slowly got up and dressed. I meant to walk with her to her dorm. I didn't like the feeling leftover from our little prayer meeting in Blanche Taylor's quarters. The feeling around their plucking out of eyes and chopping off of hands was too intense, too real. Like Lucy, I had expected them to come after us, and the thought of her alone in those long, dark hallways was enough to make the hair prickle on the back of my neck.

Before we left, I checked the cylinder in the .38 Smith & Wesson and dropped it into my pants pocket for our little walk.

Lucy and I were easy together down the hallway and out to the stairwell. Not talking very much but still understanding. Connected beneath the surface in some manner that was slowly unfolding. On the stairs, she reached out and slipped her hand behind my elbow in a way that belied how strong she was, how independent.

We were walking along companionably in the breezeway when we came up behind Lucy's friend Ezra in his orderly's uniform, carrying a bucket of cleaning supplies. His twisted back slowed him down some, so we caught up with him just before the morgue, where he did the oddest thing. He stopped at the entrance as if going in to clean, glanced up at me from his habitual stoop, and then smiled at Lucy's whispered greeting. When we started to slip past him and go on down the passage, he reached out his free hand and captured my wrist. The gesture was too slight to be threatening, and I didn't react except to bend over so I could see his face. Then, with the barest motion imaginable, so slight that I might have imagined it, he nodded toward the door to the morgue. Without speaking, he was telling me to go inside.

Together, Lucy and I pushed the door open and held it for Ezra, but the wizened little man limped on down the hallway, mysterious as always.

There was no living person in the morgue, but there was a body on the metal gurney. In the room next door, the teaching theater, a door slammed. I slipped over to the connecting doorway and looked quickly into the theater. No one.

Lucy was already bent over the corpse on the cart, studying it intently. It was the body of a thin, bearded man, whose face and hands were deeply tanned. The remainder of his body would have been pale, I thought, except that it had the same hot pink appearance that James Thompson's corpse had exhibited before it spent most of a night and a day soaking in the inlet.

"Where's Mabel?" I asked Lucy, meaning her friend who normally would have been working the midnight shift in the morgue. She shrugged her shoulders to say she didn't know and slowly began going over the body almost inch by inch, searching for any clue.

I turned away and methodically began pulling out the refrigerated drawers to see who or what else might be hidden there. In the bottom row, in the same drawer where the pregnant Hebrew girl had lain, I found a second corpse. I pulled out the drawer on its silent rollers and saw the face of a woman who, like the man, had lived much in the sun. Nut brown with wild, wiry black hair. Her eyes were half open, revealing the half-moons of faded brown irises.

There was a tag wired to the big toe of one of her splayed, calloused feet. The tag read "Servian Gypsy (Rome)" and then underneath in the same ink written by the same hand were the letters "PG." I recalled Ludmila Kuchar's serious aid-worker's voice when I'd asked her what the examiner's chalk sign for pregnancy was and she'd replied with *PG*. "PG and you go to the isolation," she'd explained. She hadn't said "PG and you go to the morgue," but then what did she know.

I folded the sheet down slowly and carefully over the "Servian" Gypsy woman, and there it was, her round belly. Though low and relatively small, the globe of flesh that would have become a darting, daring Gypsy girl or boy was obvious on her thin frame. I placed my hand gently against her belly, where the tiny corpse of her unborn baby would be, and it was winter cold, just like the rest of her.

Like the bearded man on the gurney, her face and hands were the brown of an old copper penny, but the rest of her skin—including the skin on her swollen belly—would have been pale in contrast if it hadn't been transformed into a patchy pink . . . the fading pink of a boiled lobster.

I was loathe to touch her face, but even so, I knew I had to find out, so I ran my fingers through her wild black hair, just over her temple and around her ear. And there it was, the swollen lump where someone had bashed the side of her head to knock her out.

"He tried to fight them off," Lucy said behind me.

Leaving the drawer open, I turned back to the man on the gurney. She showed me the dried blood under his fingernails, the badly broken finger on his right hand, the bruises on his throat, and not one but two nasty, swollen lumps under his hair, one of which was split open. "His scalp is still oozing," I said when my fingers found the contusion.

"I don't understand it," she said.

We left them just as we'd found them.

Between there and the nurses' dormitory, I slowly put two and two together. They hadn't come after us the night before because they'd been busy elsewhere.

"Fish to fry," I said grimly to Lucy when we were almost to her quarters.

"What?"

I nodded back toward the morgue. "Our friends who are protecting the purity of the nation had bigger fish than us to fry last night."

She nodded. She'd had the same thought.

And when we parted ways, her to her dorm and me to return to the morgue, I handed her the pistol to carry with her. She squeezed my hand and took the gun without a moment's hesitation.

According to my old, beat-up Elgin, it was a little after one in the morning, the darkest part of a dark night, and I wanted to see what would happen to the body on the gurney in the morgue. Would it sit there moldering till morning, or would someone return to deal with it? What the hell had happened to Mabel, or whoever was assigned to duty in the morgue overnight? God forbid they had disappeared. . . . And who had gone out the door of the autopsy theater just as we came in? That door didn't slam on its own.

And Ezra? Good old spooky Ezra with his oiled hair and his dark, Indian face. I needed to know what he knew, and apparently, he couldn't even talk.

Instead of marching resolutely down the main breezeway, I found an exterior door that was unlocked and slipped outside into the night, determined to come at the morgue and the autopsy theater from some other angle. It was a windy night in the harbor, clouds chasing each other across the face of a three-quarter moon and white tips on steel-gray, nighttime waves. The smell of salt was even stronger in the air than usual. I skirted the edges of the pavilions between the dormitory wing and the morgue, keeping in the shadows and listening for anything—guards that should be there and ghouls that shouldn't.

When I came to the south wall of the building containing the morgue and the theater, I found two outside doors, one that must have led into the space behind the morgue's wall of drawers, which presumably held a refrigeration unit and other machinery. That door was firmly locked. The second door led into what I assumed was the back of the autopsy theater, and—surprise, surprise—it wasn't just unlocked, it was propped slightly open with a handy chunk of mortar wedged against the bottom of the frame. Somebody didn't want the door to swing shut.

Which served me just fine. When I paused at the door to listen, I could hear muffled voices, which seemed to suggest whoever it was wasn't right inside the door and probably wasn't in the theater. I slipped inside, carefully easing the exterior door open a few inches and nestling it back again as soundlessly as possible. I was in a space that I'd never seen before, the storage and preparation room behind the exam theater perhaps. I had left my pencil flashlight back at the psych ward—a mistake I wouldn't make again—but the door into the theater was also standing ajar by a few inches, and a solid bar of electric light from inside showed me enough of where I was to ease over to the door and listen.

I could hear the voices more clearly now. It was two men talking and even laughing. Not in the theater . . . in the morgue itself. I said a silent prayer that the hinges on my door were well oiled and eased it open a foot so I could see into part of the theater, but more importantly, could make out what they were saying.

The two men were joking about the man's body Lucy and I had examined earlier.

"Was he fried or boiled? Baked or fricasseed?"

"Damned Gypsy . . . fought like a wild man," one said. A pause and they both grunted. "Heavier than he looks."

They were moving the corpse, they had to be. From the gurney to the drawer? The drawer itself was too silent on its intricate wheels for me to know for sure, but then there was the faint whoosh of the door closing into the wall. "He'll keep," one said, and they laughed again. "Like leftover steak in the fuckin' Frigidaire."

Then the gurney—one squeaky wheel to warn me, thank God—was coming my way through the open passage from the morgue to the theater. So I slipped out the way I came, through the outside door into the night, not pausing to see my two jocular friends. I didn't need to see them because I recognized their voices.

It was Ross and Ray from Nurse Taylor's Bible study, chopping off the parts of the body politic that offended them.

CHAPTER THIRTY-NINE

There had been six people at Blanche Taylor's little prayer meeting, including the saintly nurse herself and leaving out Lucy and me. When I got back to the psych ward that night, round about three o'clock, I set up shop in one of the empty rooms along the second-floor hallway. By set up shop, I mean that I placed a fairly uncomfortable chair by the outside window. I cracked the window open five or six inches, so I could smoke. Then I loaded the 12-gauge and brought it and my last cigar down to my hard chair and open window. I wanted to sit and smoke and let the warm salt air blow in off the harbor. If some of my religious friends should come calling, I wanted to see without being seen, hear without being heard.

And I wanted to think.

I wanted to think about those six people who'd been in Saint Taylor's quarters that night. I laid the gun on a handy table where I could reach it and set about trimming and firing up the cigar. It took a few moments, as it always does, to get it burning evenly, but then I was content.

Blanche Taylor had sat to the right side of her office as we faced her. Sat primly, neatly, with her teapot and teacups before her. Her face during the time we were all together was peaceful, serene even, and full of love for her fellow man—or at least those whom she included in that number. To her left, our right, sat the young nurse dressed in her whites, also sitting primly, almost stiffly, in her chair, her legs in their white stockings crossed at the ankle. Scottie Phillips. Her blonde hair pulled so tightly back into the bun on the back of her head that it seemed to stretch her face into a mask. She had read her part of the Bible verses with real emotion, bearing down hard on the word *adultery* even as she struggled a bit with *looketh*.

Then, in between Scottie and Lucy, the older man, an orderly named—I searched my memory—Jimmy something or other. He of the gravel voice and the thick, hard hands. He hadn't been in the morgue that night with the other two, or if he was, I hadn't heard him.

Then Lucy and then me, seated side by side on the sofa.

Then Ross and Ray, who seemed to come as a matched set. Then the figure who was, in some ways, the most curious of all. Ethel Adams, the giantess who was full of love and hate all at once. Who could beam down at you with affection and simpleminded humor, all the while explaining to you that people from the hot parts of the world were barely people at all. "They breed like rabbits," she had told me, almost blushing at the words.

It was Ethel Adams who had struck herself in the face so hard that it's a wonder she hadn't loosened a tooth or two. I didn't doubt for a hot minute that she would pluck out her own eye if Jesus immigrated from the Holy Land and told her to.

So there were two questions at least that needed answering. . . . I drew on my cigar. I'd gotten distracted by memories of the prayer meeting, and I'd let my stogie almost go out. A few harsh puffs and it was glowing again, the smoke rich and savory.

Make that three questions. First question we'd had for several days, ever since we saw the strange body of James Thompson. How in the hell do you kill a human being by cooking or what . . . boiling him? Or her? The Nameless Man had suggested some sort of sterilization process, as for medical instruments. I had thought of the kitchens, but Lucy was familiar with the ovens and swore they were too small for an adult body.

Second question: How many of the six were involved in this? I'd seen, or at least heard, Ross and Ray at work, joking about the Gypsy couple as they put them away to keep in the morgue. *In the fuckin' Frigidaire.* . . . But did *they* also mean Jimmy Cain—his last name popped into my head—and Scottie Phillips as well? Did that mean Ethel Adams, God help us? And were there more? Could it be that this was an even larger conspiracy than their little prayer circle?

And the last question, which was the most disturbing of all. Ethel had said she'd pluck out her own eye if Jesus told her to. As far as I could tell, Jesus wasn't hanging around the isolation wards. So if Jesus wasn't doing the telling that made the bodies pile up, who was?

Blanche Taylor? Maybe there was someone or something behind the saint-nurse. Maybe she was only a mouthpiece for some anti-immigration nutjob who believed the god of pure blood was going to save us. At least half my mind wanted to believe that Taylor wasn't behind all of this because in almost every way, she was your grandmother personified. Or not your grandmother, because far too many grannies weren't the sweet, cookie-baking type. She was the archetype of grandmother. Her body was comfortable and matronly, always ready for a hug or a good cry. Her rather chubby hands were extended in care and comfort. Her face was radiant with goodwill, her eyes twinkling and her lips smiling. She was never not smiling.

And I confess, as I sat there in the late-night dark, puffing on a cigar and with a loaded shotgun close to hand, even I—as hardheaded and hard-hearted a man as you would want to know, bereft by the loss of Anna Ulmann—even I responded to the light in the head nurse. I was drawn to her, turned to her in the unconscious way that a flower rotates toward the sun. I didn't want her to be . . . what? A demon? A killer?

But there was another part of my mind. The part that was more closely wired to my body, the part that was slowly being brought back to life in the arms of Lucy Paul, that was warming again to the sound of her laughter. The part of me that was instinctual rather than rational, the part that knew something before knowing was strictly possible.

That part of me had known almost from the beginning that there was something vaguely rotten in the sweet perfume that surrounded the head nurse. Something cracked in her twinkling blue eyes. Something that was too loving and too pure to be quite human. She was more real than real, but also more frightening. Her and her snow-white Bible . . .

So I had my tentative answer to the third question. What we were dealing with was the Cult of St. Blanche, the Head Nurse of Island 3.

By the time my cigar had burned down perilously close to my lips, the sun was climbing over the long, low horizon to the east. It was day. I crushed the last of the spark out of the cigar butt against the window frame. Stood and stretched out my tired legs and back.

It was time for the night shift, I told myself. Time to sleep during the day and roam the halls and wards of Island 3 at night, when the cult was also out and about. Find out who its members were, find out whose job was what. Find out what it would take to kill the snake. All the answers, I told myself, were to be had at night.

Ironically, it was later that same day—when Lucy came home to the psych ward after her shift ended at five—that I learned the answer to our very first question, the one she and I had been asking ourselves since Thompson. And if she hadn't been transferred to the tuberculous ward by chance, maybe we would never have known the answer, or at least not in time to save ourselves.

CHAPTER FORTY

I t's the autoclave they use to sterilize the mattresses." Lucy was still in her whites after a long day in the TB wards. "It has to be."

"What the hell is an autoclave?"

I'd met her at the entrance to our Building E, expecting, hoping, that she'd come to me when she went off shift at five o'clock. Before answering my question, she dragged me back up the stairs to the second floor and our sanctuary at the end of the hall. Whatever an autoclave was, she didn't want to describe it out on the breezeway.

"It's a giant chamber built to hold an entire mattress." She was still out of breath from rushing up the stairs. "It's what they use when a tuberculous patient dies or even after they're released alive. To kill the TB germs, they slide the mattress into this giant autoclave and crank the door tight shut."

"Like a pressure cooker?"

She nodded, simultaneously pulling out the bobby pins that held her cap on and letting her hair down around her face. "Like a pressure cooker, only one big enough to slide a mattress into."

"Which means . . ."

"Big enough to slide a person into. Maybe even two people. Then once the door is sealed, they expose the mattress to high-pressure steam for twenty to thirty minutes."

"How hot does—"

187

"Two hundred seventy degrees, maybe even three hundred at the end. That's what the orderly who was on duty today told me."

"Good god . . ."

"I know. It would cook them alive."

I walked with Lucy down to the entrance to her dormitory, where she meant to change out of her whites and put on something "more nearly human." Before we passed down the breezeway to her dorm, however, she led me back to the base of the island, where she nodded surreptitiously at one unlabeled doorway in the annex to the office building—the laundry where, in a back room, they sterilized mattresses from the TB ward.

From there, we strolled back down to the far end of the island, to the building that contained her quarters on the third floor. She went on into the dorm, and I peeled off to wait for her outside. I stood facing the inlet, not far from where I'd witnessed the discovery of Thompson's body by the bargemen. When she came back out to meet me, she was wearing black slacks and low shoes, along with the yellow linen blouse I had come to love. She'd added just a touch of makeup, the faintest flush of rouge and a bit of lipstick.

She pointed across the swampy inlet to Island 2, where the main hospital buildings sat. "Let's go eat our supper over there," she said.

"You mean get the hell off of Isolation Island?"

She nodded. "I feel like I'm always being watched here. It makes my skin crawl."

"I'm always watching you," I confessed.

She smiled at this, lighter by a bit. "Yes, but that doesn't count. With you, it's always my ass that you're watching."

"Sure. Why not? But I have to say that sometimes my eyes do drift just a bit higher." I stared fixedly at her breasts, which caused her to laugh out loud.

"Come on, get me out of here." She reached out to take my hand but then stopped herself, part of the effect of Island 3 and the silent observers.

Staying out of the breezeway and on the grass, walking easily, quietly together. I carried the jug of Italian wine and a block of cheese, plus a pear and two hard rolls that Lucy had brought back from the city. Supper.

We crossed over to Island 2 and found a spot where we were looking back at the isolation wards, back at the place that had obsessed and haunted us both for days, seeing it from at least a little distance.

We sat on a low wall that separated the hospital grounds from the inlet. With my pocketknife, I sliced the pear and cut off bite-sized chunks of the cheese. I'd brought crockery mugs for the wine, and after Lucy had broken up the hard rolls, we had what felt like a picnic.

While we relaxed in the lingering sunlight, enjoying eating and drinking slowly now that we were off Island 3, I told her about the night before, when with the help of a good cigar, I'd broken our puzzle down into three questions.

She'd apparently solved the first with her discovery of the autoclave. "If you're right," I said, "then we know how they're killing off the people they hate."

"It has to be the autoclave," she said. "Wait till you see it. . . . And the weird thing about it is that even though the body's been cooked pink, you'd never know it was murder. There's no wound." She popped a piece of cheese into her mouth, chewed slowly, and then swallowed. "Stephen, do you think they might believe it's a merciful death? If the person's unconscious when they put them in the oven?"

"Maybe. But only if they don't wake up when the steam hits them. God help them if they do. . . ."

Which gave us both a long pause. The autoclave beggared the imagination . . . almost as if the killers planned to eat their victims.

And the second question: Who? I told her about Ross and Ray in the morgue the night before. What they'd done and said. *Just like the fuckin' Frigidaire.* And she cursed them roundly, using language she'd picked up in the army and using it well.

"You remind me of my father," I told her. "He could cuss standing up or lying down and every which way in between."

"I'd like to meet him," she said, "your father." And then she looked down. It struck me we'd avoided talking about a life after Ellis Island.

"I wish I could take you to see him," I said gently, "down there in North Carolina. I can show you where's he buried, but that's about it."

She studied my face for a long moment and then nodded. "I'm sorry," was all she said.

And the third question: Who was behind it all? The ringleader? I told Lucy my theory about the Cult of St. Blanche.

"She is scary." Lucy paused to take a sip from her cup. "The first time I met her, she hugged me. Right there, standing in the nurses' quarters. At first it was warm and sweet, but she held on too long, and after a minute, I felt like I was being smothered. I don't know . . . it's as if she's a dough made of white flour and pure water. Even so, it's hard to imagine that she could be a . . ."

"A monster?"

"Sure."

"It's all in how the others see her. If they worship her, then either she's the force behind it, or she's someone else's mouthpiece."

"So how do we find out? Is she the witch, and who's in her coven?"

"Funny you should say it that way. I'm planning to do most of my sleeping during the day and haunt the wards at night. I think that's when they do their dirty work."

"Like a vampire," she said, a smile teasing her lips.

"Like a vampire," I agreed. "With a shotgun. And I want you to carry the pistol everywhere you go."

"I can't when I'm on shift. Where in the hell would I carry it? Stuffed down my bra?"

I grinned at her. "If necessary, sister. If necessary. I can help you holster it."

She drained her cup. Her eyes gleamed, and her full lips were stained berry red by the wine. "About that vampire thing . . ." she said.

"Yes?"

"How 'bout if you bite my neck first?"

CHAPTER FORTY-ONE

That night at three in the morning, I watched from underneath a set of exterior stairs while Ross and Ray, along with a third man, carried what looked like a body out along a path to the watery part of the inlet.

They came straight down the steps over my head, stumbling and whispering curses, and I got a good look at the third man—not Jimmy Cain—along with the other two. It was a three-man job. Two to tote the corpse on what looked in the dark like a litter; one showing the way with a shaded flashlight and then peeling off to bring two concrete blocks from the construction site at the top of the inlet. I let them get to the water's edge and start to work on wiring the corpse to the blocks, two of them bent over while a third kept watch.

The lookout was mostly focused on the barge thirty feet away, where the steam shovel sat silent in the dark. Was there a watchman on the barge at night, napping in the early hours? All the better.

When they were all three intent on the job at hand, the flashlight focused on the cadaver, I walked a third of the way out to where they crouched at the water's edge and cut loose one barrel of the shotgun into the night sky. The flash popped off and they scattered like rats, one of them slipping down and splashing in the inlet.

I waited half an hour and then crept out to check out the scene. One carefully shaded pass of my pencil flash to confirm what I expected. It was the body of the Gypsy man, twisted gruesomely as they'd worked to secure him to the blocks, one pass of barbed wire cutting into his neck and the other into his thighs.

I watched the rest of the night from my post under the stairwell, but the prayer meeting boys didn't return. Then, the sawed-off 12-gauge wrapped in my jacket, I walked casually back to the psych ward. Somebody else would find the body that day, and the questions could start to circulate up the Ellis Island chain of command. Somebody besides Lucy and me would have to take note.

The answer to my second question was starting to take shape. Add this third man to the list along with Ross and Ray. Jimmy Cain would make a fourth. Now who else?

My plan was not to stop them entirely until I knew who they all were. Knew if little Scottie Phillips or big Ethel Adams was part of the pack. Or others . . . I thought there had to be others, nurses and orderlies, for their well-oiled machine to run so silently and well. I didn't mean for anyone else to die, but I for damn sure meant to keep throwing a monkey wrench into that machine till we figured out who was who, including the source, the mind, the spirit behind it all.

That was my plan. But I miscalculated. They had a plan as well. The next night, a Thursday, they came after Lucy and me like a mist of blood blown in on the wind.

I had slept that day while she worked her shift in the TB ward. Waited for her in the evening while she bathed and changed. When she came at last to the psych ward, she was somehow even more real, more present, more alive than usual. We laughed as we ate soup that she'd brought from the nurses' canteen, for once more meat and vegetables than broth.

Even when I told her what had happened the night before and how I'd stopped the three men—Ross and Ray and the thin, pale third man—from slipping the Gypsy cadaver forever under the water, even then the mood didn't tail off into fear and loathing. Somehow who we were was stouter stuff than who they were. Somehow, we still had lightness between us despite the haze of hatred surrounding us.

I wanted her, and she wanted me. That's what the laughter and the sly, whimsical smiles said. What the play between us was saying, as if our bodies were talking to each other on a frequency beneath what our ears could hear.

She kissed me when I left our room at the end of the second-floor hall. "Come home early tonight," she said, teasingly, "and wake me when you do."

"Will you let me in if I knock?"

She kissed me again. This time less of a goodbye and more of a come-hither. "I'll let you in," she whispered, though there was no one else to hear.

In my nighttime rambles, I went first to the laundry, where the autoclave waited. The laundry was dark and silent behind a locked door. I circled almost the entire facility on the outside, keeping to the shadows, the shotgun by my side. Paused for a long while near the building that housed the head nurse's quarters, watching and waiting.

A storm was brewing, the air heavy with the scent of rain coming in from the ocean. Wind tossing restlessly in the few trees. When the first heavy drops came flying down, I gave up on the grounds and slipped inside. Then I sat for a while in the stairwell on the second floor above the morgue, looking for our prayer meeting friends, male or female, angel or demon, wherever I might find them. Thunder in the night air, and lightning lit up the bottom of the stairwell below from time to time.

Shortly after midnight, when the thunder abated and the entirety of Island 3 seemed as quiet as . . . well, a tomb, I gave up and, with warm thoughts of Lucy Paul waiting sleepily for me, I made my way back to Building E.

The lights were off in the second-floor hallway. I had left them on. From thirty feet away, I could see that the door to our room was standing wide open. Suddenly, just then, I couldn't breathe.

I ran with what seemed like nightmare slowness. Voice, seeking a voice, gasping, calling her name.

The bolted door had been smashed from the frame and swung loosely on its hinges. And when I flipped on the light switch I discovered the bed had been thrown roughly on its side, the covers scattered, the table listing on a broken leg, a crockery mug shattered on the hard floor, and . . . nothing.

She was gone.

She'd kept the .38 in the room with her that night, and it was gone as well. That probably meant that whoever took her had the gun. I stuffed a handful of shotgun shells into my pocket and slipped out the door and at a jog down the hallway, paused briefly to listen for anyone in the stairwell, and then leaped down the stairs. My mind was racing, red with fury, slick with horror.

It had to be the autoclave. Fifty yards away . . . I needed to go fast and quiet. I jogged rather than sprinted, trying to control my breath. Just short of the laundry, I paused long enough to break open the shotgun and check the double load of buckshot that would kill in a tight space.

The door to the laundry was closed, but the knob turned in my hand. The autoclave was in a small room of its own inside the larger laundry. I eased the door open and slipped inside. I could see light from a half-open doorway in the left corner of the room, which led into the space where Lucy had told me they cooked the mattresses. I could hear voices and a spurt of laughter.

I eased around the large tables in the middle of the laundry and closer to the doorway, sliding my feet as noiselessly as possible along the linoleum floor. Close enough to hear the deep, gravelly voice of Jimmy Cain and one of the others, Ray or Ross, talking. What I heard almost choked me.

"She's a nig, I'm tellin' ya," Cain said to the other one. "Look at her."

"You for sure? She never struck me as no nig."

"She's brown right down to her crack. She's a nig, and we never even knew it."

Holding my breath, I eased closer to the door. It was open six inches or so.

"Well, ain't that ironic. She *is* a nigger. . . ."

I heard a muffled voice call out something from farther inside the complex. A third voice.

"Lift her up and slide her in," Cain again. "Time to bake the cookies."

I heard one of the men grunt. I pushed open the door with my foot and raised the sawed-off shotgun to belt level. I was close, less than ten feet away. The two of them had just slid a mattress with a body on it into a large square opening in the interior wall. The one on the left—Cain—pushed shut the metal door to the opening and began to turn a large, round wheel on the door to lock it down.

The second, Ross, turned and saw me. He stepped to the right and reached toward a pile of clothes on a chair—Lucy's clothes—and came up fumbling with the .38. He tried to say something.

I shot him.

The blast was deafening.

At that range, the first barrel blew him into the wall and dropped him like a sack of something dead. Which was all he was.

I swiveled back toward Cain. He had turned to face me, one hand still on the locking mechanism and the other reaching out, palm toward me as if to ward off what was coming. "Stop and we'll let her out," he croaked, or something like that.

I shot him.

The buckshot tore through him and whanged off the metal door of the autoclave. He slid to the side and down, and I was at the door of the oven—turning, turning the round handle, slick with Cain's blood, counterclockwise to release the lock. Turning till I felt the door shudder free from its rubber gasket. Hauling it open on heavy hinges and tugging at Lucy's feet and legs. Dragging her toward me till I could reach her waist, her shoulders, pulling until she was slipping out over the edge of the mattress into my arms. Utterly naked, but her skin dry and cool.

She groaned, perhaps tried to say something. There was blood on her neck and matted in her hair, but God Almighty, she was alive.

In Print

In fact, we also have much to unlearn. A little while ago we were taught that all men were equal and that good conditions could, of themselves, quickly perfect mankind. The seductive charm of these dangerous fallacies lingers and makes us loath to put them resolutely aside.

Fortunately, we now know the truth. At last we have been vouch-safed clear insight into the laws of life. We now know that men are not, and never will be, equal. We know that environment and education can develop only what heredity brings. We know that the acquirements of individuals are either not inherited at all or are inherited in so slight a degree as to make no perceptible difference from generation to generation. In other words: we now know that heredity is paramount in human evolution, all other things being secondary factors.

This basic truth is already accepted by large numbers of think-ing men and women all over the civilized world, and if it becomes firmly fixed in the popular consciousness it will work nothing short of a revolution in the ordering of the world's affairs.

For race-betterment is such an intensely *practical* matter! When peoples come to realize that the *quality* of the population is the source of all their prosperity, progress, security, and even existence; when they realize that a single genius may be worth more in actual dol-lars than a dozen gold-mines, while, conversely, racial decline spells material impoverishment and decay; when such things are really believed, we shall see much-abused "eugenics" actually moulding social programmes and political policies. Were the white world to-day really convinced of the supreme importance of race-values, how long would it take to stop debasing immigration, reform social abuses that are killing out the fittest strains, and put an end to the feuds which have just sent us through hell and threaten to send us promptly back again? . . .

Within the white world, migrations of lower human types like those which have worked such havoc in the United States must be rigorously curtailed. Such migrations upset standards, sterilize better stocks, increase low types, and compromise national futures more than war, revolutions, or native deterioration.

from The Rising Tide of Color
Against White World-Supremacy
by Lothrop Stoddard
(1920)

PART THREE

CHAPTER FORTY-TWO

The Nameless Man's name was James "Jack" Durand. Associate director of the Bureau of Investigation, Department of Justice.

It took a double shooting in the Ellis Island Contagious Disease Hospital laundry, along with the dramatic rescue of a nurse who was about to be cooked alive, to bring him out of anonymity. Him and three other BOI agents who worked for him, including the man I had known only as Santa—he of the ready grin and sack of guns.

I killed James Cain and Ross Donald a few hours after midnight on Thursday, August 26. A shotgun in close quarters reverberates like cannon fire, and there were armed guards from across the three islands in the laundry within ten minutes. Despite my BOI identification, they took me into custody and took Lucy away on a stretcher—to the General Hospital on Island 2 and not Island 3. At least they listened to my strident demands on that count.

They held me under guard till the afternoon when Santa—real name Adam Fussell—arrived wearing a suit and tie. Having gotten a telegram from James Durand in Washington, they released me into Fussell's custody. I never saw the telegram, but apparently, it was strongly worded. It was the first hint I had that Jack Durand, formerly my Nameless friend, was someone to be reckoned with.

Even with that, it was agreed that I was not to leave the island until there had been a formal inquiry. So with some renewed sense of the irony involved, Fussell moved into the psychopathic ward with me.

He unpacked his duffel of personal things in the cell next to mine, and that evening he had a scotch while I had two, the first of which I dropped straight down my throat without bothering to sip. Over a second drink (for him) and third (for me), we agreed that our names were Adam and Stephen.

By Saturday afternoon, Jack Durand and his assistant were scheduled to arrive, plus a BOI attorney to defend me—if I needed defending—in whatever form of inquiry Commissioner Wallis needed. While we waited for the rest of the team on Saturday morning, I convinced Adam I had to see Lucy. Since he couldn't let me out of his sight, we set out together to navigate the complexities of Island 2.

We found her in a private room in the General Hospital. A male orderly was seated in a chair outside the door to her room, with orders not to allow any visitors except medical staff. Adam dealt with him by showing him his own credentials as well as mine and explaining that we were there to investigate the attack. When he still looked doubtful, Adam lifted him up by the arm and steered him down the hall ten feet or so, where their conversation continued but with more force from Adam and less resistance from the orderly.

I slipped quietly into her room and eased the door shut behind me. A petite, red-haired nurse was seated at the foot of the bed. When she saw me, her face clouded for an instant and then she smiled. "Are you Stephen?" she whispered. And when I nodded reassuringly, her smile broadened even more. She stood up and beckoned me forward. "She's been asking about you since yesterday." Her voice was still low.

The blinds were closed, and the light low in the room. I could just see that Lucy's head was bandaged. When I leaned closer, I could make out that her eyes were closed and the cheek below one eye was bruised black.

"Is she asleep?" I whispered.

"I'm not asleep," she said. "The light hurts my eyes."

The little redhead grinned and, in a more normal voice, said, "I'm going to step outside for a few minutes and let you two talk." And then to me, "Not too much light just yet, and not too loud."

"Is she . . ."

"She has a concussion, and she doesn't remember some things, but she'll be fine in a few days. And Stephen . . ."

"Yes?" I answered without taking my eyes off what I could see of Lucy's face.

"Remember, voice low and no hard questions just yet. Tell her how lovely she looks." She touched my arm and left, closing the door quietly behind her.

Lucy smiled. Her eyes were still closed, but that whimsical smile that was all her came and went. Her eyes flickered and then opened, slowly, including the one that was bruised. "That's Maureen," she said.

"Maureen left us for a few minutes."

"That's because I've probably told her way too much about us." Her voice was husky, and she continued to blink as her eyes struggled to adjust to the scant light in the room.

I sat down on the edge of the bed and, when she reached out, took her hand. "You look lovely," I said. Which she did even though her eyes didn't quite match; one of her pupils was larger than the other.

She giggled. "Sure I do. Like I was run over by a truck."

"No, you do. For right now, alive is lovely. . . . Just breathing is enough." I lifted her hand and kissed it.

"Oh, Stephen, I know you're mad at me."

"For what?"

"I couldn't shoot those men. I had the pistol in my hand, and they were breaking down the door to our room. I pointed it straight at the first one through, I don't remember which." Her voice was getting louder, and I placed my fingers over her lips. She smiled against my hand and nodded ever so slightly. Continued but more quietly. "I tried so hard to make myself pull the trigger, just like you told me, but I froze. I couldn't . . ."

I leaned closer. "It's okay, Lucy. I shot them for you."

She smiled. "I love you," she whispered.

"Why are you crying?"

"I'm not crying. I don't cry."

"Shhh. Your eyes are watering then."

"I can't help myself. My head hurts still, and I've been having bad dreams. I dreamed that you were . . ."

"I'm right here. Holding your hand."

"I didn't mean to say that . . ." Her eyes were closing again.

There was a polite tapping at the door, Maureen coming back.

"What? That you love me?"

She nodded. Again, that faint, whimsical smile. "Don't want to scare you," she murmured and then pulled my hand to her lips so she could nibble my fingers.

"I'm not scared of you," I said, smiling down at her closed eyes.

And then Maureen was in the room, clearing her throat and tapping me on the shoulder. "Time for you to go," she said, "so she can rest." And then to Lucy, "Let him go, honey. He can come back this evening if they'll let him."

The first interview with the formerly Nameless Man, James Durand, was not so sweet and didn't involve any hand-holding. At least not literally.

Adam sat at the end of the Building E corridor, under the sign for the psychopathic ward, so that we wouldn't be interrupted during our deliberations. Four of us sat around a table in one of the empty ward rooms. Durand and the BOI attorney on one side asking questions, the other agent beside me at the table, transcribing my long and winding statement in a lightning-quick shorthand.

Durand was the same pale, nondescript human being he'd always been, and it was hard to think of him with a name and a rank, for it was obvious the other two deferred to him. But as the interview wore on into the afternoon, and he smiled occasionally on my account, he became more human, at least to me.

The attorney, on the other hand, was all business from beginning to end, taking notes and interjecting a question when Durand would let him. He was a dark-complexioned number with a stocky body and a good-looking head that was going a little jowly with middle age. He had a deep voice that he made intentionally deeper just to sound more menacing. He wanted to menace me, but Durand was running the show, and he knew better than to cross Durand. When he did get to talk, he took on the appearance of a bulldog on a leash.

The third man was neither here nor there, but he was pleasant enough when I got ahead of him a few times in my storytelling and he had to ask me to repeat something. And when he read sections back to me for confirmation, his voice was tight and efficient but friendly when I corrected him.

Durand had me tell the entire tale from the moment I first stepped off the ferry and into the Great Hall, where I ran into Ludmila Kuchar, who toured me around her giant letter E. He more or less let me tell it straight through without too many interruptions, stopping only at names and descriptions of people. He was particularly interested in Nurse Blanche Taylor, the local saint, and in the others who'd been in the Bible study: Ethel Adams, Scottie Phillips, Ray Candler or Chandler. And when we came to him, the thin, pale man who was part of the squad who'd helped carry the Gypsy man's body to the lagoon.

"Let me have their names and descriptions on a separate list," he told the recorder. "Printed so I can read it. No, make it two lists. One for Fussell so he can collect these children of God to be interviewed."

"If they're still here," I interjected.

He shrugged. "My guess is that our friend Ray and the other man are already gone since you can finger them for actual crimes. The women . . . hard to say. They can always deny everything except devotion to God. Add Knox to the list. We need to interview him." This last to the recorder, who was already at work on a separate sheet, printed plain. "And this joker, Sherman."

"Augustus," I said to the recorder.

Durand nodded. "Augustus. He's been here forever. Even if he camps out over on Island 1 and stays out of the hospitals, he would have heard rumors if this has been going on for a while."

And so the story went, winding its way down to its bloody conclusion in the laundry. At this point, the lawyer got more forcefully into the game, punching at me with a few hard questions.

"So you shot two unarmed men, who as far as you knew, could have just been sanitizing bedding."

"One was armed," I replied. "Remember that he'd just pulled Lucy's thirty-eight out of her clothes."

He shrugged. "So you say. The other man, however . . ." He glanced at his own notes. "This Cain, he was unarmed."

I nodded. "Sure."

"And you killed him even though he was trying to negotiate with you."

"He said something. But you need to understand that he'd just locked down the autoclave door and, as far as I knew, could have tripped the switch that would have cooked Lucy alive."

"But you didn't know that for sure. You—"

"Your damn tie's too tight around that neck of yours," I said, none too friendly. "You're not listening. I knew that there was a person inside their oven. I'd seen what that oven could do to a human being. I'd heard what they were saying as they slid her in, and based on every available piece of evidence, knew it had to be Lucy Paul." I was tired and hoarse and could feel my face overheating.

"Perhaps, but—"

"Perhaps nothing. If you'd been there, I'd have shot you too."

Durand held up his hand. "That's enough." He turned to the lawyer, who had started to stand. "Sit down and rest your law books. He did what he had to do. And if he hadn't, we'd have another corpse on our hands. One of ours."

"I need to ask him about his personal relationship with Miss Paul."

Durand shook his head. "Not today. We've had enough for one

day." He looked at his watch. "You've got what you need to defend him in any inquiry that Wallis wants to hold, and you know it. Besides, we've got other things to worry about. You go write up your defense attorney notes and see if you can find anything for us to eat." And to the recorder, "When can you give me a clean transcript?"

"Morning. First thing."

"Then do it. Find a room down the hall and dive in. I'll need to edit it before we leave here."

They both got up to go, the attorney reluctantly—still straining against his leash—the recorder with a grin and a wink for me.

When they were both well down the hall, Durand got up and closed the door behind them. He got two cigars out of his coat and laid them on the table between us. And as he searched his pockets for matches, said, "All right, Stephen, tell me about the woman."

CHAPTER FORTY-THREE

"Why should I tell you about Ms. Paul? I just learned your name." I was half teasing, but only half.

He grinned. "My friends call me Jack."

"Not James?"

He found a book of matches in a coat pocket and tossed them onto the table with the cigars. "Nope. James is for lawyers like that jackass who just left."

"Okay, Jack. Is this a personal conversation or professional?"

"I know you've got a knife in your pocket. Trim those cigars for us." He hung his jacket on the back of his chair and sat back down. "Personal. For now, at least, it's personal."

One other time, he had brought me a cigar. It was when he had visited me behind bars when I was on trial for murder in North Carolina. That time, my face was a bruised and battered pulp, and my mouth was sore, but the smoke . . . I remembered the smoke, and it was delicious.

I carefully trimmed the cigars and handed his over. When I picked up the matches, he said, "You first. I have a feeling you need it more." I nodded and smiled. It took only two matches to get mine going, and I tossed the book to him as I puffed away to set the flame.

"Last time we did this," I said, "you didn't have a name."

He nodded, working on his own stogie. Then, in between puffs, "That's a problem, really. I was low enough on the totem pole then; I could afford not to own a name. Now I've moved up next door to the

210

director, and I have to talk to reporters and such. Sit in meetings till my ass goes numb."

"You don't like reporters?"

He shrugged. "Better than lawyers."

"Like our friend . . ." I pointed down the hall in the direction the bulldog had taken when he left.

He grinned. "Oh, he's not so bad. But yes, like him."

We smoked in silence for a moment, letting the tension left over from the day slowly drain away.

"Why do you need to know about Lucy?" I asked after a bit.

"Two reasons. First reason, I need to be sure there's nothing in your relationship with her that clouded your judgment, caused you to be careless, put this whole operation at risk."

"That sounds professional, Jack."

"It is, in a way. But if that was my main purpose, then I would have asked when the lawyer was in the room, and the reply would have been part of your official statement."

"What's the second reason?"

"Personal, that one is . . ." He shrugged and regarded the slowly growing ash on the tip of his cigar. "The minute I sent you over here, I started to feel guilty. I don't traffic so much in guilt, and I didn't like the feeling. Then, when I saw you at Brady's Saloon and it started to become clear that this whole operation was a stinking mess, I let you talk me into sending you back."

"No guilt there," I said. "I chose it."

"Yeah, but it didn't seem to me you were in your right mind. That Anna Ulmann woman maybe. But you seemed like a man driving way too fast on a dark road. Hell-bent on destruction. Last couple of outings, you seemed like a man happy to be alive, wanting to stay alive if you could. But when I saw you at the Algonquin, you were restless. Fidgety. And by the time I saw you at Brady's, the fuse was lit and burning. I needed you to come in here and take this problem off my list, sure, but I should never have let you come back alone."

"I wasn't alone," I said. "I was with her."

He smiled. "Well then, tell it, damn you. So I'll feel better."

"The first part is easy. The professional part. I got myself involved with her. Emotionally even more than physically. How did you put it? My judgment was clouded. I probably put the whole operation at risk. And I was one careless son of a bitch . . . at least some of the time."

He frowned.

"But then, on the other hand, when things were at their worst, she kept me from finding enough rope to hang myself. And she was the one who helped figure it all out. She was the one who discovered the autoclave. I suppose you could say that for the past few weeks, we've made a team. Partners."

He grinned. "When you weren't in bed together."

"Well hell, Jack. We did some pretty solid work there too."

He laughed out loud. Which, when you think about it, was astonishing. Not only did he have a name—he had a sense of humor.

"Fair enough," he said eventually. "Now tell me the personal side of it. Why you wanted to hang yourself, and how she saved you."

I stared hard at him, puzzled where to begin. "You'd think we were friends," I muttered.

"We might just be that," he said. "I haven't got many, and I'm probably lousy at it."

And so, as our cigars burned down, I told him, leaving out only the most lascivious details. Some things are too private, even for friends.

CHAPTER FORTY-FOUR

The next morning, Sunday, I walked over to Island 2 with Adam Fussell in tow. Back in the psych ward, Jack Durand was reading and editing the transcript from the hours-long deposition taken down the day before. The bulldog attorney had been sent out to find and request Monday interviews with most of the characters I'd told them about.

The same orderly sat outside Lucy's door as the morning before, and he was happy to walk to the end of the hallway with Adam. The redhead from the day before was not sitting in the room that morning, however. Lucy was alone.

I shut the door to the hallway and sat down on the edge of the bed. Her eyes were closed, but she was smiling. "Have they abandoned you?" I asked.

"You don't have to whisper," she said in almost her normal tone of voice. Her dark eyes blinked open, and the smile turned into a grin. "I'm past the observation stage," she added. "I was throwing up yesterday morning, but I feel better today. Maureen still checks on me, but they're no longer afraid that I'm going to drift off into a coma."

"What did they hit you with?" I asked.

She shook her head slightly. "Will you open the blinds, please, just a little. Let me see how my eyes do with the light."

I rose and did as she asked, watching her face as I fiddled with the cords to the venetian blinds. Slowly let night turn to day inside the room. "A little less," she said. More fiddling turned day back into early morning, light that was more soft than glaring. "Perfect," she said.

I pulled the one chair in the room from the foot of her bed to the side opposite the windows, sat, and reached for her hand again.

"Did you just ask me what they hit me with?" she asked. "My mind still drifts a little."

"Yes, but don't talk about it if you—"

"I can't remember," she interrupted me. She paused. "There were two of them. . . . When I wouldn't respond to a knock on the door, they kicked it in and then came crashing into the room. I think I heard a third voice later in the laundry, but I'm not sure. I held the gun straight on them. Aimed straight at their belt buckles. I tried so hard to pull the trigger that my hands shook. But I hesitated . . . and they were on me. They tore through the room, slammed me up against the wall . . . hard . . . and one of them swung something. Swung his arm, and . . . that's it. Everything stops there. Until . . ."

"Until what?"

"Until I was inside this box. Shut up inside something like . . . it felt like a coffin. I thought I was dead, maybe, and in my coffin. And then there was thunder. I swear to God, thunder. And you opened the end of the coffin and pulled me out."

"Shhh. That's enough. Don't think about it now. Think about . . ." I glanced around the room. "Think about morning. Think about . . ."

"It was the autoclave, wasn't it? Tell me the truth. They were going to boil me, weren't they?"

I hesitated.

"The truth!"

"Yes."

"Fuckers!" she said quietly.

"They were that."

"Were?"

"They're dead now." She'd forgotten the day before when I'd told her I'd shot them.

She stared into my face. "Good," she said after a moment.

I massaged the hand I held—her warm palm, her strong, blunt fingers—with both of mine and began slowly to move up her arm, rubbing away at the nightmare, or so I imagined.

"You could get in bed with me," she suggested. "Play doctor."

I smiled at her. "Not yet. Not with those two, your guard and my guard, standing out in the hall."

"Then tell me a story. Tell me something from North Carolina. From your life down there that you haven't told anybody else in New York, including . . . I can't remember her name . . . the photographer bitch."

"Did you just wink at me?"

"I tried to." She laughed. "I'm trying to get my skills back."

We stared at each other for a long moment, and the color of her eyes—in this light, a sort of burnt umber—reminded me of something from my life before, reminded me of someone.

"I'm going to shut my eyes," she said softly. "Rest them for a bit. And you tell . . ."

"My brother is a Negro named Prince Garner," I said.

"Tell me the story of Prince Garner," she whispered.

"No, he really is. Not my brother by blood. But once upon a time . . . we were married to sisters. He was married to Dora, who was the Black daughter of James Rumbough, the owner of the Mountain Park Hotel where I worked as a boy and as a man. I was married to one of Rumbough's official white daughters, an overbred bitch of a woman who wanted me to dress better than I knew how and learn country club manners."

Her eyes popped open. "Is any of this true?"

"All of it."

"You never told me you were married." Her voice had an edge, more like herself before . . .

"We never got that far back. Plus you never asked."

"Do you have any children?"

215

I knew we were on dangerous ground, and I went slow. "A little boy"—I paused to squeeze her hand—"named James, after his grandfather."

"Where is—"

"He died of infant cholera. Four years old." My own voice was hoarse, though I was only whispering, for speaking of the boy choked me.

"Oh my god. And all this time, I've been complaining about . . ." Now it was she gripping my hand. She rolled on her side toward me.

"Hush. Just hush, Lucy. Close your eyes, and I'll tell you the story of Prince Garner."

She sighed deeply. Again. And then let her eyes close.

It took me a bit, but I started over. "James Rumbough was a great man but also a hard man. He fathered seven children with his wife and one daughter with his wife's maid, a sweet woman named Mary Henderson. During the Civil War, when she was still a slave."

"Bastard."

"Rumbough? Well, he was that. And he was a lot of other things, including a substitute father to me at times."

"Still a bastard," she said. "Tell me more . . ."

"The white daughters, most of them, were haughty and mean. Society girls. But the Black daughter, Dora, was sweet and quiet. Rumbough built her a home of her own there in Hot Springs and, rumor has it, found her a husband—a large, funny man with a deep voice and a deep soul named—"

"Prince?"

"Prince Garner."

"Because he was a prince?"

"No, I think it was his actual given name. But he was, and still is, everything his name implies. A sort of Mexican bandit with a wide sense of humor."

"Is he Black?"

"I already told you," I said gently. "My brother is a Negro named Prince."

She nodded, settling in, her head comfortable on the pillow.

"So Prince and I had parallel lives, I guess you would say. He was married to Dora, and they had a fine life, though she wanted children and there never were any. And I was married to one of the white daughters. Sadie was her name. And we had a child who died."

"Stephen . . . ?"

"We had a little boy who died in my arms. And after he was buried, it was as if everything good between us died with him. We lived more and more apart, and then she divorced me, sometime around 1910."

"Did you lose your job at the hotel?"

"At Mountain Park? No, her father more or less sided with me. He knew what . . . she was like. And so I continued on with my life, drinking too much from time to time. Prince, along with his Dora, they adopted me. Spring, summer, Thanksgiving, Christmas. Prince and I became best friends, very like brothers for real, not just brothers by law, and we survived the war together. And that's the end of the story."

"Stephen," she said my name again.

"Hmmm?"

"Any other secrets you'd like to tell?"

CHAPTER FORTY-FIVE

Secrets.

The formal inquiry into the shooting deaths of Ross Donald and James Cain was set for Tuesday morning, August 31, in Commissioner Wallis's chambers. Which gave Jack Durand all of Monday to interrogate possible coconspirators and other Ellis Island personnel.

Jack explained to me on Sunday afternoon that he wanted me to come into each interview approximately halfway through to confront anything misleading or false in what was offered by way of testimony. They would begin at the bottom and work their way up the chain. Scottie Phillips to Ethel Adams to Blanche Taylor and then Knox and Sherman. Ray Chandler was nowhere to be found, but authorities in the city were already on the lookout for him.

And when he asked me what I thought we should ask, I brought up the third man.

"The thin, pale-skinned man who helped carry the Gypsy?"

"Yeah, him. Plus Lucy says there was also a third man the night they took her."

Jack nodded. "You said the same. That you heard someone deeper in the laundry, maybe behind the autoclave. Was it Chandler?"

"I don't know."

"Can Miss Paul identify him?"

"No. Or at least not yet. Her memory is coming back day by day."

"So I make it there's a third man, pale and thin, and possibly a fourth since we don't know who else was in the laundry."

I nodded.

"Well, then, perhaps our friends will tell us. . . ."

Scottie Phillips made for an interesting start to the day. She seemed to have shrunk since the prayer meeting. She was young compared to most of the nurses on the island, early to mid-twenties, with dull, yellow hair pulled back into a tight bun underneath her nurse's cap. Ruddy complexion with freckles that tended to disappear when she blushed, which she did a lot.

When Adam brought me into the room on the first floor of Building E, she'd already been in with Jack and the bulldog lawyer for most of an hour. Adam whispered in my ear just before he opened the door. "Just follow the boss's lead and lay it on thick."

The lawyer left the room by the same door as I went in. He had a smile on his face—the first I'd seen there—and I had the strange feeling that he'd been charmed by Miss Phillips.

She was seated opposite Jack Durand across a plain oak table in a hard, straight chair. Even so, she managed to appear prim. Dressed head to toe in starched white, including the white stockings that covered her carefully crossed ankles. She smiled wanly at me when I came in.

I sat down at one end of the table with Jack to my left and the nurse to my right.

Jack started the fun and games. "Nurse Phillips here is the most innocent person I've ever met," he said. "She doesn't seem to know anything about kidnapping or murder. She only does what she's told and goes home to her dormitory every evening to read her Bible and pray for the Second Coming."

"She's lying," I said to him.

"Do tell. About what?"

"Not knowing. She may read her Bible till the cover falls off, but that doesn't mean she never looks up to see what the hell is going on. Did you ask her about Nurse Taylor?"

"The head nurse. Miss Phillips here seems to think she's an angel come from above."

I turned to face Scottie Phillips. "More like the whore of Babylon," I said straight into her startled face, which slowly turned brick red.

"Keep her name out of your filthy mouth," she said, all but choking over the words.

"I don't believe I will do that," I replied. "Somebody needs to start telling the truth about this goddamned place, and I believe I'm the man for the job. Your angel Nurse Taylor is heading up a ring of killers who destroy innocent people who are only trying to somehow get into this country and make a better life." I was warming to my task, and even I was surprised at the fury that was boiling up inside me. "Many of them young . . . innocent . . . girls who just want to give their babies a new life, a better life than they could ever have had where they came from. Hell, girls your age, girls just like you!"

"How dare you!" she hissed. "You say innocent like they hadn't been . . . fornicators. Harlots. Already degraded their bodies and sold their souls to the devil . . . or they never would have been with child in the first place."

"So they needed to die?"

She froze. Her mouth was moving, she was forming words but wouldn't quite let them emerge. She glanced down into her lap, where her hands clenched and unclenched spasmodically.

"Nurse Taylor . . . Nurse says . . . said they needed to be punished. Not killed, just punished."

"For their sins?"

She nodded harshly. "Yes, for their sins."

"How were they punished?"

"I saw it only once," she said after a pause. "Mostly the men . . ."

"Mostly the men carried out the punishment?"

220

She nodded.

"Were they punished in the laundry? Were their sins burned away?"

She looked up, suddenly desperate. Her eyes went first to Jack and then back to me. "Don't you . . . it's purgatory," was all she said. And would say no more.

A few minutes later, Jack told her she could go back to her quarters, was free to resume her duties but could not, under any circumstances, leave the island.

When we were alone in the room, I asked him what he thought. "I think Taylor uses her as bait to draw the men she wants into her little group."

"What?"

"You haven't done this as long as I have." He shrugged. "And you weren't raised a Catholic."

"Like you?"

"Like me. Although nobody in the Bureau knows that, so you might keep it under your hat. Purgatory is where you go to suffer till you qualify for heaven. That poor, addled girl may well think they were only burning away the residue of sin when they stuck people in the oven."

"She can't be that simpleminded."

"Probably not, but she's carrying around a lot of guilt of her own. Guilt and fear."

"Is that what makes you think she was . . . what did you call it . . . bait?"

He nodded. "I think that down deep she was telling us that she's in purgatory. She's suffering for something she did or was made to do."

"Christ."

"I know," he said grimly. "It may be that your mind isn't dark enough to see through all of this," he added. "For which you should be grateful."

I sat in from the beginning of the interview with Ethel Adams. And it was like night and day from that of Scottie Phillips. For one thing, Ethel was glad to see me. She hugged me when Adam Fussell led her into the room, which was like being wrapped in a feather bed. When she first sat down, I asked her to list for me all of the people from the island who had attended the private Bible study in Nurse Taylor's quarters, which she did—slowly, laboriously—printing the names on a sheet of ruled paper.

Jack let me do most of the talking at first, and Ethel happily told us about the bad and desperate people who were trying to get into the country. Russians, Polacks, Ukrainians, Lithuanians, even some of the Italians. I asked about Jews, and she explained that Jews were "dark-skinned people at heart."

"Not quite African black-dark," she went on, "but dark-skinned people who want to be white." Dark-skinned people brought us round to one of her very favorite topics, the Gypsies, and when I asked her about them, she dove in headfirst.

"The Gypsies are not even one thing," she cried. "They ain't Jews, they ain't Catholics, they ain't Eastern . . ." She looked back and forth from me to Jack, suddenly stymied. "Orthodox?" Jack guessed.

"That's it." She glowed at him. "They ain't that Eastern Orthodox neither, whatever in the world that is. They ain't even a nationality. They ain't Slovakian or Romanian. Not really. They're some kind of mongrel tribe all their own, and they have the morals of alley cats. I've already explained this to Stephen . . . Mr. Robbins. The Gypsies are the biggest threat of all." She lowered her voice to speak in confidence. "Here's what I think. If we don't deport all these awful Bolsheviks and Communists and Jews, then someday—and I mean someday soon—we're all gonna end up American Gypsies."

"Why Gypsies?" I asked.

"I mean we're all just gonna be one brown tribe of people, all blended up out of every god-awful blood and plasma you can imagine. There won't be no marriage at all and hardly any family. It will be the way cavemen lived, huddled around campfires while all of our great Western culture is ground down to dust."

"How do we stop that from happening?" I asked her.

"We have to keep them out," she said, shaking her head sadly. "I don't hold with violence, I really don't. Whatever those men were doing, I understand that you had to stop them, but there has got to be a way to keep our blood pure."

"What about homosexuals?" Jack asked suddenly.

"You mean like men with . . . men and women . . ."

"With women." Jack nodded encouragingly. "Should we keep them out as well?"

Ethel Adams's already large eyes spread wide. "Oh, my Jesus," she said. "I don't know. Do we even have homosexuals here in America?"

Jack looked down at this point. He had to in order to hide the smile on his face.

"What do you think, Ethel?" I asked.

"I don't think there's any such thing as an American homosexual. . . ." There was a perplexed frown on her face that suddenly brightened into revelation. "Or if there is, it's not that bad because they can't have no children."

"Then they're not a threat?"

She shook her head, no, passionately. "Nope. They can't reproduce. The American race is safe from them."

It went on from there for a bit. And then, almost casually, Jack slipped in the question I'd been waiting for. "What do you think Blanche Taylor believes about all of this?" he asked Ethel.

She brightened yet again. "Nurse Blanche Taylor is a woman of God, a Christian saint. There has never been a mean thought to cross that dear woman's mind. And if there was, you can rest assured, Mr. Durand, that she just shook it right out." She shook her own head violently to demonstrate. "Just shook that evil thought right on out of there."

"Do you think she would accept God's children into our country if—"

"Why of course she would!"

"If they were Jews or Gypsies or Catholics."

That brought Ethel up short. And Ethel Adams perplexed was a fascinating sight. Her large, happy, disingenuous face screwed up in thought. "I think that she would pity them," she said finally, "for they ain't Christians. Not like we mean Christian."

"Would she forgive them for that?" I asked, for it seemed to me an odd and tangled question.

"I think so . . ."

"Would God forgive them . . . for not being Christians, I mean?"

"Oh no." She was on safer ground here. "God will forgive anything, but you've got to come to the foot of the cross and accept Jesus as your own personal savior. Are you saved, Stephen?"

I opened my mouth to answer, but Jack cleared his throat, tired of Ethel's twisty theology.

"Ethel, you said that Nurse Taylor was a Christian saint and that she would take pity on the unwashed horde from . . . hell . . . everywhere. But would she let them into the country?"

Ethel shook her head sadly. "Well, Mr. Durand, you know, she wouldn't. She couldn't let in the heathen peoples of the world because they would replace us. She has shared with me in private conversation"—she paused to let us absorb just how proud she was of her private parlay with the saint—"told me in my own ear that in three generations, there wouldn't be any Christian, white people left in America. We'd all be replaced."

CHAPTER FORTY-SIX

Nurse Blanche Taylor. Saint Blanche.

Before she went into the interrogation room that afternoon, I asked her to perform the same simple task that we'd asked Ethel Adams—to list for me the island personnel who'd attended her Bible studies.

"Even if they've been there only once?" she asked.

"Even if they've been there only once," I said.

She smiled benevolently at me and quickly wrote out a list in beautiful, precise cursive. Not too surprisingly, her list contained the names of those who'd been in attendance the night Lucy and I were there. Just those names, including ours, and no more. It wasn't her first mistake, but it was a mistake, for Ethel Adams's list held an additional name . . . a man's name.

After that, the whole episode took on a surreal quality. I waited while Jack and the bulldog lawyer interviewed her. Half, maybe three-quarters of an hour. And this time, I was waiting with a prop. Two props actually—Ciara McManaway's carpetbag and her shawl.

They were sitting on a side table in the anteroom when the lawyer came out, which was my signal to go in. The odd thing was that the bulldog, whom I hadn't seen smile except at Scottie Phillips, was all but glowing. "What a damn fine woman that is," he said to me, with a tone bordering on awe. "She reminds me of my own mother, the way she . . . she radiates love for the people of the world."

"Not all the people of the world," I offered.

He shook his square head roughly at me. "You be respectful," he cried. "That woman is far above people like you and me. She is the soul of understanding. I would trust her with . . ."

"With what?"

"With the power to say who goes and who stays. The power to separate the sheep from the goats."

Good God, I thought, the bulldog is perilously close to quoting the Bible.

"I'll be gentle," I promised him. Sure I will, I thought. I wrapped the shawl around my shoulders and experienced the powerful déjà-vu sense of the young woman herself and of the night Lucy and I first touched her things. Sweat and brine, onions and potatoes, a peat fire on a stone hearth in old Ireland—all these things coursed through me. I picked up the bag and walked into the interview room.

Once there, I closed the door firmly behind me and turned the dead-bolt. Then I sat without speaking on a bench against the wall by the door. Sat with the carpetbag clutched firmly in my lap, exactly as I'd seen Lucy pantomime the scene days before, a human echo of when she, Lucy, had seen Ciara McManaway outside the door of Blanche Taylor's office.

I breathed deeply, nervously, as a young pregnant girl might when faced with a personality as gigantic as Taylor's. And in breathing, pulled into my lungs the fog and rain of County Galway, on that storm-battered western coast. Felt for a brief moment my own stomach toss and turn on shipboard as my baby grew increasingly insistent, increasingly restless. That baby made of my blood and my skin. My seasickness. And my relief to again find land. Sitting there, I knew all of that, and I knew what it was to be a ghost.

"Dear Stephen, what in the world are you doing?" It was Taylor's voice but not her usual silver cordiality. There was a hint of anxiety stitched into her words.

"What do you think he's doing, Miss Taylor?" Jack asked in that plain conversational tone he had. Curious but not pressing.

"Why, I don't know. He's acting awfully strange. Are you certain that he's alright?"

"Oh, he's just fine. He wanted you to see all that remained of the McManaway girl's possessions. All she had in the world when she landed on this godforsaken rock and got sent over to the isolation wards."

"But—"

"Don't pretend for a goddamn minute that you never saw her or her things before," I said. Low but harsh.

"I don't recall that bag or that . . ."

"Shawl? Here, let me help you." I sat the bag on the floor, got up, and walked over to where she sat. I brought the heavy woolen shawl off my own shoulders and wrapped it around hers. "There," I said. "Does that help? They say smells are a powerful aid to memory."

"Oh . . . oh," she was clutching at the shawl as though it might strangle her, and after getting her fists into it, threw it convulsively to the floor. "Nasty thing," she muttered. "It smells to high heaven."

"It does," I agreed. "Smells of life. Food and fire, sex and the ocean. All the myriad things that made up that young woman's life before you killed her."

"Why, I never would . . . could do such a thing."

"With your own hands, probably not. Using the hands of others, you'd do it in a red-hot minute. I didn't see Ciara McManaway's body before it disappeared, but if your goons put her into that goddamn autoclave and cooked her and her baby to death, then there's no punishment too severe."

"Oh, Stephen, my dear, dear man. Your wits have left you entirely. I would never be party to such a monstrous act. I gather that our friends Ross and poor, poor Jimmy went badly astray and took some of what we said—you'll recall what *we* said that night at Bible study—in a literal rather than figurative sense. Mr. Durand says that they tried to harm Miss Paul, and I'm horrified, horrified to think about what they did."

"If that's even remotely true, you'll be relieved to hear that I dispatched them to their maker."

"God forgive you for what you had to do. I know I have."

Jack Durand laughed out loud. "Pardon me, ma'am, but why in the hell does it matter if you forgive him? If the commissioner's inquiry acquits him, he can go on about his business. Do you have some special telegraph line direct to God?"

"Oh, no, Mr. Durand. No, no. I'm just a humble servant, dedicated to the health and well-being of the poor and downtrodden on this earth. I base my service on the Bible, it is true, but the New Testament teaches the humility of our Lord. I believe in moral behavior and the rule of law."

"Well, your boys, Ross and Jimmy, they broke the law, and Robbins here put them down like rabid dogs."

"The divine law."

"What?"

"I believe in the divine law. It trumps our more savage attempts to establish order."

Jack looked at me. "Did she say *savage?*"

"She did."

"Well, ma'am, that's an odd tune for you to play. If Robbins here is right, and I've never known him to be far wrong, you have inspired a ring of killers who believe that by destroying certain kinds of immigrants, they are maintaining the sanctity and purity of the American race."

"That, Mr. Durand, is preposterous. I am a simple woman who desires only the best for our way of life. I could never inspire—"

"I'm not done," he said peremptorily. "I'm not done talking, and I'm not done with you. Nobody here thinks you personally committed murder. Nobody here thinks you smashed some defenseless girl over the head with two rocks in a sock. Hell, nobody here thinks you stuffed a semiconscious human being into a mattress oven and cooked them to death. But everybody in this room knows you're behind it.

You're the heart and soul of it. And one way or another, you're leaving this island. Between us, Robbins and I will see to that."

"But this is my life's work."

"You mean your death's work," I said.

"Oh, Stephen, you could not be more in error."

"You're confined to your quarters till further notice," Jack barked. "You can talk to that Adams woman if you so desire. She won't understand half of what passes out of your mouth anyway. But no one else." He glanced at his watch. "Agent Fussell will escort you there now. And there will be a guard at your door twenty-four hours a day till I figure out what in the hell to do with you."

Nurse Taylor stood and slowly, deliberately drew herself up to her full height. "It is very likely that the two of you will burn in hell," she said. "But I will pray for you without ceasing, in hopes that eventually you will be saved by the light of truth and return to the true service of our nation."

When she had made her regal exit and Adam Fussell had taken her in tow, both Jack Durand and I collapsed back into our chairs. "Talk about a goddamn force of nature," he muttered after a moment.

"She may be a witch," I said eventually. "Where I come from, we have witches."

He laughed, and I joined him. The bulldog attorney poked his head into the room and acted like he wanted to join us. "Get the hell out of here," Jack told him roughly. "Go somewhere and scratch some part of your anatomy. Come back in an hour . . . with a bottle of something hard to drink and a plate of something hot to eat." And a moment after he left, to me, "Goddamn him anyway."

"You're awful hard on him," I offered by way of conversation, not really caring one way or another.

"Deserves it." Jack stared balefully back at me. "He's a spy."

"Who's he spying on? Surely not me?"

He shook his head. "No, you don't matter so much, at least not yet. He's mostly interested in me and whether I walk the party line."

"I thought he worked for you."

"He does, and because of that, he still has to follow orders. But his loyalty is to a young firebrand named Ed Hoover who runs something called the Radical Division. Ever heard of them?"

"Nope."

"Be glad. Hoover was the one who ran the deportations through here last year. Then it was about getting rid of the Bolsheviks and Wobblies. Now it's about keeping out the undesirables. He would love our Saint Blanche of the Wards. And if we're going to pry her loose from here—let alone send her to prison—we've got to get it done before he and his damn politicians get involved."

CHAPTER FORTY-SEVEN

We changed our strategy for the afternoon interviews. Instead of dragging Knox and Sherman into Building E, Jack decided we'd learn more from seeing them in their own lairs. Jack dispatched the bulldog attorney to Island 1 to telegraph the BOI office in the city. They were to issue warrants for Ray Chandler and the extra name that appeared on Ethel Adams's list of prayer meeting attendees—Adolph Becker. We would meet the bulldog midafternoon at Sherman's office on the main island.

It gained us another hour of time without the lawyer growling and taking his notes, and we spent the hour with Dr. Howard Knox. His secretary, she of the platinum hair, was waiting for us, balanced precariously on stiletto heels, and ushered us straight into Knox's office.

The interview was relatively short and relatively sweet. Knox played the same tune he'd played with me from the beginning. He was an administrator, he was overworked, he shuffled paper all day, which kept him from the wards and kept him from pursuing his own research interests and, "if the truth were known," from participating in the true mission of Ellis Island.

"How do you define the mission?" Jack asked, again in his offhand, apparently friendly way.

"I'm not sure how Commissioner Wallis will define our work," Knox replied, "but I see us as having two purposes. One is to separate those who are suited to life in America and can contribute to the quality of that life from those who are not suited. The second is to help the well-suited find their way successfully into the mainstream of America."

"Those who are not suited?" Jack again.

"Sadly, to send them back. To return them from whence they came."

Jack glanced at me, and I picked up the thread. "You mentioned your own research interests earlier, Doctor. Is that the work you've done with intelligence testing?"

For the first time since I'd met him, Knox perked up. Sat up straighter and reached out toward me with one long, thin hand. "Yes, of course," he cried.

"I've taken one of your tests." I smiled encouragingly back at him. "And I was fascinated with the way in which you've created assessments that don't use language."

"That's right, that's right. They are linguistically and culturally neutral. They can be administered through pantomime. My dream is that we will no longer exclude the talented individual just because he doesn't speak English or recognize mainstream European cultural icons. I have written a pamphlet explaining the primary elements of my work. Would you like a copy?"

"I would love a copy," I said. "But for the moment, Agent Durand and I are primarily interested in why those who are excluded for intellectual deficiency are sent back."

"We believe that part of the purpose of immigration control is to build the moral and economic fiber of America," Knox said genially. "Note that I said both moral *and* economic. Both are a form of strength. The purpose of our various instruments is the sorting out of those potential immigrants who might, because of their mental makeup, find it impossible to succeed in America. Indeed, who might become a burden to the state, or—and this is important—produce offspring that will require care in prisons, asylums, or other institutions."

"Those who pass stand a good chance of making America stronger, those who fail . . ."

"Those who fail, the technical word for them is *imbecile*, will likely weaken the state. We pull individuals out of line in the main hall who appear dull, stupid, apathetic—you know the type—and test them for feeblemindedness. And if they repeatedly fail the tests I've developed, we can assume they are very likely to breed a next generation who will require the care of the state. Thus, weakening both our moral and economic well-being."

Knox handed me a copy of his pamphlet on the way out of the office, and I promised to read it.

When Jack and I were back on the breezeway, he grinned at me. "So how'd you make out with Knox's intelligence test?" he asked.

"Failed miserably."

"Imbecile," he said affably. "Knox would ship your ass back to North Carolina for feeblemindedness."

"Do you think he knows what Taylor and her coven are up to?"

"Nah. He's clueless. Maybe intentionally clueless, but clueless."

An hour later, when we arrived in the anteroom to Augustus Sherman's office, we could hear him in animated conversation with someone through the barely open door. Jack glanced at me and mouthed the name "Armstrong."

"Who?"

"The lawyer." And as soon as he said it, I could hear the gruff tone in the voice that was carrying on with Sherman. Bulldog gruff, but at least with Sherman, animated, enthusiastic even.

I knocked, and we went in. It was immediately obvious what had inspired the bulldog's enthusiasm. Sherman had a collection of his photographs spread out on the desk, and they were of subjects I'd never seen before—from the unusual to the deformed.

A Russian giant over eight feet tall dwarfing the two inspectors he stood between. A tiny Burmese dwarf dressed in an impeccable suit. A man with arms and legs growing out of his abdomen. A dwarfish "Hindoo" man with two microcephalics, apparently from India.

Sherman was beaming at the bulldog, Armstrong, and they were chuckling at the various manifestations of the human form that had arrived on Ellis Island seeking some sort of better life.

"What in hell . . ." The bulldog was pointing at the photos. "What in hell do they think they're going to do, find work in a circus? The Bowery Freak Show?"

Sherman shrugged and pointed with his monocle at a photo of three men from the SS Adriatic dated April 14, 1911. All with dark-brown skin. One was "Perumall Sammy," the unfortunate man with the congenital deformity of the stomach, the miniature arm and legs growing out of his abdomen hidden beneath his garments in this photo. Another was "Subramaino Pillay," the dwarf from another photo, who was wearing a coat that reached almost to his feet and a traditional turban.

"They are surely to God freaks," Armstrong declared and fell again into raucous laughter. "Who would let them into the country?"

"The giant and the tiny Burmese man, who would have come to just above the giant's knees, by the way, they were both allowed in as entertainers, oddities that would attract a crowd. The others? Well, I don't recall what happened to them. The color of their skin didn't help their cause, of course."

"I should say not," Armstrong chortled. "Imagine if . . . if any of these characters should have fathered children of their own. What in God's name would they have been like?"

"Well . . ." Sherman leaned over the desk. "It's funny you should say that. Here is a photo that all of you gentlemen will find interesting." He handed round a print, apparently of a man in a dark suit, with a dark slouch hat pulled down over his face. Spectacles almost completely hidden under the brim of the hat. The faintest mustache over a mouth drawn tightly horizontal. "What do you make of that?"

"What's so freakish about that?" Armstrong the Bulldog asked. "An elderly man trying to grow a mustache."

"It's not a man," Sherman replied. "It's a woman named Mary Johnson, who attempted to enter the country from Canada in 1908. She'd already lived in the US for thirty years and was returning from a trip abroad. The medical examination revealed that she was no man at all."

"My God," muttered Armstrong.

"But a woman who had assumed a man's identity and dressed as a man for over fifteen years."

"What a perversion on . . . on human nature," Armstrong again.

Sherman nodded. "Eventually she was allowed back into the country because she was a citizen and had already lived here for so long. She claimed that as a woman, she couldn't make a living, but as a man—"

"Make a living!" Armstrong exclaimed. "She could make a living the way women have made a living for thousands of years."

"That's enough," Jack Durand said. "From of both of you." He shook his head in disgust. "You"—he nodded to Sherman—"put away your damn photographs. They have no purchase here. And you . . ." He nodded to Armstrong. "Make yourself scarce. Go telegraph your friend Hoover and tell him that if you don't come back, it's because I threw you into the harbor."

"There's no need to become irate—" Sherman began.

Before Jack cut him off. "I'm beyond irate, Mr. Sherman. Irate is a civilized word. I'm disgusted with you and your rogue's gallery. These people deserve our pity, not your goddamn barroom laughter. It's only because there's a witness in the room that I don't slap that silly monocle right off your face."

"But this, sir, is art."

"Art ain't politics, you silly old fool. Put this stuff away and compose yourself. Robbins and I need to know what you knew and when about the deaths on Island 3, and you'll be lucky not to be indicted!"

I shut the door behind Armstrong, who was still chuckling to himself when he went out. Sherman was hastily cramming the photographs on his desk into a brown paper folder prominently labeled "Oddities," his hands shaking and his monocle dangling from its ribbon.

Once the prints were back in a bottom desk drawer, Sherman collapsed into his chair, which creaked under the sudden weight. I walked around and stood behind him while Jack confronted him from across the desk. He went straight to the point. "Tell us about Blanche Taylor," he said.

"What do you—"

"When did she arrive here? Was she always chief of nursing? Who is she allied with in the administration? What dealings have you had with her? Everything you can think of. . . ."

From where I stood, I could see that he had two folders on his desk, legitimate personnel folders, not packages of photographs. The top one was labeled "Knox, Howard, MD." The second, when he pulled it on top, was labeled "Taylor, Blanche, RN." He opened it and glanced down at the summary sheet.

"Blanche Elizabeth Taylor came here in 1910," he began, his voice shaking at first and then slowly regaining its sonorous formality. "She came first as assistant chief of nursing in the main hospital on Island 2 and then, in 1912, became chief of nursing in the isolation hospital on Island 3."

"Where did she come from?" Jack's voice still had an edge, and a sharp one from a man who mostly spoke so softly.

Sherman looked down again. "From Bellevue Hospital in the city."

"What is her reputation on the island?"

Here Sherman paused, considering.

"You can speak candidly, Mr. Sherman. At this point, it would be in your best interest."

"Her reputation is as some sort of holy martyr, almost like an angel of the isolation wards. In the beginning of her time there, before the war, she was constantly in the wards themselves, assisting with the other nurses in caring for patients. More recently, however, I believe she has become more of an . . ."

"Administrator?" I offered, still standing behind him.

"Yes, exactly. She still attends meetings here from time to time and is meek and quiet except that she wants to begin and end with prayer and, depending on who is running the meeting, sometimes does so."

"What did she do during the war?" Jack asked.

Sherman referred to his folder again. "She was actually one of the very few nursing staff who stayed throughout. Since we were essentially shut down as an immigration station and taken over by the army and navy as a military hospital for over a year, not many of the Public Health nurses were kept on."

"But she was?"

"Yes, because it was thought that she had some expertise in mental health and could deal with those returning soldiers and sailors who suffered from . . . shell shock. Are you familiar with . . . ?"

"I know what shell shock is." Jack's voice had settled back into its accustomed, more neutral tone, and now he took things smoothly into a new direction. "What role did she play in the deportations after the war?"

"Well, now that's interesting. When Inspector Hoover and his team came to the island last year, most of us—myself included—were outraged. It was as if they were turning the island into a prison. Using us for the exact opposite purpose from what was intended. But Miss Taylor was . . . I'm not quite sure how to say this . . . Miss Taylor was elevated somehow."

"Elevated in terms of her position? Promoted?"

"No, not that. She was exhilarated. Enthralled. It was as if she'd suddenly found her true purpose. While the rest of us were shoved to the sidelines, so to speak, she was suddenly at the very center of things, working very closely with Mr. Hoover in overseeing the incarceration of the men and woman, mostly men, who were to be deported."

"Including Emma Goldman."

"Including Mrs. Goldman, yes."

"How did she react when the deportations were shut down?"

"Badly, I'm afraid. She complained bitterly to the former commissioner, and I assumed she would leave once the army was gone and Immigration officials returned. Because of her loss of administrative status if nothing else."

"But she didn't leave."

"No, she ingratiated herself with Dr. Knox, and she appears to have regained something of her former influence."

"Last question, Mr. Sherman, and we'll let you get back to . . . whatever you do. Does Blanche Taylor's influence extend beyond Island 3? Into the main hospital, for example, or into the medical examinations here?"

Sherman popped the monocle out of his eye and shook his head, firmly. "No, sir. From what I understand, the doctors and nurses on Island 2 have no time for her. And our protocols here in the Great Hall are firmly established and run without any outside interference from Island 3."

Jack stood up, and following his lead, I stepped around the desk. "Thank you, Mr. Sherman," Jack offered. "You've told us a great deal."

Jack didn't speak when we left Sherman's office, and I left him to his private thoughts as we wound our way back down to the first floor of the Great Hall and out a side door to the corridor that would take us back to Island 3.

Once we were out of earshot from anyone who might understand what we were saying, he asked me quietly what I thought.

"I think that if what he says is accurate, Blanche Taylor discovered her purpose in life during the war," I replied.

He nodded. "Loved the deportations, even though they were essentially illegal. And now she's running her own private brand of deportations undercover, except that she's sending those she doesn't favor to an oven rather than back to some other country."

"In her mind," I said grimly, "she's sending them to hell."

CHAPTER FORTY-EIGHT

Lucy Paul was sitting up in a chair beside the window of her room when I went to see her that evening, the evening before the inquiry. It was the first time I had seen her sitting up since her attack.

The orderly who'd been guarding her door had been dismissed, and since I was no longer being followed around by my friend Adam, we were alone. It felt strange to be alone again with Lucy. Though it had been only a few days since I'd pulled her out of the autoclave, so much had happened that it felt like weeks had flown.

She was staring out the window at the brick wall of another wing of the hospital. I was standing silently just inside the door, watching her, wondering what she was feeling, not wanting to startle her.

"I know you're there," she said suddenly. "Watching me the way you do." She turned her head and smiled. There was still a bandage above one ear, but her head was no longer wrapped in gauze and her face was less swollen. She was herself.

Then the redhead, Maureen, was in the room, bustling past me and bending over Lucy to stare into her face. "How are they?" Lucy asked her, and I realized Maureen was examining her eyes.

"Better. The pupils almost match and will by tomorrow. . . . Are you still sure you want to go for a walk?"

Lucy nodded slowly, and I got the sense that sudden movement still threw her.

"Then we'll let Stephen here take you down to the porch. That far and no farther."

Maureen helped her to her feet and made her pull a thick white robe on over her gown and then tied it at the waist.

"Miss Paul is ready for your date," she said to me with a grin. "And it's a good thing you got here when you did, or she likely would have come looking for you." And then whispered to me in passing, "Go slow. She's still not steady on her feet."

The wide porch at the end of the ward was an open space where patients could breathe fresh, salt air during the day, one of the hospital's thoroughly modern innovations. As it was supper time in the ward, it was completely empty except for Lucy and me. I pulled two chairs up to the railing facing away from Island 3 and the lagoon and toward the Great Hall and the open harbor beyond.

"How are you truly?" I asked her after we sat down.

She rolled her head slowly from side to side and smiled at me. "Close. Close but not quite right. My head still feels empty at times. Other times, full of . . . I don't know . . . full of pressure. Sick to my stomach some, but not bad."

"Do you remember?" Even as I said it, I realized there were things I hoped she didn't recall. Would never recall.

"Some," she said. "I remember that I screamed your name when they broke into the room, and that they laughed at me. Called me a bitch before they took me. I remember they hit me with a billy club. I covered my face with my hands, but they hit me again. I dreamed about it last night. The first time I've had anything like a normal dream since that night."

"What did you dream?"

"That I was locked in the autoclave again, scratching to get out, and you were coming to save me from far, far away. You knew I needed you and you were running, trying as hard as you could to get to me, but you . . . it was as if you were stuck in a thick fog, fighting to push your way through, and it was getting harder and harder for me to breathe."

"What happened?"

"I woke up." She reached over and took my hand. "So you must have broken through. Saved me again . . . last night in the middle of the night."

"I'm glad your mind is coming back, but we need to find you something else to dream about."

"Look," she said, pointing with her other hand. "Just at the edge of the building." There was the ghost of the moon, half full, coming from the east, even though the sky behind the Great Hall to the west was still brimful of light. "I'd like to dream about the moon."

When she said it, her voice so full and plaintive, I felt the sudden twinge of deep memory, because I had dreamed about the moon. Sometime in the past few nights, dreamed it and forgotten it till that moment.

"I have a dream to give you," I said and edged my chair closer to hers. She wrapped my left hand in both of hers, nestling it into her lap.

"Tell it," she said. "Give it to me."

"My favorite moon of all," I said, "has always been the October full moon. In the mountains back home. The Cherokee call it the Hunter's Moon."

"Because . . . ?"

"Because October is the time for hunting and preserving meat for the winter. Up home, that mostly means deer hunting and then either cooking the venison or drying it for winter months. Which is what the Cherokee do, smoke strips of meat over fires to preserve it."

"Were you a deer hunter, Stephen?"

"I was and intend to be again." The words were out of my mouth before I really thought about them, but they seemed true enough. "I find that I don't care for hunting people, at least not to kill them. . . . I'd rather hunt deer." I smiled at her.

"Did you really dream about the moon?"

"Yes, one of these last few nights. And I had forgotten till you asked for a dream and then pointed at that shadow just peeping around the side of the building. Forgotten the dream entirely until you mentioned it."

"Is a dream real if we forget it when we wake?"

"Oh yes. All dreams are real, whether we recall them or not. Just like all stories are real, whether we remember the telling. They just exist below the horizon, waiting to rise again when we need them."

"Tell me about the moon then." She nestled back into her chair and slipped my hand beneath her robe, so that it lay open on her leg, with only the thin, slippery fabric of the gown between my fingers and the warmth of her.

"I was walking across the river bridge in Hot Springs, just as the sun was setting. I stopped halfway over and paused to look around. See the river and the mountains rising above. Late October . . . it must have been October, because the trees were on fire with color. Oranges, reds, yellows . . . the mountains were painted all of those and more. That's how I knew it was fall. And while I stood there, looking out at my world, the moon appeared. Rose up out of the east, I guess, though in the dream it seemed suddenly to appear as if a lamp lit. Full and yellow and so close that it seemed I could touch it if I just reached out my hand."

"And it was full?"

"Yes, the full moon, and in the underneath of my mind, I knew it had to be the Hunter's Moon, and I was home again, after being a long time away. All my life I have been a man in search of a home, all my stories about the road back. Ever since I ran away as a boy, hoping and searching for that one place where I might rest."

"Was it comforting to be there?"

"It was everything to be there. Everything in this world. And the river, the mountains rising and surging all around, the trees. Bathed in moonlight. I felt as though I could breathe more deeply than I could anywhere else. I felt completely a part of it all."

"You were home, is what I think."

"I know. In the dream, I was home."

"I think you belong there."

"I know I do." I could sense the dampness of tears on my face. "But it's far away from here. Hard to get back to. . . ."

"Maybe not," she offered. "There are roads, you know. There are trains that go from here to there. And I'm going to dream it for you tonight . . . just like you described it."

After a bit, she pulled up her gown underneath her robe, so that my hand rested against her thigh. Just there . . . on her bare, warm skin. And then she shifted to lean over to me, so that her poor, battered head rested against my shoulder.

CHAPTER FORTY-NINE

The formal inquiry to decide if I was culpable in the deaths of James "Jimmy" Cain and Ross Donald took place on that Tuesday morning in the office of Commissioner Wallis. On one side of the desk sat Wallis, whose gout must have been bothering him that morning because he stood when we all came in but didn't move from behind his desk to greet us. With him sat Augustus Sherman, representing the island bureaucracy. Between them sat a thin, spare man from the city coroner's office. According to Jack, who understood these things, they each had something of a vote, but the final outcome was essentially up to the coroner.

I sat alone facing them, with Jack to my right seated against the wall and Armstrong to my left, also against the wall. Anyone could ask questions, but in theory, at least, the coroner would prosecute me and the bulldog Armstrong would defend me as need be. A clear case of who needs enemies when you have a bulldog for a friend.

Before we went in to take our places, I asked Jack what the possible outcomes of all this rigamarole might be. He shrugged and said that the coroner might decide that I was doing my duty as an agent of the government, and I'd walk out exonerated; on the other hand, it might go badly for some reason, and I'd be held over for a real trial in the city.

Was he worried?

He shook his head. "The only person in the room I worry about is the guy who's supposed to defend you," he muttered.

Which, as it turns out, was exactly what he should have been worried about. It took me perhaps an hour to make my initial statement, starting with a brief summary of the disappearance of Ciara McManaway and my arrival on the island. As Jack had suggested, I told the first parts in sum, without trying to convince anyone in the room of Blanche Taylor's involvement or the inner workings of her Bible study group. I also left out the more intimate parts of my relationship with Lucy Paul. We had become partners in the law enforcement trade, that was all, sharing information and insight as we pursued the same end.

I brought us up to the night of the killings, watching while both the coroner's deputy and Armstrong took notes, wondering if Armstrong's were for his shadowy boss back at the BOI. When I got to the night in question, the part of the story where I went back to the psychopathic ward and discovered that she'd been taken, Armstrong interrupted me for the first time.

"Why did you think she'd be there?" he growled at me.

"The second floor of Building E was our base of operations," I replied. "It's where we often met to discuss the progress of the case and plan our next moves."

"In the middle of the night?"

"Depending on her shift in the hospital, it was necessary to meet at all hours of the day and night. Especially since it had become obvious that the malefactors were taking people and disposing of them during the night."

"What people?"

"The immigrants who were being killed."

"Oh, them . . ." Armstrong said it with such scorn that it was obvious that he barely considered them at all. And he said it while watching the coroner for his reaction, looking for any sign of agreement.

And then on to the events in the laundry, where I'd surprised Cain and Donald in the process of loading Lucy's semiconscious body into the autoclave. Armstrong interjected again. "Were you armed?"

"Of course I was armed."

"With what?"

"A sawed-off shotgun."

"Did you assume that there might be violence?" This question from the coroner, the first time he'd spoken since we were introduced.

"Yes, because of what I'd witnessed on previous nights, in particular the attempt by these men to dispose of the Gypsy's body."

The coroner nodded, and I continued. Finished through to the shooting of Jimmy Cain and pulling Lucy's body out of the autoclave.

Armstrong: "Were there any other witnesses to the events you just described?"

Out of the corner of my eye, I could see Jack Durand shifting restlessly in his chair.

"No," I replied. "None that survived, at any rate."

Armstrong: "Because you killed them both."

I nodded.

Armstrong: "Let the record show that the witness acknowledged—"

Durand: "There is no record because this isn't a court proceeding. Get on with it."

Armstrong: "If I understood you correctly, you shot Donald when he threatened you with a thirty-eight caliber revolver that was taken from Miss Paul. Would you characterize that action as self-defense?"

Me: "Yes. He was aiming the pistol at me."

Armstrong: "And you shot Cain even though he was trying to plead for his life?"

I considered before answering: "He was trying to say something. I'm not sure what exactly."

Armstrong: "But you didn't give him time to explain himself, did you? You didn't give him the opportunity to even finish a sentence . . ."

Me: "No, I didn't, and I'll explain why." I could feel my face heating up just as it had the first time I'd debated this point with the bulldog.

Armstrong: "Wasn't it because you lost your temper? I submit that you were in a blood rage because of your relationship with Miss Paul and you killed a man when you could have taken him prisoner, so that he could be interviewed by the proper authorities."

Me: "That's one way of looking at it. Certainly, Miss Paul and I were friends as well as partners in the investigation. What you don't seem to grasp, mister, is that Cain had just cranked shut the door to the autoclave. It was locked, and as far as I knew at that moment, he could have set in motion the process by which she would have been boiled to death. I didn't have time to debate with Cain or take prisoners for later consideration. I had to act or see another human being killed in front of me."

Armstrong: "So you shot Mr. Cain just like you shot the sheriff of"—he referred to a separate sheet of notes from his pocket—"Madison County, North Carolina, three years ago. Also with a shotgun. Also claiming self-defense . . . as you are now claiming with Mr. Donald."

I glanced over at Jack. This wasn't something that either of us had expected.

Armstrong: "Not only that"—he was now ignoring me and speaking directly to the coroner—"Mr. Robbins previously shot and killed that same sheriff's brother some years before in front of dozens of witnesses, also with a shotgun. The man is his own judge and jury, a regular shotgun executioner."

Coroner: "You stand trial for these shootings, Mr. Robbins?"

Me: "Yes, sir."

Coroner: "Were you acquitted?"

Me: "Yes. In the first instance, the man I shot was threatening a woman who was in my employ with a corn knife. In the second case, the sheriff had just given me this"—I pointed to my face—"and was drawing down on me with his pistol."

Coroner: "Violent part of the world you come from, Mr. Robbins."

Me: "Yes, sir. On occasion, it is."

At this point, Jack Durand stood up and nodded to the three men on the other side of the desk. "I'd like to suggest we take a break," he said. He looked at his watch. "We've been at this for almost two hours, and our star witness might like to catch his breath."

The coroner nodded. Wallis and Sherman, both of whom had remained silent throughout, agreed, and we all stood up. Jack went out into the hall and whispered something to Fussell, who left immediately, intent on some mission.

In the hallway between sessions, Sherman approached me, though tentatively. "I thought that man, Armstrong, was supposed to defend you," he whispered.

I nodded. "So did I in the beginning, but apparently he's a henchman of some guy named Ed Hoover, who oversaw your deportations."

Sherman adjusted the monocle in his eye to regard me more closely. "God help you if he's involved," he muttered.

When we reconvened thirty minutes later, taking the same positions in the room, Jack Durand himself placed a second chair beside mine and, with Wallis's permission, took the commissioner's overcoat from the rack, folded it carefully, and placed it on the seat. When I glanced questioningly at him, he said only that he thought we needed a second witness to help us get at the truth.

And then, just as Wallis himself sat down, there was some commotion behind me, and Adam Fussell brought Lucy into the room. All of those present—all men—leaped to their feet, even Armstrong.

She was still wearing her hospital gown and slippers, as well as the thick robe that I'd seen her in the night before. She was pale beneath the natural buff of her skin, drained from the exertion of climbing all those stairs, even with Fussell's help. The vestiges of her black eye stood out all the more against her wan face, and someone—Maureen perhaps—had rewrapped her head in gauze.

Holding on to Fussell's arm for support, she half bowed, half curtsied to Wallis and the coroner. I held her chair while Fussell lowered her gently down on the well-padded coat that served as a cushion.

She didn't make eye contact with me in the beginning but focused her attention on the three men on the other side of the desk. The coroner asked Jack to introduce her.

Durand: "This is Miss Lucy Paul, on special assignment from the United States Public Health Service and the American Medical Association. She has been working in the isolation wards on Ellis Island for almost seven months, simultaneously fulfilling her duties as a ward nurse and investigating why the number of deaths and disappearances on Island 3 has remained so high since the Public Health Service returned to the island hospitals after the war. She is a decorated veteran of the US Army Medical Corps."

Coroner: "I'm just curious, Mr. Durand. Why did you invite her to attend the inquiry? We originally agreed that the only witness we would need is Mr. Robbins."

Durand: "Earlier in the proceedings, Mr. Armstrong pointed out that since there were no other witnesses to the events that took place on the night that Cain and Donald died, you wouldn't be able to corroborate Robbins's story. He seemed to think that was a problem. So I sent Special Agent Fussell to inquire whether Miss Paul was up to answering your questions, and she got up from her hospital bed to come over here."

Coroner: "Miss Paul, we're very grateful for your help, and I promise this will be brief."

Lucy gave a short, cogent explanation of events leading up to the night she was taken. I confess that as she talked, I began to glow on the inside, as her account matched mine so closely that you would have thought we'd rehearsed it, even though all either of us did that day was tell the truth. Even Armstrong was puzzled how to attack her. At one point, he tried again to suggest some impropriety on our part.

Armstrong: "Miss Paul, isn't it true that you and Robbins here became more than just professional acquaintances, that you—"

Paul: "We became friends."

Armstrong: "But didn't you spend . . . with him several times in . . ."

Paul: "The night? Are you asking me if I spent the night with the man?" The tone of her voice was rising in that way I knew only too well. "The answer is not just yes, you little man. The answer is *yes, of course.* We spent the night several times in the morgue, examining the bodies of the poor, unfortunate victims. We spent the night in the baggage storeroom identifying and examining the luggage of those who had died, searching for clues to their identity. We spent the night following the members of Nurse Taylor's little confederation. We spent the night working. What was it exactly you were trying to imply, Mr. Armstrong?"

Armstrong: "I'm sure I meant no disrespect. I merely—"

Paul: "You meant nothing but disrespect. Both to me and to this man"—she reached over and gripped my arm briefly, the only time she touched me during the proceeding—"who saved my life on your *night in question.* If he hadn't trailed my kidnappers to the laundry and stopped them when he did, you'd be holding this inquiry into my death, not theirs, and you"—she nodded to Armstrong—"would be blaming him for that rather than this."

At this point, she bent forward and gasped, overcome briefly by her own ferocity, and then leaned slowly back in her chair. Wallis said to Jack, "Don't you think that's enough?"

Jack nodded and said, "Do you have any further questions for Miss Paul, Armstrong?" He phrased it as a question, but his tone made it clear that Armstrong was done.

He got the message. He only shook his head.

Adam Fussell came forward again—nimbly and quietly for such a big man—to help Lucy to her feet and walk with her out of the room. Again, she didn't look at me, gave no sign of any sort of connection.

There was a long pause, and then, before anyone else chose to pick up the thread of the discussion, the coroner's deputy spoke.

Coroner: "Anyone else have anything to say with regard to Mr. Robbins's culpability in these deaths?"

Armstrong: "I think he should be bound over for trial in the deliberate murder of James Cain. I believe I've made that clear."

Coroner: "Is that the considered opinion of the BOI, Mr. Durand?"

Durand: "Of course not. Armstrong is just arguing a case to see how far he can push it. This man acted well within his duty and should be released to get on with the job at hand."

Coroner: "Mr. Wallis, Mr. Sherman, anything to add?"

They both shook their heads.

Coroner: "I've heard enough then. Especially from you, Armstrong. What you may not know is that both my parents immigrated through this building forty-five years ago, both from County Clare when the Irish were widely considered to be the scum of the earth. And I sit here today, somehow having made something of myself.

"I concur with Mr. Durand. Stephen Robbins, you are hereby acquitted of any wrongdoing in the deaths of Ross Donald and James Cain. Our formal proceedings are adjourned.

"But before we go, I'd like to hear what you, Mr. Robbins, might have to say *off* the record. You've taken your lumps today, all but had your character assassinated here in this room. Even so, I'd like to know what you think about this place now that you've seen it from the inside out." He waved one arm as if to indicate all of Ellis Island, looming around us. "What do you make of America's great doorway?"

He caught me completely by surprise, so he got my unguarded answer. Having Lucy so unexpectedly there, and in such close physical proximity, had raised up a tumult inside me and loosened my tongue.

"There is something inside all of us that loves to hate" is how I began.

CHAPTER FIFTY

None of you except Mr. Durand knows this, but during the war, I was the inspector general of the German internment camp at Hot Springs, North Carolina. A hell of a long way from here and not just in miles. Even so, the internment camp during the war years reminds me of Ellis Island now. A huge anthill of a place with thousands of aliens living out their day-to-day lives in one of the most isolated places in the eastern United States. German civilians, mostly the crews of merchant marine and passenger ships, cooped up inside the fences we'd built around our hotel grounds.

"The mountain people were fascinated with the internees, called them the *Germanies* . . . as in *what them Germanies like who live inside that fence?* And the German officers and sailors were just as fascinated with the local people. You see, we employed dozens upon dozens of Madison County men and women as camp guards, cooks, general handymen . . . what you would call orderlies. There were very few regular army soldiers, just average people trying to make a living and survive the winter.

"What was fascinating about the whole place was that after a few seasons had come and gone—summer, fall, winter—almost everybody involved had gotten to know and like each other. Learned to speak to each other in a sort of German English accompanied by a few gestures and a lot of laughing and pointing. Even with the war raging in Europe and the bodies of American boys killed in the trenches starting to show up on the railroad platform, there wasn't much hatred in our little town. It was almost like we were an island of peace in an ocean of bloodlust."

Armstrong interrupted me. "There was obviously some violence. You shot your own sheriff."

"Well, someone shot him. And right after he almost tore my face off with his pistol barrel. But that fight was between two or three Americans, and for my part, I was protecting a German sailor when it happened. My point is that we human beings seem to need hatred. Not as Germans or Africans or Asians, not as Christians or Jews or Muslims, but as just plain people. There is something in us that craves hatred, and one race, one type—as Sherman likes to call it—is no more subject to it than another. People with pale skin want to hate people with dark skin and vice versa. People with blue eyes want to hate people with brown eyes.

"And yet . . . what the internment camp showed me is that given time and enough food to eat, we're also capable of better. I know it sounds funny coming from me. Armstrong over there thinks I'm nothing but a hired killer. But I once told a *New York Times* reporter that what the world needed was just kindness, simple human kindness. He laughed at me, of course, and called me a damn fool. Said I had no business running an internment camp, which could well be. But as for the larger issue, maybe I was right about the human species. Maybe there'd be less killing if there was more kindness."

I paused, having gotten lost inside my memories. The coroner had asked me about Ellis Island, not the internment camp. "What I think, sir, in response to your question, is that Ellis Island seems balanced on a knife's edge. This comes in part, Sherman, from something you said to me the first time we ever met. Something that has stuck in my mind. You were talking about life here during the war and the deportations that were rammed through here after. You said that this beautiful place was intended to infuse America with the new blood that keeps it vital, not as some giant sewage station to flush those we hate out of our house. And you said it with passion, with conviction."

Sherman was nodding, remembering.

"This island is like my internment camp because both are human institutions that became, in time, like the world in miniature." I formed a ball with my two hands to suggest by gesture a small version of the globe. "For most of the time my Germans were inside the Hot Springs camp, we were able to make that little, isolated world a friendly place despite the fact that our two nations were at war and, on the surface at least, the Germans were as different from our mountain people as two groups could possibly be. The same race hatreds are at work here, whether some of us want to admit it or not. So, Mr. Coroner, the question is . . . which will it be? Will Ellis be an island of hate or an island of kindness?"

"Which is it now?" he asked quietly. "Now that you've looked at it from the inside for a month, which is it?"

"Both," I said. "Balanced on that thin knife's edge, while we try to make up our mind who we are going to be."

There was a long pause, broken by a scornful guffaw from Armstrong. "That reporter was right!" He jabbed his finger at me. "You *are* a fool. If Ellis Island is a knife blade, then it ought to be used to cut *them* to pieces, not us."

I didn't even bother to look at Armstrong, but Wallis did. Wallis stared at him for a long moment and then said something interesting, something that proved he'd been listening. "I've run prisons and I've run halfway houses," the commissioner said. "And I don't intend this place to become any kind of prison. If you worked for me, Mr. Armstrong, you'd be unemployed by morning."

The meeting broke up shortly after. I shook the hand of each man present except Armstrong, who didn't offer. Jack Durand leaned close when we grasped hands. "You going to visit your nurse?" he murmured. When I nodded, he followed with, "Wait for me in the hall for a few minutes. Compare notes before you go."

While waiting, I wandered over to the railing above the Great Hall two floors below. The hall was once again full, flooded by boatloads of that day's immigrants, already shepherded into lines before the examiner's desks. At the far end of the hall, I could see Ludmila Kuchar, dressed again in her peasant garb from Eastern Europe, talking earnestly with several mothers in the women and children's line. The doctors were at work doing their quick once-overs, and the chalk was being applied to the lapels of dozens of men and women.

Then Jack was beside me, watching the crowds below. "How many do you think will get in?" he asked.

"Most of them, according to Sherman. Say, sixty percent. Maybe twenty percent get sent straight back and another twenty to the hospitals for one reason or another."

He glanced at his watch. "It's almost noon. I need to telegram Washington." He paused to consider. "Let's play it this way. You go visit Miss Paul, and when you do, thank her for me. I'll let my boss know where we stand and talk to Wallis. Meet me back at the psych ward around three."

"What about Armstrong?"

"That SOB will be on the next ferry. We're done with him."

"When are you leaving, you and Fussell?"

"By tonight." He paused again, still staring down at the crowd of eager, fearful humanity, straining forward to meet a future they couldn't imagine.

"What do you think causes it?" he asked quietly. "The hatred you were talking about."

"Has to be fear," I said. "You can't love something you fear. Or someone you fear."

"And the fear breeds hatred." He didn't state it as a question.

But I replied anyway. "The fear justifies the hatred, doesn't it? Renders it righteous somehow."

He nodded.

"I know what you're thinking," I said after a moment. "Nurse Taylor."

"Yeah." He shrugged his shoulders. "If we didn't have that damn saint on Island 3 to deal with, I'd send you on home."

CHAPTER FIFTY-ONE

When I got to Lucy's hospital room that afternoon, an older nurse I hadn't seen before stopped me just before I went in. "Quietly now, she's resting," she whispered, her hand on my arm. "They had her over to the Great Hall testifying about her attack, and she's worn to a frazzle."

I nodded and placed a finger over my lips to show that I understood.

The shades were pulled, and Lucy was curled under a sheet with her eyes closed in the semidark room. I lifted a chair to her bedside and sat down as quietly as I could. Someone, perhaps Lucy herself, had unwrapped the gauze from her head, and even in the darkened room, I could tell that she had her natural color back. Her hair, where it hadn't been shorn on one side for the bandage, was wild and dark on the pillow.

Her breath ran deep and slow, and I imagined her fully asleep, dreaming perhaps. After a moment, though, she pushed one arm out from under the sheet and reached out to me. She didn't open her eyes but knew someone was close by. I imagined she knew it was me.

I took her hand, those strong, blunt fingers, and held it loosely as her arm relaxed again, down against the bed. I could feel myself easing a bit then too, exhaling after the long trial of the day. Letting my shoulders sag, rolling my head to ease the tension in my neck.

"Stephen?" she said quietly. Not asking if it was me; she seemed to know it was. Rather saying my name as if a question was to follow.

"Yes," I replied after a moment. "I'm here." I expected her to ask if I'd been declared innocent, turned loose from the inquiry, but she didn't.

After a pause long enough that I wondered if she'd fallen more deeply asleep, she spoke again quietly. "Did Anna ever have children? . . . Your child I mean?"

"No." I again had the sense that I was speaking to her in her sleep, as if I were a part of some dream she was having. "She had a miscarriage," I murmured, intending to tell the whole truth of it. "A late miscarriage."

"Were you there?"

I knew what she meant. "No, I was still in North Carolina, and I never knew till later."

She nodded ever so slightly, her head moving on the pillow. And then, a moment later, squeezed my hand. "I thought there was something," she muttered.

There was another lapse of time in which, without moving, she seemed to rise within herself, resurface from a deeper place where she had lain resting. I can't say how I knew she was waking, yet I was sure she was coming closer. Then she rolled onto her back and stretched her legs out beneath the sheet. Arched her back and yawned, the wide, lazy yawn of one returning . . . but slowly, like a dog uncurling from a nap.

Her arms were limp beside her on the sheet as she lay waking. She wriggled the fingers of both hands, almost as if they were coming alive themselves, those fingers, and then ran both hands slowly up over her stomach to cup her own breasts sensuously through her gown. "That is *you* sitting there, isn't it?" Her eyes were still closed, but she spoke in a more normal tone of voice.

"It is," I said with a smile.

"Good . . ." Her wonderful black eyes blinked open and steadied against the half-light. She turned her head to look at me. "I may be coming back to life," she said easily, naturally.

"You damn well better."

We both smiled.

"I heard what you told me," she said.

I shrugged.

"No, I need to say this, and we can move on. . . . I hate it for her that she lost her child. No woman deserves that. But I'm also glad. For it would have tied you to her. . . . You'd be there, and neither of us would be here."

I nodded in agreement and smiled into the deep pools of her eyes. "It's best that we're here now, I agree, though it was a twisty damn road we had to take getting here."

More smiles. And some laughter.

When I left an hour later, I met the same nurse in the hallway who'd shushed me when I went in. "How is she?" I asked. "I mean, medically?" The woman smiled. "Still some nausea, and we're not sure why, but the headaches are gone," she replied. "They're going to release her in the morning, and if she wants, she can go back to work in a day or two."

I'm not sure how that pronouncement played into my late afternoon conversation with Jack Durand. He and I walked outside on the south side of the Island 3 buildings and found a spot just at the edge of the breakwater to smoke a cheroot. We were facing Liberty Island, where the statue loomed.

"You can't really see her face from here, can you?" Jack said as he puffed to get his Havana going.

"I've noticed that." I paused to pull the smoke out of my own cigar. "I've often wondered since I've been here just what sort of face she's showing the world. Come here to find your dreams, or stay the hell away; we don't want you."

He chuckled, again reminding me that over the past few days, he'd taken on a downright human attitude. At least in moments like this. "Listen, Stephen," he said after a moment. "If you were a regular agent, I'd pull you out of here. Take you with me back to Washington tonight and leave Fussell to deal with Taylor and her tribe. In fact, Bureau protocol requires it."

"But you don't want to do that." I'm not sure if what I said was a question or a statement.

"Well hell, I'm not even sure what *want* has to do with it. Part of me is still sorry I let you wander into this mess in the first place. I thought it was just a case of one missing Irish woman, remember, and you did look bored as hell working in that hotel."

"The Algonquin."

"Right, the Algonquin. But at least if you were still there, you wouldn't be dealing with the serial killing cult of some modern-day Christian saint."

It struck us both at the same instant that the way he'd said it sounded exactly like the cover of *True Detective* magazine, adorned by a colorful drawing of a crazed nurse with insane eyes clutching a bloodstained knife. We both started laughing, all the strain of the past few days pouring out of us along with throats full of cigar smoke.

"Way I see it then," I said after both of us caught our breath, "I've got to stay here till we can figure out what to do with Taylor. What did Wallis say about her?"

"He's too new," Jack replied, suddenly grim again. "Said he just got here himself, and both Sherman and Knox warned him that Taylor was so well entrenched that if he fired her, he might lose half the nurses on Island 3. Said he wasn't well-enough established yet to make a move like that."

"Did he say he'd pray about it?"

"Hell yes. Pray for a solution. And at the same time, pray for you and Miss . . . Paul. Pray for me and the mayor and the governor."

"Lucy . . . Her first name's Lucy."

He nodded. "Lot on my mind," he confessed. "Couldn't remember."

"So we're back to where we started. I've got to stay till we can figure out what to do with her."

"I reached that conclusion too," he said after a moment. "Though I don't like it. You were never trained for this type of work."

"Maybe I'm just a goddamned natural," I said.

He grinned. "Maybe you are. . . . So here's how I see it, Mr. Natural. We let Taylor off house arrest. Let her and the giant woman . . ."

"Ethel Adams."

"Let her and Adams go on about their business. You and Miss Lucy . . ." He paused and glanced at me. "Is she part of this deal as well, or is she ready to go home?"

"She's in. I'm not sure she has what you'd call a home anyway."

"Well, you and Miss Lucy lie low. Stay out of their way as far as official channels go but watch every step they take unofficially. We'll leave the thirty-eight with you."

"Not the shotgun?" I was half ribbing him.

"Hell no. I'm tired of having to explain why you just shot somebody else with a damn shotgun."

"So you're telling me to fade into the background and spy on them."

"Sure. Whatever the hell that means in a place as confined as this. If we give Knox and Wallis something like proof, something that ties Taylor directly to a death, then Wallis will have to act."

"Prosecute her?"

"Just throw her off the island, if nothing else, or lock her up in a psych ward of her own. I can't imagine the jury that would convict the woman, once she started smiling and quoting the Bible at them."

"Then we need to give her enough rope to hang herself."

"You got it. But just be damn sure she doesn't wrap it around your neck."

CHAPTER FIFTY-TWO

I helped Adam Fussell pack up the last bit of their gear that evening while Jack met with Knox for the last time. As promised, he broke down the shotgun and stowed it in his own duffel bag. When I complained that he was taking my best friend, he shook his head. "You need to come into the modern times," he said. "Where's that chopper I brought over to you?"

When I looked blank, he laughed. "You know, the tommy gun, the Chicago typewriter, the annihilator. That big nurse take it away from you?"

I went down the hall to where Lucy and I had hidden the tommy gun and brought both it and the ammo drum back to Adam, who proceeded to give me a quick, down-and-dirty lesson. How to snap the drum in place, pull back the operating bolt on top, and turn it loose. "Hold on tight to both grips if and when you do fire it," he said. "Big, old forty-five caliber shells at six hundred rpm. Noise like you wouldn't believe."

"I still like my shotgun," I muttered.

"No, you don't. You're about to join the twentieth century. But I will tell you this—I don't know that I'd teach this one to Miss Paul. It's not a woman's gun. Too damn heavy."

"You don't know this woman. . . . But even so, she's too kind-hearted to use it."

"Too much the nurse," he agreed. "But you, on the other hand . . ."

I thanked him for rehanging the door to the room I had shared with Lucy. During his spare time, he'd taken down one of the doors that fit from down the hall and screwed into the doorframe of what we jokingly called my cell.

And then Jack was back. It was almost dark, well after the last ferry. When I asked him how they planned to get back to the mainland, he just laughed. "Help us carry this stuff down to the end of the island beside the staff residence and you'll see for yourself."

Full dark by the time we got down to the breakwater rocks, where a small motorboat waited in the chop. No running lights, and the two crewmen dressed all in black. While Fussell was tossing over their baggage, Jack paused for one last word. "I told Knox that you and the Paul dame were going to do a staffing review for a week or so, make an inventory for the Immigration and Public Health Services. He should collaborate where he can, as your report will help him get back up to full complement."

"He agree to that?"

Jack shrugged and grinned. "Acted as if he did. . . . You watch your back and get us that damn nurse." And then they were aboard and out into the harbor. Black faded into black, and then even the noise of the motor went away.

When I got back to my home sweet home on the second floor of Building E, I found a last present from Adam, another bottle of the bonded scotch, twin sister to the one he'd brought us a week before when he delivered the duffel full of armament.

The bottle confirmed where I wanted to go and what I wanted to do. First, though, just to let my instincts settle, I built myself a drink out of what few materials I had to work with. A dusty glass from the cupboard, a splash of tap water from the sink in the lavatory, and two fingers of scotch—stir and consider. It was hot enough to burn and easy enough to swallow.

It had been a hell of a long day, starting at nine that morning with the formal inquiry that had turned into something like a trial, at least for me. Whispers with Lucy followed by a cigar with Jack Durand, no longer the Nameless Man. And finally, toting and loading the cavalry that had come to our rescue into an all but invisible motor launch off the breakwater rocks in the dark.

I figured I smelled like all of that—trial, whispers, cigar, and salt spray—so I anointed my glass with a little more scotch and a thimble full of water before stripping down to wash. Which I did, with strong soap, cold water, and a rough cloth that I found in the bathing room. After a good scrub and the last sip from the glass, I scraped the stubble off my face, brushed my teeth, and put on clean clothes starting with undershorts and working my way out to a fresh shirt.

I found a paper sack for the bottle, slipped down the Building E stairs, and headed for the main hospital on Island 2. I didn't know if Lucy Paul would be asleep or awake. I didn't care.

Almost midnight.

I tried to ease past the nurses' station on Lucy's hall without being spotted, but Maureen the redhead was on duty, and she looked up from her magazine as I was just in front of her. She smiled at me, and the smile became a grin when she saw the shape of the bag I was carrying.

She cut her eyes down the hall to indicate Lucy's room, asking me if I was going there.

I nodded. I held out the bag toward her to ask if she wanted a nip of whatever was inside to help her through the long night. She shook her head ever so briefly, no. She was being good and not drinking on duty.

Then she winked and gestured with her head toward Lucy's room, telling me to go on. An entire conversation without a word being spoken.

I eased Lucy's door open and slipped through. Eased it even more quietly shut behind me, letting the tiny tongue of the latch click into the socket in the door frame. The blinds were pulled tight shut, but there was a nightlight in the far corner of the room, which gave off just enough illumination for me to make out Lucy's shape under the thin blanket on the bed.

I tiptoed forward, literally tiptoed with the bottle of scotch clutched in one hand, to see if she was awake. One step and then two—

"It took you long enough to get here," she said. Quietly but firmly. "Make a girl wait all damn night."

"Want a drink?" I asked, trying to match her wiseass tone through my smile.

"What is it?"

"Scotch. Good stuff."

"Maybe. . . . Later."

I took another step forward and set the bottle down under the edge of the bed where it wouldn't get knocked over in the dark.

"Why are you dressed?" she asked when I straightened.

"'Cause I usually don't skulk around hospital corridors naked."

"Too bad. Take it off."

"It?"

"All of it."

And while I was undressing, throwing my clothes carelessly onto the chair beside her bed, she asked me if I'd talked to Durand before he left.

"Yes, and we have an assignment."

"Hmmm? What is it?" If she'd been a cat, she would have been purring.

"Lie low. Spy on Taylor till she incriminates herself."

"Lie low?" She almost giggled.

I was straightening up from pushing my shorts down to the floor, hoping she couldn't see in the thin light just how aroused I was. Or maybe hoping she could see. . . .

"Undercover work," I said hoarsely.

She tossed the sheet and thin blanket down on my side of her bed. "Then get in and get to work," she said. "If you're up to it."

She must have known I was coming; she'd already taken off her gown.

CHAPTER FIFTY-THREE

M aureen—it must have been Maureen—woke us by tapping on the door the next morning. Early . . . when we were both still tousled in sleep and in each other. I dressed as quickly as I could find my clothes, which was complicated by Lucy tugging on my hand or my arm to delay me, embarrass me.

I even remembered the bottle under the bed—not to kick it over and to take it with me.

A kiss, and then a little more of a kiss, before I pulled away. "I'll see you later," she whispered. "At the house." And we both knew she meant the psych ward.

When she arrived later that morning at Building E, we spent a few hours comparing notes, figuratively speaking. What Fussell had told her versus what Jack had told me. The scuttlebutt she'd heard from the nurses and orderlies in the main hospital laid alongside what I'd seen and heard while she was recovering. The fabric of reality after the night of her attack—sewn up into something whole.

As we did the back-and-forth, weaving various threads of thought and sight and sound, two things emerged that were more question than answer, more doubt than certainty. One was the role of Scottie Phillips inside the workings of Blanche Taylor's dark drama. When I told Lucy what the Phillips woman had said about purgatory, she looked confused. I explained Jack's theory that in the Catholic tradition, purgatory meant the burning away of impurities, the purging of sin from an individual soul so that it could float up to heaven.

"So the damn autoclave was some kind of purgatory?" Lucy asked incredulously.

"In the Phillips woman's mind. We couldn't tell whether Taylor had intentionally planted that thought or whether she'd dreamed it up on her own to justify boiling people to death."

"Crazy little simpering bitch," Lucy said in an undertone. "What was her role then? To go around saying her rosary and . . . wait, was she ever part of the crew that actually took victims from the wards and stuffed them in the oven?"

"We don't know. We never got that far with her, but it was obvious she knew what was happening."

"Makes sense that they would need her help to get some of the victims out of the units where they were being treated. Or if not her, some other nurse that people recognized. You can't just go waltzing into any wing of a hospital, wave at the nurses and orderlies on duty and roll out one of the patients. They had to have a system of some sort."

"There's more. Jack suggested that from the way she reacted when we questioned her, that she herself was torn up by guilt . . . and that maybe . . ."

"Maybe what? That Taylor was using her to attract the male orderlies they needed? That she was screwing them?"

I shook my head in wonder. "That's exactly what he thought. Why am I the last to catch on to—"

"Because, Stephen dear, there are ways in which you are still the innocent country boy from the hills. And because you were so busy at the prayer meeting showing off your Bible skills that you didn't notice how the men in the room kept looking at little Miss Phillips."

"But I thought she was . . ."

"Sitting all prim and proper, with her white-clad knees pressed demurely together? Looking down at her hands folded in her lap? Don't be such a child, Stephen. Some men love that look."

"Didn't do anything for me."

That brought a grin. "No, you seem to require a more direct approach."

And then there was Adolph Becker. Before Jack and Adam Fussell left the island, I'd heard Fussell report to Jack that Ray Chandler had escaped to the mainland, quite probably on the first ferry out the morning after I'd shot Cain and Donald. But in the little time he'd had to ask around, he discovered that an orderly named Adolph Becker was still employed in the isolation wards. This was all news to Lucy. I described for her the thin, pale man whom I'd seen only in the dark on the night they'd tried to dump the Gypsy's body. Told her that, "I heard a third voice several times that didn't belong to Chandler, including in the laundry the night that . . ."

"They tried to boil me alive and you saved me."

"Yes, that night. There was a third person, sounded like a man, on the other side of the autoclave. But once I pulled you out, I forgot about him till later."

"You never told me what I was wearing when you pulled me out."

"Your skin."

"So they stripped me before stuffing me in there?"

I nodded.

"And touched me, no doubt."

"Maybe."

"Bastards. I'm glad you killed them."

"I'd do it again."

She smiled. "I know you would."

It was a strangely intimate moment. Staring at each other over a table in the room next to our bedroom cell in the psych ward. A sad moment and tough. Yet loving in a way. Wartime loving.

"So we have two places to start," I said eventually, after the tide of emotion between us ebbed a bit. "Two people to follow back to the source."

"I'll take Scottie Phillips," Lucy replied. "A cute little trick like her can fool a man—obviously—but she can't fool another woman."

"Then I'll take this Adolph Becker. See if he might be the man I saw."

"And what do we do with them?"

"Find out what role Taylor actually played. Did she order the killings? Did she take part? Can we find enough to get rid of her?"

"Send her home to Jesus?"

"Well, maybe. Or at least get her off the island."

"Aren't you forgetting somebody?"

"Who?"

"Fee-fi-fo-fum. Don't leave her out. She was at that prayer meeting too."

We agreed on a return to normalcy for the days or weeks we had left on Island 3. Lucy would seem to move back into the nurses' quarters once she'd been assigned a ward. "Just for appearances' sake," she said firmly. "I still don't feel entirely . . ."

"Safe?"

She nodded. "And I want to keep an eye on you."

We also agreed that we'd pretend to do the personnel review that Jack had given Knox as our cover. That way, we decided, we had a good reason to dig into who did what on Island 3. Who, besides Scottie Phillips and Adolph Becker, might lead us back to Ethel Adams and Blanche Taylor?

We started that afternoon together in Knox's office, or at least in the meeting room beside his office, where the personnel records were kept.

To Knox's credit, and even that of Melissa, his secretary, the isolation hospital records were carefully organized. If you wanted to chase down individual nurses or orderlies, their files were neatly arranged in alphabetical order.

I pulled *Cain, James* from the filing cabinet containing the letter C and scanned a brief history of the man and his employment.

PREVIOUS EMPLOYMENT: City Hospitals (Bellevue)

EDUCA: Army Medical Corp, Medic

RECCD BY: Blanche Taylor, Head of Nursing

REFERENCE(S):

HEIGHT: 5' 8"

WEIGHT: 145-150

EYES: blue

AGE at EMPLOY: 47

START DATE: 13 July 1919

ASSIGN: Measles Ward F, Influenza J

EVAL: Superior

TERMINATION: Death / Aug 1920

"Anything unusual about this?" I asked Lucy, with the file open before us on the table.

"Nothing that I can see," she muttered. "Let's look at mine to compare."

NAME: Paul, Lucy Jane

PREVIOUS EMPLOYMENT: American Medical Assoc

EDUCA: Army Medical Corp

RECCD BY: Randall Davis, MD (AMA)

REFERENCE(S):

HEIGHT: 5' 7"

WEIGHT: 130

EYES: black

AGE at EMPLOY: 36

START DATE: 1 January 1920

ASSIGN: Trachoma, Influenza J / Roaming

EVAL: Sufficient

TERMINATION:

"Who's Randall Davis, MD?"

"Head of Malpractice Investigations, AMA. He's who sent me here in the first place."

"Do you report to him?"

"By mail, once a month. Telegraph in between. I sent him a summary when I went into the city on my day off."

"Did you have him check to see if I was who I said I was?"

"Of course." Lucy smiled. "Just like you and Durand checked on me. . . . Stephen, wonder why *black*?"

"Your eyes? They are black, at least in most lights."

"But they're normally recorded as brown. Nobody has truly black eyes."

"You come the closest of anyone I've seen." I glanced down at Jimmy Cain's file. "Cain's are recorded as plain old blue. Let's pull the others."

We laid out on the table six files: Cain, along with *Adams, Ethel*; *Becker, Adolph*; *Chandler, Ray*; *Donald, Ross*; *Phillips, Scottie*.

"What do you see?"

"All of them except Becker worked for the city hospitals. Does it mean anything?"

"Maybe," I said. "Saint Taylor worked at Bellevue before the war."

"All were received . . . or what . . . recommended by Taylor, head of nursing."

"Jesus, Lucy, every damn one of them has blue eyes."

"Why would that . . . matter . . . ?" You could see her working it out in her mind. "Didn't Ezra keep . . . ?"

"Pointing at his eyes. At my eyes . . . your eyes. Trying to tell us something that we were too stupid to see."

"Are the eyes the marker for . . . ?"

"For some sort of racial purity maybe, or at least a certain racial type."

"Nordic," Lucy said.

"Nordic?"

"Remember the book that Durand sent over with the guns and the scotch. *The Passing of the Great Race* by somebody . . . Grant. According to him, the pure white American breed that we're supposed to do everything we can to protect is not just European, it's Nordic."

"No brown eyes allowed?"

"There have to be some admitted to the club because it's so common, but maybe blue eyes are supposed to be . . . what . . . ? Pure?"

I pointed to my face. "Like these?" I asked, unable to resist.

"You're about as impure as they come. Despite your eyes."

"Next time we see Sherman, we'll ask him about the eyes," I said. "He has all sorts of theories about racial features."

Somehow, what had almost been funny, flirtatious even, suddenly wasn't. Sherman and his family faces, his racial traits. Eye color and hair. Skin tone and texture.

"Do these tell us where we can find Scottie Phillips and the man Becker?" I asked Lucy, suddenly feeling cold and hollow.

She nodded, having caught my mood. Picked up first one file and then the other. "Little Scottie is on the influenza ward. I'll wander down there afterwhile and take a peek at the schedule, see when her shift is. Becker is . . . you'll like this . . . assigned to the laundry. Graveyard shift."

"Are you serious? Graveyard!"

"That's what it says. Look for yourself."

We placed all the files except Lucy's into one empty drawer in the bottom of the last cabinet, imagining that we'd be back to study them further. Lucy left to trace Scottie Phillips, and I walked down to the foot of the island, intending to ask Nurse Blanche Taylor if I could see any personnel records kept in her office. I didn't find Taylor, but I did find Ethel Adams.

She was seated at a regular-sized desk in the anteroom to Taylor's quarters. She dwarfed the desk, and I was reminded of a tale that I had read years before on a snowy winter night in North Carolina. Something about Gulliver and his travails. She was trying to make sense of the large white Bible that we'd handled at the prayer meeting.

Ethel told me that Nurse Taylor had gone into the city that morning and was expected back on the last ferry. When I asked her about personnel records, she said that everything she knew about was kept in Knox's office, and without my even asking, told me that she couldn't let me inside Taylor's private rooms—emphasis on the word *private*.

"What are you reading about?" I sat down in the only other chair.

"I'm trying to figure out about the Jews," she said, almost plaintively. "Can you help me?"

"What are you trying to make out?"

"Why everyone seems to be so upset with them. Hate them even."

"Is it just because they're different?" I asked her.

"When I worked over on Island 1 before the war, they came through by the boatloads, and even though they dressed funny and covered their heads, and some of the men had big, scratchy beards, that didn't make them any different from half the people from that part of the world."

"What does Nurse Taylor say?"

Her brow creased in consternation. "She says they killed our Lord."

"Jesus? I believe it was the Roman soldiers who did that."

"I know. . . . I studied about it in here."

"I don't know what to tell you. Look in the book of Deuteronomy."

"What book is that?" She looked around the room, as if expecting a library to appear.

"It's in your Bible there, way back at the beginning. Chapter seven or thereabouts."

I stood, thumbed through the ornate, gilded Bible for her, back to the early books, and pointed out Deuteronomy. Turned over a few pages to the seventh chapter, till I found what I thought was there. Pointed it out.

"How come you know so much about the Bible, Stephen?" she asked. "You being such a tough guy."

"Who said I was a tough guy?"

"It's the way you talk sometimes. And you shot poor Ray and Jimmy."

"I did. They didn't leave me any choice."

She nodded sadly, and if I'm not mistaken, a giant tear might have even begun to form in her eye.

"I know about the Bible," I said, "because where I grew up, in a cabin way, far back in the mountains, it was the only book we could get our hands on. For a long time, it was read the Bible or not read at all. I have a cousin named Jedidiah who can recite whole chapters by heart."

"What does Deuteronomy say?" she asked after a moment. And it was then that I realized she was struggling in part to understand things because she could just barely read.

"It says that the Jews are God's special people. Raised above all the people on the face of the earth. This may not make any sense to you, but Jesus himself was a Jew."

"Then why on earth . . . ?"

"Because people are meaner than hell sometimes," I said. "The meanest animal that ever existed to our own kind."

She stared at me for a long moment. "I'm confused," she admitted. She did look deeply troubled.

"Why?"

"Because Miss Taylor ain't mean. Not a drop of it."

"And . . . ?"

"And she hates you worse than anything, worse than any old Jew or Gentile that ever lived."

CHAPTER FIFTY-FOUR

It helped that I still had the bandage on my scalp. That scared her. She kept talking as if I had come back from the dead. Nobody ever escaped the oven but me. Half the time talking under her breath about me and half the time talking to me." Lucy was describing her conversation with Scottie Phillips while we ate some supper she'd brought back from the canteen. "At first, when I found her coming off her shift in the flu ward, I didn't think she'd even look at me, but I walked her all the way upstairs to her room and followed her inside, so she didn't have much choice."

"Was she afraid of you?"

"Not that I was going to punch her in the nose, if that's what you mean, but it's like she was afraid of who I was. Like I was a ghost of someone she thought she'd never have to look at again."

"What did she say about—"

"Don't interrupt, let me tell it. Her roommate was on duty, so it was just the two of us with the door closed. Sitting across from each other on the two beds. She started out by pretending she didn't know who I was, and I reminded her that we'd met at the Bible study. Then she pretended that she didn't know what had happened to my head, and I reminded her that her friends had knocked me out and almost boiled me alive. It was spooky, Stephen. It was like peeling back the layers of an onion to see her try one thing and then another, giving up on one lie and then trying again. Sometimes she would cry and sometimes not, but eventually, she admitted she knew what happened to me, knew what happened when Chandler and the others took some girl away."

"All girls?"

"She seemed to think so. Pregnant girls mostly, and then lately, a few men who knew too much or posed a threat to them."

"Like the Gypsy who caught them with his wife."

"Probably. But mostly she was sad and ashamed. She asked me twice if I had come to punish her for her sins. Said it exactly like that. And so finally, I asked her what her sins were. Told her that if she confessed them to me, then she wouldn't have to be punished. That I had the power to forgive her."

"You're a genius."

"Glad you noticed."

"And . . ."

"She slept with the men."

There was a long pause, as I wasn't sure what to say. "All . . . ?"

"All of them. At first, she was just supposed to flirt with them, with whoever Taylor figured out she needed to join the Congregation. By the way, that's what they call their little gang—the Congregation. So Taylor would identify someone she thought would make a valuable member, and if it was a man, she'd send little Scottie to flirt with him and invite him to Bible study. If they weren't interested in the Bible, Scottie would act like there might be a little extra incentive, a little private time together afterward. One way or another, most of those she invited showed up, and it was her sacred duty to walk one or another back to his dorm . . . or her dorm, if her roommate was out."

"Sacred duty!"

"She said that—*sacred duty*—about a dozen times. It was her sacred duty to bring these men to Christ. That's how it was explained to her in the beginning by both Taylor and Adams. That they were heathens who needed to be washed in the blood. Do people actually say that, Stephen, *washed in the blood*?"

"Oh yes. Washed in the blood of the lamb, or washed in Jesus's blood."

"Nasty. You'd think nurses would . . . Anyway, in the beginning, it was just flirting. Holy flirting, she called it. And then there was some kissing and heavy petting if one of the men wouldn't do what Taylor wanted or if he threatened to leave the Congregation. I think she said it was holy flirting, then innocent kissing, then something like chaste touching, and then finally sanctified intercourse. Blessed by Blanche Taylor."

"Good God . . ."

"Oh, it gets better. Miss Saint Nurse Taylor liked to watch."

"No, she didn't."

Lucy nodded. "Several times, she had Scottie meet one of the men, I think it was Chandler, in her office where we had the Bible study. The way Scottie described it, it was a sacred place, and that sofa was the altar. And afterward, after the union, she realized that the door was cracked open and that someone had been watching her perform."

"The union?"

"That what she calls sex—the union—along with it being sanctified or holy or righteous."

"She volunteered all of this? You didn't have to twist her arm or poke her in the eye?" "She was confessing, Stephen. And once she started, it was like a dam broke. It came pouring out of her. She wanted to tell it all, including what the men did to her. It was weird and awful and fascinating all at the same time."

"You said that Taylor and Adams both told her it was . . . what? Sacred?"

"Her sacred duty. And yes, Adams is in it up to her fat neck. She probably believes whatever Taylor tells her comes straight from above and carries the orders from the saint down to other members of the Congregation. Scottie called Adams the Messenger."

"What's she going to do now? Scottie, I mean . . ."

"Well, first of all, I forgave her. We both had a good cry, and I hugged her and told her that she was forgiven all her sins. And after we got through sniffling and forgiving, I told her to get the hell off the island."

"She have a place to go?"

"Not really, but her family is in Brooklyn, and I told her I'd help her find a job in the city. Or you would. . . ."

"Will she go?"

"I think so. If we can keep Taylor and Adams away from her for a few days. . . . Stephen?"

"Yes?"

"Do you know what the creepiest part of all was?"

"Taylor watching them on the couch?"

Lucy nodded. "Hell yes, screwing on the sofa, sex on the altar, just because some righteous old woman orders you to do it while she watches. . . . The Taylor broad probably sitting in the dark licking her lips. . . . Before we tackle your friend Becker, I need a drink. A double."

I bought Lucy that drink out of Fussell's nice bottle of scotch, a double for her and a single for me. I was on edge from the day's events, and I wanted to keep that edge right up till midnight when Adolph Becker's shift began at the laundry.

While we savored the scotch, I checked the .38. It hadn't been fired since it came to the island in Fussell's duffel bag, and I wanted to be sure it was serviceable before we went calling on Becker. I unloaded it, checked the barrel and cylinder, and then reloaded. Lucy watched moodily, sipping her drink, while I did all of this. I figured it reminded her of the night she intended to fire and couldn't.

When I got up to lay the pistol beside my folded jacket on our spare bunk, she suddenly asked me where the tommy gun was.

"In the cabinet across the hall." I pointed. "Under a pile of blankets. Why? You planning to use it for something?"

"Maybe. I haven't been alone at night since . . . There was always somebody around at the hospital. I'm not sure I can . . ."

I knew what she meant. The dark of the night is a strange country when you don't know what might come screeching out of it. "You want me to show you how to fire it?" I paused. "Just in case?"

She nodded and raised her glass. "Think of me as your very own gun moll," she said, trying to lighten the mood.

I brought the chopper from the other room, along with the drum magazine containing the .45 caliber shells. Showed her how to unlock the slot and insert the drum before pulling back the bolt on top to set the firing mechanism.

"Then cut loose?" she asked, mimicking the motion of mowing down imaginary enemies. Still playing the gangster moll with her empty glass in one hand.

"Fussell said to hold on tight to both grips if you ever do pull the trigger," I said, smiling at her antics. "Otherwise, you'll be lying on your back shooting at the ceiling."

"I have a better idea," she said. "How 'bout you just don't leave me alone at night till we both get off this damn island?"

CHAPTER FIFTY-FIVE

I could sense Lucy's growing distress as we approached the laundry where she'd almost died. So much so, that I asked her if she wanted to wait outside even though it was almost two in the morning.

She shook her head, at first slowly as if unsure and then with increasing vehemence. "Hell no," she muttered. "I want to see where it all happened, and I want to be there when you talk to him."

We walked in on a stack of mattresses in the room where I'd shot Donald and Cain. The door to the autoclave was open, and a thin man in an orderly's uniform was busy feeding the top two mattresses from the pile into the autoclave. His back was to us, and the only immediate detail we could see was his thin blond hair. The mattresses in, he pushed the round door shut and began spinning the handle to lock it closed. Lucy grabbed my arm and began to squeeze, tighter and tighter as the handle spun. The door mechanism clicked, and the man then reached up to flip several switches to the right of the door, studied several gauges for a moment, and then pulled down hard on a lever just at shoulder height. Lucy was almost panting, and I put one arm around her shoulders to steady her.

Then the figure turned, and in that movement, I felt certain he was the man I'd seen helping carry the Gypsy's body out to the lagoon. From ten feet away and in the bright light of the laundry, he had a thin, muscular neck and a pale, scarred face. But that's not what sent a shiver through me and wrung a gasp out of Lucy.

It was his eyes.

He was wearing thick glasses with dark rims, which didn't at all hide the fact that one of his two eyes tremored constantly in its socket, as if charged with some sort of crazed electricity. The other eye—the right—held steady, and it was with that eye that he regarded us. "Who the hell are you?" he said quietly, with a definite European accent. German, I thought.

The eye that was focused on us was blue, a gunmetal blue that reminded you of something hard like a ball bearing. The iris of the second eye, the quivering eye, was dark brown, as if it had been ripped from some other face and jammed unsuccessfully into this one.

"You know who I am," I said. "And your name is Adolph Becker. I saw you the night that you helped your friends carry the Gypsy's body out to the lagoon."

Becker smiled. "That was you fire off that gun shot." His English was stiff, formal almost, but broken in places. "Same damn gun that killed my friends . . . right here in this room."

I nodded. "That was me."

"Where's your gun shot tonight?" He pronounced the words *gun shot* in two rock-hard syllables. "You don't mean to shoot me too?"

I stepped forward, pulled the .38 out of my belt and laid it casually on the tabletop. "No, not tonight, not unless you force my hand, like your friends did."

He smiled again, which was difficult to even see in his fractured face. "This your girlfriend there? The one they claim was in the oven?" He gestured behind him with his head to indicate the autoclave.

"Oh, I was in it," Lucy said, her voice hard, her anger having revived her.

"Well, miss, maybe so, but I did not put you there. Them other two men, they put you in there." He shrugged. "I didn't have nothing to do with that."

"Where were you?" she asked. "You could have stopped them."

"I am taking a break. Gone out the back door to roll myself cigarette. Two cigarettes."

"Was that the agreement?" I asked. "You make yourself scarce and don't ask any questions?"

He nodded. "Whenever the men needed to use the oven, I needed a smoke."

"Who told you they were coming?"

"You mean who was boss?"

"Sure. Who told you what to do?"

"The Messenger let me know when they were coming. Even what time they come. Why I think you already know that?"

"The Messenger is Ethel Adams?" Lucy's harsh tone.

He nodded. "See, why do you ask me what you already know?"

"Who told Ethel?" I asked. "Who was her boss?"

"That woman they all call Saint," he said. "You already know this too."

"How did you get involved?" I asked, but he only stared with that hard blue eye, the dark eye quivering madly, uncontrollably.

"Did Scottie Phillips pull you into it, into the circle?" Lucy asked.

He grinned. "Oh yes," he said. "She pull me."

"Did you sleep with her?" I asked.

And he snorted some sort of laugh. "Do you mean did I . . . screw her? Finally, something you not know. Think about it, Herr Robbins. Why not . . . ? Pretty American girl and . . . you guess what?" He turned his head slightly to focus his blue eye on Lucy. "She like it how I do it."

"Bastard," Lucy muttered. "I can tell you right now that she didn't like it one damn bit." She glanced down at the pistol on the table, and for a moment, I thought she might pick it up.

Becker shrugged. "Then she very good fake."

"Will you testify?" I said to Becker suddenly.

"What you mean? Testify?"

"Will you say in court before a judge what you just told us?"

"Why would I do that?"

"Because Scottie Phillips is no longer selling herself for the Saint," Lucy said, changing course in a way that didn't occur to me. "No more free American girl just for taking a cigarette break at the right time of the night."

He seemed to consider. His good blue eye—if you can call it that—blinked rapidly. "Scottie is no more?" he said, focused now on Lucy.

"Scottie is no more."

"And if I speak in court, they will not . . . jail me?"

"If you speak in court, and name who the Messenger is and who the Saint is," I said. "Explain to the judge what they did and how they did it, then no, they will not jail you."

"And if I don't speak the judge?"

I picked up the pistol. "Then you are of no use to us."

His ball-bearing eye was now focused firmly on my right hand and the gun it held. The .38 wasn't pointing directly at him, but he could see it plain, and I figured he was not far away when I'd killed two men more or less where he was standing. The paint that was meant to cover their bloodstains was still fresh on the wall.

"I would like to assist," he said slowly. "I would like to . . ."

"Testify?"

"Yes. I like to testify . . . if that would help you."

"It would help us. And we would help you. . . . Here's the plan, Adolph. I want you to keep right on doing what you normally do. Don't leave the island. But stay away from Blanche Taylor and Ethel Adams."

"And Scottie Phillips," Lucy added.

"And Scottie Phillips. Stay the hell away from anybody that had anything to do with the Congregation. Don't talk to them. Don't even look at them. And when the time comes for you to testify, we will let you know."

"And no jail?"

"No jail for you."

He looked up then with his one blue eye and used it to make contact, first with Lucy and then me. He nodded solemnly. "I will do what you say me to do," he said. "And here is my . . . for you."

"Gift?" Lucy suggested.

"No gift . . . warning. Be careful the Messenger."

CHAPTER FIFTY-SIX

Lucy and I had coffee the next morning in the nurses' canteen. Coffee and what the orderly who served breakfast cheerfully claimed was oatmeal. The coffee was better than the mush . . . black and hot. Strong enough to stir the blood even though we'd had only three or four hours' sleep.

We were both quiet as we sipped that coffee, for we both knew that Blanche Taylor was next. There was no one else left on our list, no other place to go.

"You afraid of her?" Lucy said finally.

"Hell yes." I shrugged. I got up, fetched the glass pot from the warmer and poured us both a half a cup more. "When I was a kid in the mountains, my grandma told me that if you stared into a snake's eyes, it could hypnotize you. You'd freeze, couldn't move, and the snake would bite you or slither away, either one."

"So she's a snake?"

"Sure. She has that power. Her eyes, her voice. Especially her voice."

"If you freeze up, what am I supposed to do?"

I smiled. "I don't aim to freeze up. I aim to bite."

"Just in case." Her tone was serious.

"If I freeze, you attack. If you freeze, I attack. That's why there's two of us."

That brought a smile, a real smile, from Lucy's mouth and her chocolate eyes. Maybe the first smile of the morning. "Fair enough. . . .

Oh, and Stephen, one more thing. If she offers us anything to drink, don't accept it."

"You mean that tea she's always brewing up to salve what ails you?"

"That's what I mean. When I first came here, the other nurses told me—late at night when we were sitting up talking—that she put things in the tea."

"Poison?"

"Maybe. Or potions to make you sleepy or complacent. Drugs to make you do her bidding. We all giggled like schoolgirls when they told it, like it was some kind of pajama party bullshit, but still, we laughed because it was scary true."

"Then let's go see the wicked witch of Island 3," I said. "And not touch the poisoned cup to our lips."

It was as if she expected us.

Ethel Adams was there, in the anteroom to Taylor's quarters, where I'd seen her the day before. She led us into Taylor's office without speaking a word, which was strange in and of itself. Then she shut the door behind us, leaving us alone in that odd room that was both den and office, the room where the Bible study and so much else had taken place during the previous weeks.

A cheerful voice, chirping almost, called out from the inner room that "I'll just be a minute. Finishing touches." Blanche Taylor's voice.

We sat down on the couch side by side, just where we'd sat the night of the prayer meeting, and I believe we both had the same thought at exactly the same moment. From where we sat, there was a clear line of sight to the inner door. Someone standing inside it looking out could see anything that occurred on that sofa.

"We're sitting on the goddamn altar," Lucy whispered.

"Sacred union," I replied.

Then the door opened wide, and the Saint was in the room with us. She was unchanged from the first time I met her. Perfectly dressed and made up. Every gray hair in place, the white nurse's uniform meticulously pressed and starched. The large silver cross pinned to her blouse. Even her white nurse's shoes polished to a sort of modest perfection.

Her ruddy complexion was open and glowing. She could not have been happier to see us, it said. Maybe she had aged a bit from the strain of the kill-or-be-killed weeks, but if so, she had become your grandmother rather than your aunt. Homemade cookies on a china plate along with the unconditional love.

"I so hoped you'd come to visit," she said, "and I thought to make tea for us. Strong tea for this early morning."

"No thanks," Lucy and I said almost simultaneously.

"We've both had our coffee," Lucy added.

I picked up the thread. "We need to discuss something very serious with you. No social amenities."

"Do you mind if I have a sip then," she said, "to clear my thoughts." She didn't wait on a reply but went to the side table and poured out her tea into a china cup. Placed the cup delicately onto its saucer and added two sugar cubes before stirring.

She arranged herself across from us in her typical chair, her well-upholstered throne, with the cup on the padded arm. I could feel both of us, Lucy as well as me, being drawn in, fascinated by the one-woman show being staged just five or six feet away.

But then she misplayed. "I am so glad," she said to Lucy, "to see you up and about, recovered from that horrible incident in the laundry. It's the answer to my fervent prayers."

"No thanks to you," Lucy said. Low in her throat.

"Whatever do you mean? Stephen, what does she mean?"

"She means that the men who attacked her were acting under your orders."

"But that's impossible." Infinite surprise. Infinite concern. "I would never hurt any of God's creations." It was as if she'd completely forgotten the accusations that Jack Durand and I had flung in her face the week before.

"Not you personally," I started. "Not you with your own two hands, but—"

Lucy cut me off. She'd had enough. "You sanctimonious bitch," she snarled. "Don't pretend with us. Those two men you sent knocked me cold with a billy club, carried me senseless down to the laundry, stripped the clothes off of me, touched me—do you know what I mean when I say touched me? Of course you do. And then they stuffed me into an oven to cook me to death." She paused but only because she was out of breath. Panting almost.

"But surely you don't think I would sanction such atrocities?" She reached up to place her fingers delicately on the cross at her throat.

I started to speak, but Lucy wasn't done. "Don't you think I'm one of God's creations?" she barked. "Or James Thompson? Or Ciara McManaway? Or the dozens of others. Poor, pregnant girls who only wanted a home, any safe place to give birth and raise a child." There was a sob in Lucy's voice now. What had started in raw anger stirred now with sadness.

"Not this place," Taylor said calmly. "Not this place unless they have a husband. A father for that child you're feeling so sorry for. This place . . . is a place where families matter. Where we do things in a calm, Christian manner. I don't condone what those poor, misguided men were doing, but I do understand it. America is a sacred place, where God's anointed people can make a home based on Biblical values. And where they will remain safe from the foreign corruption that people like you seem bent on allowing into our country."

"Only one problem," I said. "What those poor, misguided sons of bitches were doing was murder. Over and over . . . murder."

"But don't you see, I was trying to stop them. I had them here"—she spread her arms wide—"in my own home to try to influence them for the good. To teach them Christian forgiveness. To help them find a better way."

It was such an outrageously bold lie that you had to almost admire it. Almost. "Nice try," I said. "But Scottie Phillips says different. Adolph Becker says different. And when we track down Ray Chandler, he'll no doubt say different as well. You had them call you the Saint, and you ran the Congregation from right here in what you call your home."

That brought her to a pause. But not for long. "You'll never find Mr. Chandler," she replied. "He's gone for good. That leaves poor, misguided Scottie, a tramp off the streets. And that Kraut stowaway Becker. If those are your star witnesses, then . . ." She shrugged. "I believe I'll sit right here and put my faith in the Lord."

Lucy was growling again, deep in her throat. "Pimp," she muttered.

"What did you say?"

"You pimped that poor girl out to the men you needed to do your bidding. And while you may not want to believe it, she's the kind of witness that twelve good men in a New York jury box will just love. They will pity her, even salivate over her, and you'll go to the chair. Will the Lord protect you when they flip the switch on you up in Albany?"

Her veneer finally cracked. "Why, you little whore! You and that man beside you stewing in a rancid cot up in the psychopathic ward of all places. You have no right to say anything to me. God will—"

"You'd like to see it, wouldn't you?" I interrupted her.

"What?"

"He means you'd like to watch us stewing, wouldn't you?"

There was a long pause. Lucy reached over and slipped her left hand inside my elbow. Taylor tried to take a sip from her china cup, but her hand was shaking so badly that the brown tea spilled all over her immaculate bosom. The cup clattered when she placed it back down onto the saucer. Her face was quivering, her nerves broken now.

"I'll leave," she offered eventually, when she'd regained some composure.

"Leave?"

"I'll leave the island."

"Not return," Lucy said. Calm now.

Taylor nodded. "And not return."

"You've got three days to clear out," I said. "And God help them wherever you go."

CHAPTER FIFTY-SEVEN

And that was that, Lucy Paul and I told ourselves. That was our victory over the head nurse of Island 3, the witch saint who'd sent no telling how many girls and women to their deaths over the months. Along with the men who'd tried to protect them.

She wasn't going to prison, or to the electric chair that Lucy'd threatened her with, and that seemed anticlimactic. Less than we'd bargained for and yet more as well. For it was as if a weight had been lifted off both of us. When we left Taylor's office that morning in early September, we weren't sure what we should do next . . . or where we should go.

We strolled outside for a bit on the south side of Island 3, where we could actually see the Statue of Liberty bathed in midmorning sunshine a half mile away. We both laughed a bit when we caught each other staring at it. "That's us," Lucy said.

"Free, you mean?"

She nodded and grinned. "Free from all this," she said. She waved her arm to indicate Island 3 and the rest of Ellis Island behind it. "Free and alive." And then after a bit. "What is there left to do?"

"I should walk over to Island 1 and telegraph Jack Durand," I said.

"I'll go with you. I should do the same to Randall Davis."

"Tell him you're done?"

"Hell yes, done. And then what?"

"I think I'd like to take a nap," I said, staring at her. "I was up all night."

"Alone?"

"No, you were with me."

"I mean take your nap alone . . . ?"

"God no."

And so we did, rather slowly actually. Strolled over to Island 1 and took turns composing telegrams to Jack and to her Dr. Davis. Mystery solved(.) Culprits identified(.) Head Nurse Blanche Taylor leaving Ellis(.) And so on. Simple words for weeks of desperation.

"Should we report to Wallis?" she asked me when we were back outside the main hall, watching yet another ferry disgorge its wave of hungry, anxious human beings. Bravely facing a huge, dirty, and very new world.

"Wallis and Knox," I replied. "But that feels like tomorrow. Let's leave something for tomorrow."

We bought hot dogs, of all things, from a vendor with a steaming cart. And from another vendor, paper cups of lemonade. Sat together on the rocks out at the eastern point of Island 1 to have our picnic lunch. Where I'd sat weeks before in the fog, smoking a cigar and dreaming about my father.

"Were you asleep?" Lucy asked, for I was telling her about the dream.

"No, I don't think so. I was awake but lost in the fog and wondering how in the wide world I ended up here, trying to make sense of what had happened to Ciara McManaway."

"Did your father speak to you?"

I nodded. "Funny you should say that. He did speak to me."

"What did he tell you?"

And there we were, having drifted without meaning to up against the future. Mine versus hers. "He told me to come home when I was done here," I admitted.

She sighed. "Will you? Go home I mean. . . ."

"I don't know, Lucy. I confess that I want to. If Jack doesn't have

293

another missing person he wants me to find, I might go see the mountains again. Visit up home."

We drifted by silent mutual consent back to Island 3, still walking slowly, as we had all the afternoon before us, and beyond that, the long September evening. Tomorrow, we agreed, we would check on Scottie Phillips to be sure that she could find a life in the city. Remind Adolph Becker not to disappear. See if the Saint was packing up her belongings. Tomorrow was soon enough for all of that. And the next day . . .

Lucy took my arm, blatantly, publicly, as we walked down the long breezeway to Building E. And then, when we turned into the pavilion, she started up the steps ahead of me, making music with her hips. I reached up to play that music, caress it, and by the time we reached the top of the stairs and shut the hallway door behind us, we were clinging to each other. There was a happy, groping intensity to that walk from one end of the psych ward to the other. We stopped twice for kisses that went as far and deep as kisses alone can go.

We began to undress in the doorway to the last room on the left, our room. Undress ourselves and each other indiscriminately. Running our hands over each other's bodies beneath our clothes, even as we found ways to discard clothing.

Skin.

Breath.

Teeth . . . and tongues.

Thigh.

Hard flesh and . . . soft.

Damp . . .

Pliant. Yielding.

Warm . . . to the touch.

Longer, slower . . . fierce possessive . . . that sweet, wild convergence.

It was as if we swallowed each other whole. And afterward there were tears.

"Why are you crying?" I whispered into her ear.

"I'm not crying. I don't cry."

"Then why . . ."

"What if that's the last time?"

"It's not, darling. There's tonight."

"And tomorrow."

"That's right. Tomorrow."

We dozed then. Exhausted from the night before and the morning's collision with Taylor. From our own soft collusion. From all of that, we dozed. And when I drifted slowly awake, much later in that day, I asked her what she would do. After the tomorrow that we were holding in front of us . . .

"I need to see my mother," she said, the practical side of her returning. "Make sure she has enough money. Make sure she'll be okay this winter."

"Still in New Jersey? The western part that looks like mountains?"

"Hmmm, that part. Still on a farm that's too far from town. My brother is nearby, but he's a brother, not a sister."

"And he doesn't check on her."

"Not like he should. Not enough to suit me."

"And then back to the AMA and Dr. Davis? More mysteries to solve?"

She nodded but slowly. "Maybe. . . . Maybe all the mysteries are solved," she said and rolled over against me. Resting, savoring the moment, and refusing to think too far ahead.

We scrounged together a very nice supper that evening. Two pieces of beef from the doctors' mess, where such as we were not normally allowed. Some potatoes mashed with butter and salt from the nurses' canteen. Some not bad red wine and a bar of chocolate sent over by

Maureen and Lucy's nurse friends from the Island 2 hospital. A feast that we celebrated outside on one of the rough picnic tables that faced the lagoon.

One of the things I'd always loved about Lucy was how she relished her food. The beef and the potatoes, butter and salt. Washed with gulps rather than sips of wine. The conversation delayed by the food. Smiles, then grins, then laughter, subsiding again into smiles, and the food warmed us and the wine shone upon us.

"You know what, Stephen Robbins," Lucy said around one mouthful. "In the end, I'm just glad to be alive." She paused to swallow. "I almost wasn't, you know. And stretched out on a dirty mattress flirting with death is enough to make you appreciate life."

"You didn't say that in the beginning, you know. You said that way back in England when that sorry bastard killed your baby that you wished you had died."

"I know. I did wish it. Even stared long and hard at the cabinet full of drugs and considered killing myself. But you know what, Stephen, it's a long damn way from England to here."

We clinked our mugs together, a silent toast to how far away that time and place was. A swallow of wine. "Are you glad to be alive?" she asked. "After what that photographer bitch did to you?"

"I'm past that," I said, sure that it was true. "So far past it, I don't even think she is a bitch. Just a woman chasing fame and fortune."

"Fucking fame and fortune?"

I had to smile. "That too."

"Then here's to our fame and fortune. What we have tonight and tomorrow, right here." Cups again, again a swallow.

We had recovered our spirits, Lucy and I. Neither willing to say anything about the life after. About parting . . . leaving . . . separating. What we would mean when we waved to each other from dock to ferry and shouted, "See you around sometime." We'd mean something without being sure what. And we'd be tough about it.

We were close enough by then—friends as much as lovers—that when we made our way back to the psych ward that night, shut the door to the hallway (maybe for the last time), and shut the door to our room for the night (probably for the last time), we stripped down to our skin. Left a couple of candles burning and slipped into our sad, old cot. For the last time?

Half-drunk with wine, we curled comfortably into each other, willing to sleep because we knew that we'd never make it through the whole night without waking up. Making our twin bodies into one body . . .

We were right; our instincts were sound. We each stirred early in the morning, when the light through the window was the faintest pink and objects began to take shape. First to go one at a time down to the lavatory and then to luxuriate ourselves back into bed for a sort of languorous, half-sad and half-glorious lovemaking. Not screwing now but making love. The beginning of our leave taking.

And so we were locked into that most private, flowing place, my insistent flesh becoming hers, when the door to our room opened.

"Don't stop on our account. I can see just fine from here." The words emanated from a dark form in the doorway. The voice and the form of Blanche Taylor.

Everything then is fast.

I pull back from Lucy, choking with fury. Push to my feet and turn to face her Sainthood, my erection wilting as I stand.

Snarl at her like an animal caged. "Bitch." Step forward. "Wicked . . . sanctimonious . . . bitch."

I mean to be between her and Lucy, protect her naked body with my own. Though I can hear Lucy on her feet behind me. Cursing.

"Get my hands around your neck, and I'll wring it till you choke," I'm shouting now at the Saint.

I stalk forward, hands curling into fists.

She steps back, I think to run, but only to let the giantess step through the door. Ethel Adams fiercely weeping, her eyes quite mad.

"You can't speak to her like that," she cries and swings one long arm. Hits me in the face with her open hand so hard that my head snaps over my shoulder and my feet leave the floor. Flying or falling . . .

The back of my head crunching against the metal frame of the cot. My crippled neck in jagged lightning . . . and then nothing . . .

But the sound of hammering, hammering, hammering . . .

Inside my bursting head . . .

. . . and the broken, battered world.

CHAPTER FIFTY-EIGHT

In the beginning there is crushing pain. Spasms. Pulsing and coursing pain that is like hot light burning through every awareness and any thought. No notion of a body except one outlined in darkness, dangling at the end of a rope.

The rope is my neck. Twisted.

Eventually the pounding inside my head lessens and only a coarse wind blows through the cracked and empty casing.

I'm standing on the old road that snakes up and over the Divide Mountain and down into Anderson Cove. I would like to go there. My father is buried there and lives there.

My mother and sisters, where are they . . . ? They are there. They would bury me beside my father with their weeping. Were I to go there to die . . . and visit with them.

My boots are on my feet, and my feet flash free. My old barn coat to keep the frost away. Leather and denim and wool for my skin.

I lean forward into the stony falling sway of the road and take a step. Then another. And what do I see and feel? My old dog is with me. King James, the rangy black husky-shepherd. Where did he come from, where did he go? Is with me now. He nuzzles my hand, and I stroke the thick fur of his neck.

He has met me at the gap of the mountain, as he was wont to do. The wind always blows hardest at the gap.

Another step along the road, and we are going together, King James and I, loping along with free legs and strong. He is ranging ahead to scout the terrain and then back to me for touch and song. The song of a warm dog and man—mandolin chords and the fiddle.

The road is banjo steep in places, slick with damp leaves. I can hear King bark at a squirrel or fox. When you are the King, all the world is made of foxes and squirrels. The leaf-strewn path at my feet is orange and red, yellow and gold. For a moment, I think my eyes dazzled by midday sun and the colors are inside me rather than out, but no. No, the colors are everywhere, and it is fall. Autumn in the mountains, when the air is full fresh and the trees shake off their summer skin.

King James is back again to be sure that I am with him, following him, traveling the right road down. I laugh and he barks. Though the way in is steep and rough, we know the path. It belongs to us.

A question.

I know that there is a question I'm asking. If I can. A riddle perhaps that I can't solve with my own broken head. My shattered heart. As we walk, my dog and me, I try to recall that riddle.

It is important that I remember.

But I have come so far, so very far, and try as I might, I have lost my reason along the way.

King James barks on up ahead. He is down into the valley now, fields and orchards, and he has met someone on the road. His greeting bark reassures me. My nerves, what's left of my arms and legs, my belly and back, they tell me that when I meet the answer, I'll remember the question.

Seems that the answer waits on me—here in the high, sweet bedland of home.

King is back at my side, making sure that I'm still afoot and still coming on. We are out of the trees now and into my father's wide fields, resting fallow in the slant autumn light. Up ahead I see a young couple coming along the road. I blink and they are old, slow, and crippled up. I blink again and they are all youth and strength. King James pauses at my mother's side to lick her hand before racing beyond them up the cove.

Meeting them, I know the question.

"Must I live or die?" I ask. And in the long moment that follows, a harsh wind roars through the gap above to shiver the orchard trees.

"Why live, of course," my mother says. Surprised by the question. "I surely didn't conceive of you to die."

"But it hurts so," I say, my bones suddenly tired and chilled from the brutal wind. "This life."

My father laughs at such foolishness. They both do, and my fatigue falls away. I am then and there as young as they. "There is always enough light," Papa says, "to leaven the pain."

CHAPTER FIFTY-NINE

A rattling, surging movement. That didn't hurt. Though I had a body stretched out flat on some sort of bed, the bed itself was moving. Occasionally, it felt as if something—or someone—would touch my hand. First one of my hands and then the other.

Grip my hand, flex and massage my fingers, and then cling to my hand as I squeezed back. Refreshed by touch.

That didn't hurt either. Neither motion nor touch brought pain.

But the goddamn whistle. Somebody somewhere kept blowing a whistle, long and loud. Now, that hurt like fire.

"Make that damn fool stop," I said eventually. Though my lips were cracked and dry, I would speak about the whistle.

"Stop what, Stephen? What is it?" The voice that talked back was full of wonder.

"Stop blowing that whistle," I croaked.

The voice laughed. "That's the engineer. He has to blow his whistle when he comes to a crossroads, doesn't he?"

I licked my lips, and the voice wiped my face with a cold, damp rag. Wet my cracked lips. "Sip," I whispered, and there was a cup of water held precariously against my teeth.

"What kind of . . . engineer?" I was able to say a little while later.

"One on a train, Stephen," *my* voice said. For I had come to think of the person who touched my hands and replied to my questions as mine, as belonging to me.

It was, after all, a voice I thought I knew. Husky, a bit hoarse, but a woman's voice for all that. I couldn't name it, but I felt that I knew it.

I thought of another question. Though my head still hurt from time to time, I discovered that I liked to think of things. To think through the pain. "Where is this train a-going to?" I asked.

Again, the laugh. I liked to make the voice laugh. "Why, it's going south as hard and fast as ever it can. We're in Virginia now, I believe."

"South . . . ?"

"It's taking you home, Stephen. To North Carolina."

It was sometime later that the voice unwrapped my head and removed the gauze that was protecting my eyes. At night, with only one candle lit in the makeshift hospital car, as the doctors had told her that too much light would be painful to me in the beginning.

She wiped my face, and then ever so gently, my crusted eyes. The rag was warm now and wet, and it felt like some angel had made it. I blinked my eyes open slowly and was a little surprised that I could see after so long. Surprised and glad.

I smiled up at the woman who was hovering over me. She dropped her rag and took up my hand. Began to massage it much as she had been doing along the way. She's nervous, I thought.

"What the hell are you doing here?" I said to Lucy. "This far south in the middle of the night?"

That made her laugh, as I'd hoped it would. "You had to have a nurse, didn't you?"

"I need some good nursing," I admitted. "God knows."

"They didn't want to turn me loose after I chopped down that Adams bitch and chased Blanche Taylor into the lagoon, and me stark, staring naked the whole time."

"You did what?"

"But your friend Jack Durand reasoned with the authorities, and here I am. Did you know that the drum of a tommy gun holds fifty rounds?"

"No, I . . . did you kill Ethel?"

She shook her head. "No. I tried my best to kill her after she hit you, and I shot her up some, but mostly I killed the walls and ceiling like you said."

I paused, for I didn't quite know how to ask what was on my mind. "Well I'm glad you didn't kill them all . . . But why in the world did you decide to come with me?"

"Who is King James?" she asked.

"What . . . ?"

"You talked a lot when we first put you on the train some days back. Not much sense to it. Some made-up place called Anderson Cove, your dead mother and father talking. This character named King James who was yelling at you . . ."

"King James is a dog. I suspect he was barking."

"You never told me you had a dog, Stephen!"

Later, after I drifted in and out a few more times. I asked her about Saint Blanche, the witch who'd started it all. "You chased her into the lagoon?"

Lucy nodded. "I tried to shoot her too, just like that Fee-fi-fo-fum, Adams. Chased her in her whites all the way down the stairs and out to the edge of the lagoon, firing off a burst or two as we went. I thought Adams had killed you, and I was so choking furious that I totally lost track of the fact that I was naked. Finally ran out of ammo when I was at the edge of the fill and she was up to her waist in muck and water."

"Did she drown?" I said it almost wistfully.

"Hell no, but your boss, Durand, has her in custody in New York and intends to try her despite the politicians, her and Adams both."

"I might just love you," I said. "A little."

"Even though I can't shoot straight?"

"Even though . . ."

Later again. In the night.

She wouldn't let me move my head or neck much. Not yet. But she did manage to lay down beside me with her head on my chest, my arm around her. Her holding my stray hand against her side. And as the Norfolk Southern locomotive drilled on down the line, carrying us farther south and west, we whispered a bit to each other, she and I. And so morning broke inside our rattling, clacking train car. Broke open so slowly and peacefully that the dawning light didn't pain me as she feared it would.

I may have dozed a bit. I suspect we both did, lulled by the sound of the train spooling off its miles and the faint knit and purl of light pulsing around us. We were stretching back into awareness again when it occurred to me that she still hadn't answered me.

"That's all fine, Lucy," I whispered into her hair. So fine, in fact, that her body beside mine was causing its own kind of resurrection. "God knows, I'm glad to be alive. But you never said just why *you* decided to come south."

She sat up, rather roughly in fact, not bothering now about my head and neck. "Don't you want me?" she said suspiciously.

"Well, damn it to hell . . . of course I want you. Need you, want you, require you. All of it." I started to raise up off the pillow despite my neck, but she leaned on my chest to hold me down.

Her frown faded. To be replaced with a rueful grin that I'd never seen before. "To tell you the truth," she whispered as the morning light poured in around us. "I was wrong about something, mistaken about my own body . . ." Her face was only inches now from mine, her raven eyes gleaming. "And I thought I ought to stick with the father."

"What father?"

"The father of my child."

ABOUT THE AUTHOR

Terry Roberts is the author of three celebrated novels: *A Short Time to Stay Here* (winner of the Willie Morris Prize for Southern Fiction and the Sir Walter Raleigh Award for Fiction); *That Bright Land* (winner of the Thomas Wolfe Literary Award, the James Still Award for Writing About the Appalachian South and the Sir Walter Raleigh Award for Fiction); and most recently, *The Holy Ghost Speakeasy and Revival* (a finalist for the 2019 Sir Walter Raleigh Award for Fiction).

Roberts is a lifelong teacher and educational reformer as well as an award-winning novelist. He is a native of the mountains of Western North Carolina—born and bred. His ancestors include six generations of mountain farmers, as well as the bootleggers and preachers who appear in his novels. He was raised close by his grandmother, Belva Anderson Roberts, who was born in 1888 and passed down to him the magic of the past along with the grit and humor of mountain storytelling.

Currently, Roberts is the Director of the National Paideia Center and lives in Asheville, North Carolina with his wife, Lynn.

ACKNOWLEDGMENTS

W hen I was a boy growing up in the mountains of Western North
Carolina, my father was a devoted reader of classic, hardboiled
detective fiction: Dashiell Hammett, Raymond Chandler, James M.
Cain, James Thompson, Ross McDonald and so on. If you're going to
be snowed in on top of a mountain for a week or so, one could do worse
than such a bookshelf, especially if you discovered a bottle of good
bourbon hidden behind the books. *My Mistress' Eyes Are Raven Black*
was composed in the shadow of these distinctly American writers.

It was also written to address a distinctly American dilemma.
What is America after all, and who will be allowed to come here?
Almost all of us are immigrants by blood in one way or another—
some willing and many unwilling. And yet ... we are prone to hate
the late arrivals, especially if their skin is of a different hue. America
in the 1920s was a hotbed of eugenics and race hatred, which calls out
in blistering terms to America of the 2020s.

Which brings us to Ellis Island, which stands here for all the
various points of entry into the United States where migrant peoples
are judged and sorted. There are a number of excellent histories of
Ellis Island in general, and especially its renewed role in American
immigration policies after World War I. Among those, I kept Vincent
J. Cannato's *American Passage: The History of Ellis Island* close at hand
while working out the historical background for this story. Augustus
F. Sherman's photographs permeate *My Mistress' Eyes Are Raven Black*,

thanks in large part to the Aperture volume titled *Augustus F. Sherman: Ellis Island Portraits 1905-1920*, with its excellent introductory essay by Peter Mesenholler. I cannot recommend this book highly enough. Most of the captions to the photos as described here come from the brief, often cryptic notes that Sherman himself jotted on the prints.

Among those who were extremely helpful during the recreation of Ellis Island in 1920 were Barry Moreno and Jeff Dosik at the Ellis Island Museum of Immigration; and Wendy Ikoku, who read and reread the manuscript with her sharp eye for detail. Many thanks to my agent, Margaret Sutherland Brown, for believing in this book from the first time she saw it. A deep bow, as always, to the team at Turner Publishing who have brought it to life.

And of course, Lynn, who spent many months discussing xenophobia, eugenics, and tommy guns at the supper table. You've no idea how patient and funny she is!

Back to where it all began—with dad and his stack of well-worn paperbacks. Think of a snowy mountain night and the wind whipping around the eaves of the old farmhouse at the foot of Baird Mountain. Dad is propped up in bed, wearing his robe backwards like an extra blanket with arms. Clutched in his hand is a paperback with a gaudy, highly suggestive cover: perhaps something 90 proof or stronger by Raymond Chandler. The dark night and the winter wind contribute to the mix. Now that, dear friend, is some fine writing and some good reading.